Dance With My Heart

A Southland Romance

By Meda White

Dance With My Heart
Copyright © 2014 Meda White

Editor: Andrea Grimm Dickinson
Cover Artist: Kari Ayasha, Cover to Cover Designs

This is a work of fiction. Names, characters, places and occurrences are a product of the author's imagination. Any resemblance to actual persons, living or dead, places or occurrences, is purely coincidental.

ISBN: 1941287085
ISBN-13: 978-1-941287-08-8

DEDICATION

To my brother from another mother, thank you for the inspiration. My imagination might be more dangerous than some of your missions.

ACKNOWLEDGMENTS

A big hug and thank you to the real-life heroes and heroines who serve or have served in the U.S. Military, Law Enforcement, Firefighters, and First Responders.

Chapter One

Jane Dillon braced for action when she heard Breck Stanton's name announced for Best Male Actor. Applause erupted and fans screamed. From her position backstage, she could only see a portion of the auditorium. The shadowy figure on the highest balcony level, a member of the security detail she served with, moved along the side wall.

When Breck jogged up the stairs on the side of the stage closest to her, Jane shifted her feet and wiggled her fingers, adjusting her grip on her gun. She inched closer while scanning the part of the audience she could see.

An infrared beam flashed, and she hit her coms button with her left hand, unsheathing her pistol with her right.

"Red alert." She ran onto the stage as a shot rang out. "Down! Get down!"

The clear glass podium fractured with spider

veins from the hit. Cheers turned to screams as panic ensued among the audience members. Jane moved between Breck and the shooter. She wasn't tall enough to block a head shot if Breck had been upright, but he was crouched down behind the remains of the shattered podium.

"Move your ass, Breck." Her voice matched the firmness of her grip as she grabbed his arm and started moving him to the right side of the stage. "Stay low."

Initially, he gave her a wide-eyed look, but then moved with her to get to cover. When they were almost clear, she felt the impact of the round as it grazed her back. It made her stagger, but didn't knock her down. The force pushed her into Breck who wrapped his free arm around her and pulled her backstage with him.

God, please don't let him be hit. Why didn't we insist he wear body armor?

Her breath came short and quick. "Keep moving. Third door on the left."

She knew all of the hiding places and escape routes from having thoroughly checked the area she was assigned. When they were safe inside the utility closet, she turned to Breck.

"Are you hit?" She holstered her gun and removed her black jacket, the word SECURITY printed across the back in big, white letters.

He shook his head and frowned as his eyebrows knit together. "Jane?"

"I'm with B&B. We're going to get you out of here." She hit her coms button. "Asset secure. About to move."

"Roger that, Dillon. We're after the shooter. Take the mark to a secure location," Joe, her boss and team leader, said.

"Roger."

She pulled off her Kevlar vest and checked to see where the round had hit. The material that covered her upper right back was abraded, but not punctured.

Shit, that was close. She silently thanked her guardian angel as she pulled at the vest's Velcro side seams.

Breck stared at her with his mouth slightly open, catching his breath.

"You're okay. Take a deep breath." She unfastened the vest's shoulder straps. "Take your coat off."

He did as she directed, and she secured the vest over his shoulders. It was too small for him, but it covered his heart and lungs. Because it was unisex, it wasn't her vest of choice for personal use, but she'd brought it specifically for this reason, in case he needed it. He was the one with the stalker and a bull's-eye on his ass.

He put his coat on over the vest as she pulled her jacket on.

As soon as she zipped up, Breck's lips covered hers. He kissed her hard, backing her into the door. She returned the kiss for a second, until her brain gained control over her hormones. Placing her hands on his chest, she pushed gently. He took the cue to disengage.

"We have to move fast. My SUV is near the rear exit."

He nodded, and she took her pistol out of her thigh rig.

Jane had Breck out of the building and almost safely to the SUV when she heard the report of a gun. She crouched low to the ground and pulled Breck's arm, so he would mimic her movement.

They were at the rear of the passenger side of the SUV, and she needed to get him to cover on the other side of the vehicle.

When they'd almost cleared the back bumper, another crack ripped through the night air. Breck pitched forward, and Jane used his momentum to move him sideways, out of the line of fire.

The shooter was on the roof of the building they'd just exited, and she relayed this information to Joe. She wanted to reposition and return fire, but her primary objective was the safety of her asset, and he'd just been shot.

She opened the rear door on the driver's side and helped Breck inside, telling him to stay down. He was practically on the floor, which was good.

Sliding behind the wheel, she barely had the engine cranked before she stood on the accelerator.

***

Danny Baker wanted to be on the ground in Los Angeles dressed in tactical gear with the comfort of his gun in his grip. Instead, he was in the air somewhere over the Midwest. He paced the narrow aisle of the jet his sister, Liz, had gifted him with when he got out of the Navy and settled on the West coast.

His fingers fluttered by his sides with nervous

energy as his imagination ran through possible scenarios of tonight's awards ceremony. He checked his watch, and let out a long breath. It was underway.

The safety of one of Hollywood's most famous actors had recently been threatened, and Breck had come to B&B Security for help.

Danny wondered who might be angry enough with Breck to threaten his life. The man was a talented actor, so Danny didn't think Breck would have any trouble getting through the awards ceremony as if nothing were amiss. It would've been best if he'd skipped the function entirely, but the actor's agent had insisted Breck be there to accept if he won. They also thought it was important to maintain the appearance of normalcy, even though things were not normal at all.

At first, Danny had hoped the threats on Breck's life were idle ones, but after the break in, vandalism, and near vehicular homicide, he knew better. The escalation of violence proved the stalker to be dangerous. The home security specialists from B&B had since made Breck's beach house as secure as possible, and he now had a security team near him at all times.

Joe had been handling the situation while Danny dealt with family issues in Georgia. After years of working together, Danny trusted his business partner had things under control. Most of their men were military, two were former Special Forces. Then, there was the woman.

Danny fought back the growl in his throat. She was the newest hire, a former SWAT member from back East. Danny hadn't met her and hated to pre-judge anyone, but women had no business in his business.

Danny refused to open her file, even though he'd had it for several weeks. He was being stubborn about it. She had two strikes against her; she was female and a Yankee. It made his Southern bred testosterone rear up in a bad way.

Breathing out on a huff, he powered up his laptop to look at the file. He needed to know what B&B had gotten into with Jane Dillon.

The picture was a black and white passport photo. Her facial structure was comprised of hard lines, softened by big eyes and full lips.

His protective instincts kicked in and his chest tightened. He didn't like that she was on a potentially dangerous assignment.

It was the principal of the matter. Men protect, women nurture. Dillon would probably shoot Danny on sight if she knew his mind. That thought was reinforced when he read the list of weapons she was trained to use.

"Oh, God."

A moan followed by vomiting got his attention.

Danny shoved the laptop into an empty seat and rushed to the back of the plane.

His sister, Liz, hunched over a small trash can, while seated on the couch. She'd gone to sleep there shortly after takeoff.

He perched next to her and rubbed a big circle on her back, while she spewed her guts out. "Oh, sweetie. Did you not take your motion sickness medicine?"

She spit and shook her head. "I've got my magic wrist bands on."

"Don't think they're working. What can I get you?"

"A new stomach. Mine's on fire." Placing the can on the floor, she put a hand over her upper abdomen.

"Let's get you in a forward facing seat, and I'll grab your toiletry bag. I know you keep a small pharmacy in there." He winked and pulled her from the sofa.

After helping her up the aisle and getting her settled, he returned to the back for supplies. He dumped the puke in the toilet and cleaned the can, in case she needed it again. She probably wouldn't eat grits and eggs again for a while, and breakfast for supper was her favorite.

When he had more than he could carry, he made his way back and knelt next to her seat. "Here you go. Wipe your face."

She took the wet washcloth. "Thank you."

Trading the cloth for a small cup of water, he said, "Rinse and spit it back."

While she did, he popped the top on a can of ginger ale. Once she started sipping the bubbly drink, he dug into her suitcase.

"You packed for a long stay, sister."

"I never know where you're gonna send me next, great-master-of-hiding-people-who-want-to-disappear."

He forced a smile, but inside he wanted to rearrange the face of a certain actor who'd ruined his sister's life.

"Let's see." He held up both of his hands, which were full with an array of medications. "You want blue pills, pink pills, fruity pills, crack, or cocaine?"

She laughed, spitting soda all over him.

He dropped the pills and made an exaggerated show of wiping his face with his entire arm. "Woman, don't make me toss you out the window.

Liz giggled and held her hand open. "Sorry, bro. Give me the antacids."

His butt vibrated as he passed the medicine.

When he checked the screen, the text message from Joe read:

Shots fired. Shooter escaped. Dillon has Stanton. Waiting to hear his condition.

Danny fell back onto his heels. The little knot in his belly erupted into a five-alarm fire.

He held his hand out to his sister. "Save me a few of those."

Chapter Two

"Where are you hit?" With both hands on the steering wheel, Jane glanced over her shoulder.

Breck didn't answer, but dragged himself up to lay on his side in the backseat. His breathing was shallow and ragged. "Back. Can't...breathe."

"Try to slow your breathing, Breck. Think shallow, but count to four to inhale, four to exhale." She reached a hand back to squeeze his arm. "We're on the way to the hospital."

"No." He exhaled loudly. "I mean, I don't think I need it. The vest."

"Keep breathing. I'll pull over to check you in a minute."

Breck counted out loud, like he'd done when learning to dance. Jane smiled at the memory of the arrogant man she'd met the day of their first lesson.

One of the people Jane had befriended upon moving to Los Angeles was Tommy the Dancer, a fellow Philly native. When he'd called her in for help with Breck's dance lessons, Tommy had told her to bring her gun.

Jane pulled into a parking garage and climbed between the front seats. "I'm going to feel your back. It may hurt, but don't hit me because I hit back." She grinned.

"Okay." He kept counting, focused on his breath.

First, she felt the back of his coat until she found the hole. Next, she slipped her hand between the coat and vest and felt the round embedded there. At last, she eased her hand under his T-shirt to feel his skin. He forced air out between his teeth.

"The round is in the vest, not you. You'll be bruised, but you don't have a bullet wound. Thank heaven for Kevlar."

He let out a sigh of relief. "You...You're like G.I. Jane or something?"

A small chuckle escaped her as she removed her hand from his back. "Call me what you will."

"I'll call you my hero. Thank you for rescuing me."

"You're going to be all right." She climbed into the driver's seat. "I'm taking you to a secure location."

"Where?"

"My place." She turned and caught him smiling.

By the time they reached Jane's house, she was starting to feel the adrenaline wane. She needed to examine Breck more closely and report in.

She pulled into her garage and jumped out of the SUV to disarm the alarm. Breck was hauling himself out of the back seat, so she put an arm around him and helped him up the stairs to the door into the house.

"So, this is your place?" Breck glanced around casually, as if he hadn't just been shot.

She nodded and wondered if she should have taken him to headquarters in the office building owned by B&B.

She would after she checked him over, but this was the safest place she knew in L.A. She was perfectly fine being unsupervised and in close proximity with one of the best looking men in Hollywood.

She led him to the guest bathroom. "Take off your coat. I'll be right back."

Stepping into her bedroom, she put her weapons on the dresser. Her next stop was the kitchen for juice. She gripped the handle of the refrigerator door harder, when she realized her hand was shaking.

It'd been a long time since someone had tried to kill her. If she didn't shut those thoughts down and put up her mental walls—think like a man—she would be on the floor in a ball in no time at all.

She inhaled hard and set her jaw.

When she reentered the bathroom, she found Breck poking his finger through the hole in his jacket, eyes wide. "I can't believe someone shot me. What did I do to deserve this?"

"Drink this." She gave him the glass. "It'll help with the shock."

While he drank, she removed the Kevlar vest and placed it in a large plastic bag.

"Let's get your shirt off."

He smirked. "I always knew you wanted to get my clothes off."

Jane smirked back. "If I wanted to see you shirtless, I could just rent one of the dozen movies you've made. I think they write in topless scenes just for you."

"They do." He smiled and raised the hem of his T-shirt.

Instead of staring at his chest and washboard abs, Jane walked around to inspect his back. It was also very well-defined. It wasn't that she didn't appreciate his efforts in the gym—she knew what it took to get a body like that—but they'd been inches from their last day on earth, and she couldn't look at him as a man. The temptation might be too much.

"How does it look?"

She lightly touched the red area just under his right shoulder blade, and goose bumps erupted on his flesh. Her skin did the same, but it was because of the near miss.

Closing her eyes, she choked down the bile coating the back of her throat. He could've been killed.

She exhaled slowly. "Not bad yet. The ribs may be cracked. It'll bruise and be sore to touch. You should ease up on your workouts for a couple of days."

Breck turned and put his hands on either side if her face before he kissed her. She had time to stop him, but she didn't and her pulse quickened. His hands moved to her hips and lifted her off the floor. Her legs automatically wrapped around him, and too late, she realized her mistake.

She wound her arms around his neck even as her head screamed, *Stop kissing your paycheck.* Her body was ready, but she couldn't continue without being honest with him.

She broke the kiss. "Breck, what you're feeling is a result of what happened tonight. Surviving makes you want to live, and sex is a great way to prove you're alive."

"I have to have you, Jane. I've wanted you for too long." He set her on the bathroom counter and removed her tank top.

Later, she'd probably regret not stopping him. But in the moment, she wanted him just as much as he wanted her. She wanted something to make her forget.

Battle lust raged in her blood, and succumbing was the only way to find release. Her heart belonged to someone else, but she could never have him again, so she would take what physical comfort she could get.

Breck carried her into her bedroom and laid her down on the bed. "Let's dance." His voice took on a husky tone that fueled something inside her.

There wasn't a lot of foreplay involved. As soon as Breck rolled the condom on, he was on her...or in her, rather. He came more quickly than she'd anticipated, but not before she turned into a quivering, orgasmic mess herself.

He collapsed his full weight on her in the seconds after release.

When he lifted himself and rolled onto his back, he pulled her close. "How did you do that?"

"Do what?" she asked.

"I haven't come that fast since high school."

"I told you. Danger. Adrenaline speeds things up a bit."

"Are you lying to make me feel better?"

"Would I lie to you?" She sat up. "I have to report in. No one can know about this, Breck. I could lose my job."

His brown eyes narrowed and a wicked gleam flashed. "I won't tell as long as you keep me happy."

"You're blackmailing me for sex? Don't women just throw themselves at you when you walk down the street?"

"Yes, but I don't want them. I want you."

"I could just shoot you myself." She got up and walked into the bathroom.

***

Jane called Joe to report that Breck was secure. She left out the part about him being naked in her bed. Her job had been to guard his body, and she'd done it a little too well.

"We tracked the perpetrator to the roof, but by the time we got there, he'd disappeared—"

"Or she," Jane interrupted.

"Right." Joe paused. "Do you mind keeping him overnight? We're having an apartment put in at the main office for this purpose, but we haven't needed it until now, and it isn't ready. I'll come by tomorrow morning to debrief you both, and since LAPD is involved, I'll take you both in to make statements."

Once she disconnected the call, she took a

moment to think. Breck was the first man she'd slept with since Karl. It'd been over a year and a half since she'd lost him. She hadn't wanted another man until now.

She fisted her hands in her hair and pulled a little as guilt and grief surged through her dead heart. *How do you move forward when you can't let go of the past?*

The explosion that had killed Karl and the rest of their team had landed her in the hospital. She hadn't woken up until two weeks later, after everyone had been buried. Her heart still ached with the loss and the missed opportunity to say goodbye.

She took a deep breath and let it out slowly, reaching deep for the strength she knew was hidden there.

She'd moved to Los Angeles for a fresh start. It was time to say goodbye to the old ghosts. She knew this thing with Breck wouldn't last past tonight, so she made up her mind to enjoy it while she could.

In the bedroom, Breck was stretched out, looking at home, and at the same time, out of place, on her bed. He was the proverbial tall, dark, and handsome. His body was hard and his eyes full of heat.

Those dark eyes watched her every move. "You are the most beautiful thing I've ever seen."

She raised an eyebrow. *Actors.*

"I'm serious." He sat up and moved to the edge of the bed. "Come here."

She walked to him and let him loosen the belt of her robe. He looked at her body with something like admiration. Her body used to be something she admired too, but no more. She held her breath, waiting for the question she knew was coming.

He surprised her by kissing her stomach before he pulled her down to straddle his thighs and took her mouth again. He pushed the robe off of her shoulders. They took their time with each other and found release together.

Afterward, he propped on his elbow and traced patterns on her torso with his fingertip. He skimmed the large scar on her right side. "Can you tell me about this?"

She closed her eyes and swallowed, trying hard not to remember, trying not to see Karl's face in her mind. It was impossible. The scar marked her body as a constant reminder of her loss.

Chapter Three

When Jane awoke the next morning, there was a hand on her left hip, and it didn't belong to her. It took her a moment to orient and remember she had a famous movie star in her bed. She got up carefully, so she wouldn't wake Breck and stood by the bed watching him sleep.

Disappointed by her own lack of professionalism, she was surprised to feel a little dirty. That was new. In the past, her support of women being comfortable with their sexuality had always trumped the right/wrong argument. Men could sleep with whomever they pleased without feeling guilty, and she'd never appreciated double standards in any area. So, why was a battle waging in her mind?

Pushing the disappointing thoughts away, she examined her conquest. The word made her laugh inside. A fine specimen, Breck was all male, all muscle and raw beauty. His dark hair was down over his forehead, and his beard growth was a day old. Not many people got to see him like this.

She preferred this natural look to the overly groomed one he had in his daily life—perfect hair, eyebrows, everything. She'd always been attracted to men who were more rugged, like Karl.

Stop comparing every man to him.

No one had known how in love they were, except his parents. They couldn't tell their co-workers and team members because she'd feared they would remove her from the team. Karl had seniority, and she'd worked her ass off to make that damn team. She hadn't been willing to give it up for love.

After she was released from the hospital following the explosion, she went to pay her respects to Karl's parents. They offered her a box of his belongings, but she only took one thing—his favorite pistol, a custom tactical piece.

She kept it in a safe place and only took it out once in a while. The grip was designed for Karl's large hands, and she couldn't bring herself to change it. For a long time, she'd slept holding onto the grip, trying to remember the feel of his hands. She didn't ever want to forget.

Jane gathered Breck's clothes and put them in the washing machine. Then she went to work out. When she bought the house, she'd set up a home gym on the lower level. She never missed a workout because she had to stay on top of her game to keep up with the men in her field.

After finishing a satisfying sweat session, she showered and dressed before she woke Breck.

She'd hoped he wouldn't join her in the shower; although, she'd fantasized about it. Their night together was over, and today, he would return home or possibly move to a new safe house, if the shooter was still at large.

After kicking the end of the bed, which jarred him awake, she backed a safe distance away to the bedroom door. "Breck, your clothes are drying, and Joe will be here soon."

He yawned and stretched while she tried to ignore the rippling muscles.

"Don't forget, we're friends, not lovers. I like my job, and I need it to pay the bills. Are you a good enough actor to pull off the ruse?" Jane appealed to his vanity.

"I assure you our love affair will be our little secret, Ginger." He sat up and reached for her. "Are you sure you can handle it?"

"If you'd like your hand to remain attached to your arm, I suggest you keep it to yourself." She almost broke into a smile when he dropped his hand to his side.

"I see you're back to being the bad-ass G.I. Jane who surprised and saved me last night. What happened to the woman who rocked my world?"

"She's gone. I've got my game face on." She winked and turned away, refraining from telling him to get over it because she needed his cooperation. Her job security was literally in his hands.

Joe called to say he was approaching, and she opened the second garage door, so he could pull in. It was a protocol she'd suggested for privacy and safety, and Joe had agreed it was a good one. Jane waited at the top of the stairs from the garage for Joe to come around the corner on the lower landing.

"Come in," she said before she noticed he wasn't alone.

She stood aside to allow Joe and the unknown man into her home. The sight of the stranger startled her because of her earlier thought about preferring rugged men.

This man was of a similar height, build, and coloring as Breck, but he was more…unrefined.

When the sexy man and his intoxicating scent invaded her personal space, her hormones surged to life causing her abdomen to tighten. That naughty feeling, like she'd done a bad thing, caught her off guard again.

Was it so terrible to bed one man and then have impure thoughts about another one the morning after? Guys did it all the time, and if she was anything, it was one of the guys.

"Jane Dillon, meet Danny Baker, your other boss," Joe said.

"Pleased to meet you." She offered her usual firm handshake.

When their hands touched, a jolt shot through her, not unlike being shocked. A warm tingle spread from him into her, as his dark green eyes looked into her soul.

His strong jaw dipped with his single nod. With one look, he seemed to know all of her secrets. Her heart raced and her suddenly dry mouth made her remember the coffee she'd made.

Releasing his hand, she motioned for them to

go into the living room. Joe did, but Danny waited for her to go before him.

Heat flared in her chest. That Southern macho crap wasn't going to fly with her.

Joe had warned her that his business partner would be resistant to accepting her due to his old-fashioned ideas. Jane should be used to it by now.

She stared at Danny until he conceded and moved in front of her. Her tenacity had served her well over the years; although, his smirk and simple head shake spoke of his displeasure.

Chapter Four

Danny stared at Jane Dillon a little too long, damn stubborn woman. The black and white photo hadn't done her justice. At about five and a half feet tall with muscle definition everywhere he looked, she was built to handle. Heat had surged through him when they'd touched.

She didn't look like a female weightlifting competitor; instead, she had the lithe, lean, well-defined muscles that come from hard work. Her shoulder length hair was strawberry blonde, and she had the most beautiful green eyes he'd ever seen, even if they were looking at him with defiance.

When he and Joe were seated in the living room, Jane went to get coffee. The moment she entered the room carrying a service tray, Breck Stanton came in wearing nothing but a towel.

"Can you rub this on my back?" Breck held a tube of sports cream. "I can't reach very well."

When Joe and Danny stood, Breck jumped,

dropped the medicine, and took a moment to wipe the surprised look off of his face.

"Joe." Breck shook hands with Danny's partner and then him. "Danny, what's up, man? Long time no see."

"What's this I hear about folks shooting at you, Breck? Let's see where you were hit." Danny kept one eye on Jane, while he noted the baseball-sized bruise on Breck's back.

"Sorry for my state of undress. Jane was nice enough to wash my clothes since I nearly wet myself when somebody shot at me. I've been in enough action movies you'd think I'd be used to it."

"It's different when the bullets are real. I'm glad you're okay, man." Danny sat next to Joe on the couch.

Jane left for a moment and came back with Breck's clothes. She put the cream on his back in front of them. "There's pain reliever in the medicine chest, if you need it."

Breck left to get dressed, and Jane poured coffee from a carafe.

"You're acquainted with Breck?" Jane passed Danny a cup.

Breck returned, pulling his shirt over his head as he spoke. "Yeah, Danny trained me for some fight scenes a few years back. He's a damn good fighter. That's how I knew to call B&B when the threats started."

Jane handed a plastic bag full of Kevlar to Joe. "Here's the round. My fingerprints will be on it, but if LAPD can get another one, we might have a lead."

Danny gritted his teeth as he examined the vest.

"Good work, Jane," Joe said. "Listen, we want to debrief you separately. Is there someplace we can go?"

The two of them went into another room.

Then Danny motioned for Breck to sit. "Tell me what happened."

Breck started his account from the time he heard the first shot. "When she shoved me into that broom closet, I thought I was going to vomit. She took off the vest she was wearing and put it on me. Thank God, or I might be dead right now."

"Was she wearing the vest over or under her shirt?" Danny tilted his head to one side.

"I don't know." Breck hesitated like he was reaching into his memory to find the answer. "I was in shock. Was she not supposed to give me her vest?"

"No, she wasn't, but if she hadn't, like you said, you'd probably be dead."

"But...she could have been killed." Breck grabbed the sides of the chair as the realization hit him. "She put herself in danger to save me."

"It was her job to protect you. I'd say she succeeded." Danny sipped his coffee and tried not to grind his teeth. *Damn, woman.* "Breck, do you have feelings for Jane?"

"She's my guardian angel. I'd propose if she weren't a lesbian."

The swallow of coffee Danny had been taking went down the wrong pipe, and he coughed violently.

Breck pounded his back. "Trust me, man. I asked her out months ago, but she shot me down. Our friend Tommy told me she was getting over losing her partner. Plus, she's never shown any interest in me, and straight women can't resist me."

When Jane returned from the other room, Danny took his cue.

"We'll be back in a few." He joined Joe at the dining table. "Why'd she give him her vest?"

"Instinct." Joe raised an eyebrow.

Danny clenched his fists. "That's all she said? It's a protocol breach."

"She pointed out that Stanton getting killed on our watch would've been bad for business."

Danny relaxed his hands. "That's true, but I still don't like it."

"You or I might've done the same thing. I gave her a warning. Next time, she'll wear two vests."

"There won't be a next time if I have anything to say about it." Danny stood and returned to the living room where he found Breck, looking much too relaxed on Jane's couch, channel surfing.

They laid out the plan for going to the police station, so Breck and Jane could give official statements.

"Joe and I will drive you and escort you into the station. We'll *all* wear Kevlar." He gave Jane a pointed look.

"Is that necessary?" Breck asked.

"The shooter is still out there. He *shouldn't* know where you'll be, but it's better to be safe than sorry."

"Or *she*," Jane said.

Danny dismissed her idea. "Women kill quietly; they don't shoot large caliber weapons."

"You must not know many women." Her voice was hard.

Danny pressed his lips into a tight line to contain his smile. He'd recently spent several months in close quarters with his step-mom, three step-sisters, and three nieces. The women he was closest to could shoot anything you put in their hands. Any Southern woman worth her salt could.

"We need to address where you should go from there, Breck." Joe was playing peacemaker. "We don't advise you to return home. If you can lay low for a couple of days, it'll give the police time to see if they can get prints or a trace on the ammo."

"I start filming a Western in New Mexico in two weeks." Breck propped his elbows on his legs.

"We'd normally put you up at Danny's place, but he currently has a guest," Joe said. "Jane, would it be all right if Breck stayed here with you for a couple of days?"

Danny didn't like the plan, but he hadn't come up with a viable alternative yet. The corner of Breck's mouth twitched at the suggestion, confirming Danny's instincts. When he looked at Jane, her expression was neutral.

"I need to get extra supplies, food. Breck needs clothes and toiletries."

"We can work that out," Joe said. "We'll compensate you for expenses incurred during this assignment."

"I'll go to Breck's place later," Danny said. "You can make a list of what you'd like me to pick up."

Chair legs scraped across the hardwood floor as Jane stood and started pacing, while she looked at Danny with narrowed eyes.

She was starting to irritate him, and it showed in his voice. "If you've got something to say, Dillon, spit it out."

"If you plan to draw out the shooter by sending a body double into Breck's place, then don't forget your body armor."

"What the hell are you talking about?" Danny stood and ran his hand through his hair. *Crazy ass woman.*

"I see what she means," Joe said. "Danny, go stand next to Breck."

The men moved next to each other.

"Danny, you could be his body double. You're the same height and build. You have the same dark hair and olive skin. It's a great idea, Jane."

"I want in," she said.

Danny and Breck spoke in unison. "No!"

Her eyebrows rose as she looked from them to Joe, causing Danny's temper to flare.

"We'll see." Joe looked apologetic.

Jane dropped her arms to her sides. "Looks like I still have to prove myself to some people. Nothing new. I'll take care of Breck like I have since the first infrared signature flashed last night."

Danny nearly flinched from the weight of the screw-you stare she aimed at him. He had three sisters and considered himself an equal rights kind of guy, for the most part. But he was also a Southern gentleman, and they kept their women out of danger. There were some jobs women shouldn't do, not that they couldn't do them, they just shouldn't.

He could hear Liz in his head. *"Yeah, Danny, keep the little woman pregnant and in the kitchen."*

That thought was especially difficult because that sister, who was currently hiding out at his place, wasn't married and couldn't have children.

"Taking care of me is a good plan, Ginger." Breck moved to put an arm around Jane.

Danny didn't like that option either. Seeing Breck touch her made his stomach burn.

Chapter Five

The drive to the police station was tense. It was stupid to be irritated because Danny had called her by her last name. It was professional, which meant it wasn't personal. It let her know her place, and she wanted to drive her fist through his chiseled jaw.

Joe drove and Danny rode in front, so they could discuss plans for a visit to Breck's place later in the day. Breck was in the back next to Jane, bouncing his knee and fidgeting.

"Do you remember that hip-hop dance we worked on?" Jane asked. She'd used hip-hop as a reward for his learning to waltz without grumbling every other step.

"I'll never forget it."

"I have a dance game for Xbox we can play later. You'll love it."

He nodded, but turned to look out the window. She put her hand on his and squeezed. She knew all too well how long it took to forget someone wanted

29

you dead.

"Let's do the dance, now, together, in our heads. Let's talk through it," she said.

His eyes were questioning as he grinned. "Okay."

She snapped her fingers. "Five, six, seven, eight…"

They did small foot movements, a few hops in their seats, as much as the seatbelts would allow, and a few hand movements, too. When Breck laughed, she knew it was working.

"It's hard to shake your ass when it's belted down to the car seat, huh?" She chortled.

"I can't do the routine without hearing your voice in my head. *Get funky.*" He mocked her.

"I didn't even realize I say stupid stuff like that." She covered her face.

"You get into it, Ginger. That's the great thing about you. You're so…passionate."

When he said the word *passionate*, she expected a cricket to chirp in the silence which followed. Joe and Danny looked back at them.

"About the dance, guys. You should see Jane do her thing. Tommy has an open floor night every week."

Jane cussed under her breath. It made them look guiltier, Breck trying to explain it away.

Too soon, they were parking. Danny took point, and Joe took the rear as they escorted Breck and Jane into the precinct. They made it in and out with no problems.

Jane was on her guard after having her motives and expertise questioned by the detectives. Not surprisingly, they'd asked inappropriate questions, like, "How was it having Breck Stanton under your roof?"

To which she'd smirked and answered, "Better than you can even imagine... He does dishes." *Bastards*. To make it worse, Danny had listened to her statement, never stood up for her, and now looked at her with pity.

Clenching her fists, she let out a long, slow breath. He better stay far away or she might be tempted to elbow the look right off his face.

On the drive back to Jane's house, Danny and Joe made plans to put a team together to stake out Breck's place. Danny was going to go in, pretending to be Breck, to see if anyone shot at him.

"Brave," Breck whispered to Jane.

"Or stupid. We walk a fine line between the two sometimes."

Breck took her hand and made circles on her palm. She started to pull away, but it was nice to be touched.

"If the shooter is there, they have a great opportunity to get her," Jane said.

"I don't want Danny to get shot, but I do want this nightmare to be over. Then, I'll take you out dancing to celebrate."

Jane didn't say no. Dancing wasn't the same thing as a date in her mind, but she would explain that to Breck later. Their night together had been wonderful, a turning point for her, but she had no intention of dating him.

***

All the team members were in position when

31

Danny arrived at Breck's place. A limo service had picked Breck up for the awards ceremony, so Danny arrived in a cab. He was wearing Breck's black coat with the hole in the back where the bullet had pierced it. Underneath, he wore Kevlar.

He didn't want to get shot. Who did? But the sooner they caught the shooter, the sooner Breck would be out of Jane's house. No matter what Breck said, Danny didn't think Jane was gay, and he sensed something wasn't above board.

The first thing Danny did after entering the house, besides force himself to breathe, was check the security system. Everything was working properly. He took the detailed list of items Breck had requested from his pocket, found a duffle bag, and started packing.

His thoughts centered on Jane. He'd learned dancing was the way to her heart, not that he wanted to go there, but it was something she cared about.

Dancing always reminded him of happy times with his mama, before she got sick. In his earliest childhood memory, he was sitting on the floor, surrounded by Lincoln Logs, watching his parents dance around the living room. When he was about five, he told his mama he wanted to dance with her, too. She taught him the steps, and every week, until she was too sick, they'd danced. His dad always pretended to be a little jealous and would cut in. Danny would give them a few minutes and then cut back in. It was a fun game they'd played.

After her death, while watching his father grieve, he'd made up his mind he would never let himself fall in love. It was too painful when the one you loved went away.

He didn't dance again for several years, until he got new sisters who were dancers. His dad had practically threatened to take Danny's life if he didn't help teach the girls the ballroom steps his mama had taught him.

Danny mentally shook off the thoughts and returned to the task at hand. An OCD person must have organized Breck's closet and dresser, because everything he asked for was right where it ought to be. When Danny's fingers gripped the black dancing shoes with the suede outsole, his thoughts returned to Jane. He wondered how she moved, and the thought disturbed him.

He refocused on how Jane was treated at the police station. He'd watched her defenses go higher with every question of her ability and integrity. Danny was sympathetic, but he'd stopped himself from reaching out to her. His gut told him she would misinterpret it for pity, and he'd regret it.

When he was ready to leave Breck's house, he called Joe for a pickup. They'd decided Danny leaving in Breck's Porsche would draw too much attention.

He made it safely into Joe's SUV and breathed a sigh of relief when no one tried to kill him.

Arriving at Jane's house, Joe pulled into her garage and left the car running while Danny took Breck's bag up to the door.

"Was there any sign of the shooter?" Breck asked.

"None. We should know more when the

ballistics report comes back."

Breck took his bag and headed for one of Jane's guest bedrooms.

Danny stopped on the top step and turned back to Jane. "I'll be here at nine in the morning to train with Stanton. Are you gonna be okay with him here by yourself?"

"Whether you choose to accept it or not, I *am* capable of taking care of myself and Breck."

Even as the faint smell of something like honeysuckle hung in the air causing desire to course through him, the door slammed with a finality that stung like a slap on the face.

Damn woman.

Chapter Six

Jane regretted letting Danny Baker know he'd gotten to her. She'd grown weary of the macho bull which always followed her, like not being allowed on the mission because she was a delicate female. When she was working, she was doing her part. On the sidelines, she had time to think and worry about everything that could go wrong. Babysitting Breck was not the assignment she wanted, but it was what she was stuck with.

Deciding she might as well make the most of it, she turned the music up, grabbed Breck, and they danced until they dropped.

When Breck collapsed to the floor, pulled her down to him, and kissed her, she let herself melt into the moment, until Danny's face intruded into her thoughts. She pushed away and rolled to her feet.

"I'm sorry, Breck. I can't. I shouldn't have done it last night. If you follow through on your threat and tell my bosses, I'll just find another job."

He stood and walked over to her, placing his hands on her shoulders. "Jane, I would never tell anyone about us without your permission. Do you regret it?"

Jane hesitated for a moment, while she decided which approach to take. Breck had been honest with her. She owed him the same respect. "No. Last night was great, but it was unprofessional of me to let it happen."

"You didn't do it by yourself. In fact, you didn't start it. I did."

"Breck, I'm just beginning to put my past behind me. I haven't fully recovered from it." She motioned to her right side. "I have scars you can see and ones you can't."

He ran his hands down her arms until he squeezed her fingers. "I'm not going to push you. I can't pretend to know what you've suffered, but I care about you. I'd like to be here for you, if you'll let me."

Her throat closed and her eyes stung as she dropped her head. "Thank you."

She didn't say more. She couldn't tell him the other reason she wouldn't take him back to her bed was Danny Baker.

***

Jane let her house guest sleep in, so she could work out and shower before Danny arrived. When Danny texted her he was on his way, she woke Breck.

"You should work out with us," Breck said.

"No thanks, I better stay away from your body

double. The two of you together might send me over the edge." *And not in a good way*.

"What's up with you and Danny?" Breck eyed her with suspicion.

"I'd like to choke the life out of him." She mimicked the motion with her hands.

"He's a good guy."

"If you say so."

Jane put together a light lunch for the three of them, unsure if Danny would stick around to eat it. She hoped he wouldn't, but she didn't want to be inhospitable.

Being around him made her uncomfortable for several reasons. The least of which was the way her body screamed in wanting. Imagining his hips moving in perfect rhythm with hers.

Must be pheromones, she reasoned with herself.

Seated at the dining table, her lunch already eaten, she looked up when Breck and Danny came into the kitchen.

"You cooked?" Breck asked.

She closed her book and stood, forcing a smile. "Baker, you're welcome to stay."

"This looks fantastic." Breck settled into a chair. "If it tastes as good, I'm going to have to marry you."

"Easy, I might say yes." She fought an eye twitch and played it off as a wink before she cleared her plate from the table, leaving the men to dine without her.

***

After lunch, Danny waited for Breck to excuse

himself to the shower, so he could talk to Jane alone. He didn't understand why he was so bothered by her easy camaraderie with Breck. As the answer flashed in his mind like a bright green neon sign, he unclenched his teeth.

He had to let the jealousy go and gain some footing with his employee. "My sister is visiting from out of town. We'd like you and Breck to come over for dinner tonight."

A mask of neutrality looked back at him from where she stood, a hip leaning on the edge of the kitchen island. "Liz?"

"I guess you read the rags."

She tilted her head and examined him. "I'm surprised she didn't tell you I escorted her from LAX to your place a few months ago."

That was news, but he kept his face disinterested. "Good, then you won't need directions."

"Do you think it's wise? Since Breck is still in danger and in hiding."

"Your house and mine are the safest places he can be. Liz is trustworthy, especially after all she's been through. What about Stanton?"

"With what Breck is going through himself, I think he'll keep his mouth shut. He'll probably also be glad to have someone to look at besides me." An almost laugh escaped her lips as she sat opposite him.

"I doubt that, but I'm sure Liz is tired of my ugly mug." He grinned.

Jane propped her elbows on the table. "I don't believe everything I read. Would you mind telling me about her situation?"

Relieved at her concern, Danny pushed his chair away from the table, so he could stretch out his legs and not kick her. He let out a long breath and began his tale, trying to include only the most basic details. Brevity was a throwback from his service in the Navy. Already, he'd noted it was a habit of hers, too.

"Liz dated Ian Clarke for a few months. I introduced them. When the tabloids found out about her money, they made Ian look like he was with her for that reason alone." Danny shook his head. "No one could get that a celebrity would love her for who she was, not because of what she could give him."

A cute little crease formed between her eyes. "Are you sure he wasn't with her because of it?"

He ground his teeth. At this rate, he'd have no enamel left by tomorrow. Everyone asked, so he wasn't angry with her specifically. "Ian didn't know about her money."

"But he looked bad in the press and had to break it off with her?" Jane played with the edge of the placemat, rubbing the fabric between her thumbs and forefingers.

"Yeah, the press is still after her. And you wouldn't believe how aggressively people ask for money if they think you have more than you need. I'm trying to keep her off the grid. Eventually, I hope to get her resettled in a new place, possibly with a slightly altered identity."

"She knows about Breck's situation?"

"I mentioned the predicament, but no names.

She suggested we invite you to dinner, so none of us would get bored with each other."

Jane's lips turned up at the corners. He'd seen her smile at Breck, but this one was for him. Heat radiated through his chest.

Dazzled. It was the strangest thing for him to think because he'd never felt it before. That's what the wide stretch of her full lips, exposing even white teeth, did to him.

He cleared his throat. "Will you explain things to Breck? He trusts you, and I think he has a thing for you."

"No, he doesn't...have a *thing* for me. Haven't you heard about me?" She cocked an eyebrow.

***

When Jane called to let Danny know she was approaching, he opened the third garage bay, so she could pull in.

Danny tucked his shirt in. "I really got off on the wrong foot with this one, Lizabelle. Wish me luck."

"You don't need luck, brother. Just be yourself."

"I think being myself is what caused the problem." Aiming a mix between a grin and a grimace at Liz, he crossed his eyes.

Danny showed Jane and Breck around the basement/garage level, which had a workout area, before bringing them upstairs to introduce them to his sister.

"Liz, you've met Jane Dillon, and this is Breck Stanton."

Liz hugged Jane. "I don't remember if I

thanked you for helping me that day. I was in a daze."

"That's why they pay me the big bucks. You've changed your hair." Jane gestured to the former red head's blonde locks.

"Yeah, a new do to throw the hounds off my trail." She patted her hair.

As soon as Liz shook Breck's hand, he started working his charm with effusive compliments.

The man has no shame. Danny twisted his lips until Jane caught him. Thankfully, Liz was a no bullshit kind of gal.

"Can I have a quick tour?" Jane asked, interrupting his thoughts. "I like to know my way out of a place."

Appreciating her training, Danny gave her the tour.

"Can I get you a beer?" Danny asked her as they returned to the kitchen.

She nodded.

A woman of few words.

Breck asked Danny to show him his collection of weapons, some of which he'd already seen downstairs.

"You wanna come?" Danny asked Jane.

Her eyes widened at the offer before her face relaxed. "No, thank you."

Danny tried not to frown as he led Breck downstairs. He was hoping for an opportunity to connect with Jane, and he was sure weapons would do it.

Chapter Seven

"How can I help?" Jane asked when she and Liz were alone in the kitchen.

"Don't you want to see Danny's toys?" Liz smiled from her place at the counter.

"I've got my own." Jane washed her hands at the kitchen sink.

"Well, I'm making spaghetti and am trying to get this Italian sausage out of the casing, so I can brown it, but it's giving me a time." Liz paled and then turned a little green. "I think I'm gonna be sick." She covered her mouth and ran out of the room.

Jane was not the motherly type because she herself had never been mothered, so rather than follow the sick woman she opened drawers and cabinets to get acquainted with the kitchen. She found an apron, put it on, and finished the sausage.

When the water for the pasta started to boil, she added the spaghetti. Vegetables were on a side counter, so she began to prepare salads on four small plates.

Liz returned to the kitchen. "Sorry about that. I don't know what's wrong with me." She puffed out a breath that made her bangs flutter. "Yeah, I do. You know about my breakup, right?"

Jane nodded. "I'm sorry you had to go through that, especially so publicly."

"It's my own fault. I'm not always such a mess. After my divorce, I couldn't eat, and I lost a lot of weight. This time, I can't stop eating. I'm gaining weight, and I'm nauseated all the time." She wiped at a stray tear. "Broken hearts suck."

Jane paused in the middle of slicing a tomato. "Is there a possibility you could be pregnant?"

"No chance of that. I couldn't get pregnant when I was married years ago. The doctors told me it was highly unlikely I could conceive naturally."

"But not impossible." Jane raised an eyebrow.

Liz gasped and raised her fingers to her lips. "I can't be. It just isn't poss— It's just my luck actually—get dumped for something stupid and find out I'm miraculously pregnant." Another tear made its way down her cheek.

"Do you want me to get your brother?" Jane wasn't good with tears.

Liz shook her head from side to side as her big blue eyes overflowed. "It's not possible; it can't be." She wiped her face with her hand. "He doesn't even want kids."

"I thought he married that model because she's pregnant."

Liz pointed to the back door. "They live right

over there. Backyard neighbors." She let out a humorless laugh before she covered her face, sobbing uncontrollably.

Jane went into medic mode, treat what you can. She surveyed the refrigerator for something sugary without caffeine. In a moment, she had the shaken woman sipping orange juice. "What can I do?"

"Please don't say anything to Danny, not until I know for sure." She slurped the juice and wiped her eyes with a paper towel. "Would you help me, Jane? Can you get me a home pregnancy test? Maybe I can come to your house with Danny tomorrow and take it while he and Breck work out?"

Jane didn't like getting in the middle of other people's problems, but her heart went out to Liz. She'd never wanted kids herself, but when the surgeon who'd removed the shrapnel from her right side told her she had ovary damage, she was surprised to feel like she'd lost something—an opportunity maybe.

She'd lost it anyway, when she lost Karl.

Plus, if Danny knew Liz might be pregnant, he'd just assign Jane to go get a pregnancy test anyway. He'd think it was a fitting assignment for a woman. *The jerk.*

When Danny returned from showing off his toys to Breck, dinner was on the table, and Jane and Liz were sitting at the bar talking.

"Why didn't you come get us?" Danny asked Liz.

"We're just having some girl talk." Liz stood to get salad dressing out of the fridge.

44

"You been crying?" Danny spoke in a low voice to his sister.

Jane moved away, so it wouldn't seem like she was eavesdropping, but she did wonder how a tough guy like Danny would handle a crying woman.

"Listen, I know you need someone to talk to, but Jane might demand a pay raise for having to listen to girly problems. She's so tough I bet she's the heartbreaker where she comes from," Danny said.

Sarcasm and distraction. *Typical*. Men didn't address emotional problems head on. But, according to her therapist, neither did she.

"Jane wouldn't do that, but if she did, I'd pay her a bonus or something." Liz folded and refolded the hand towel by the sink.

"She didn't hit on you, did she?" Danny's voice was a loud whisper.

Steam was coming out of Jane's ears, so she was glad Breck came into the room to distract her. If she listened to Danny any longer, she might pour hot Bolognese sauce on his handsome head.

***

The next day, Danny observed his sister and Jane interact as they made lunch. Liz was relaxed; a state he hadn't seen her in for a long time. He credited Jane for that and wondered what her secret was?

He hadn't really thought Jane was hitting on Liz, and his sister reminded him the sexual orientation of his employees was none of his business. Normally, he would agree, but since Jane had Breck in her house, it concerned him for reasons he didn't want to explore.

Danny couldn't ignore the distance Jane maintained between herself and him. She was probably still upset with him from their first meeting when he'd told her she couldn't go to Breck's house with the team. Some women could really hold a grudge.

He wanted the same easy relationship everyone else shared with her, and he wanted another smile. The thought of it made his heart rate pick up.

Watching the women together gave him an idea.

If Jane knew his real motivation, she would shoot him. His plan would help Liz, with the added benefit of getting Breck out of Jane's house. He would run the idea by Liz first. Then he could approach Jane about her new assignment.

It was good to be the boss. One corner of his mouth turned up as he sipped water from a bottle.

On the drive home, Danny cleared his throat. "You and Jane get along all right?"

The dreamy look on Liz's face faded when she turned to him, brows furrowed. "Yeah. Why?"

"I'm working out your future. At least for the next few months until people stop coming out of the woodwork for a story or a handout." He pulled the car into the garage.

"Before you make too many plans, there's something I should tell you." She wiped her eyes.

He hated it when she cried, and she'd been doing way too much of that lately. He ought to march across the yard and make Ian Clarke cry like a little girl. "Bastard."

Her eyes widened. "What?"

"Nothing, I'm pissed off on your behalf. What is it? What do you want to tell me?"

She swallowed hard. "I'm pregnant."

"Shut the hell up." He took the keys out of the ignition and got out of the truck.

When she didn't follow, he halted his forward progression toward the kitchen and turned back. Her shoulders shook violently, her face in her hands. He opened the door and wrapped his arms around her.

"Lizabelle, I'm sorry. I just know you've always wanted kids and couldn't have them. I thought you were teasing me." He patted her head. "What makes you think you're pregnant?"

She struggled to catch her breath. "The three different pregnancy tests I took at Jane's house."

His body tensed. "Jane had pregnancy tests at her house? Why?"

"Because she suspected yesterday and I asked her to get them for me. I didn't want to upset anyone...you, if there was nothing to it." Her breath hitched again.

"Well, this is great. I'm gonna be an uncle...again." He hugged her tighter before he cleared his throat. "When you're ready to tell Ian, I'll be by your side."

She shook her head and pulled away. "I'm not telling Ian. Ever." She locked her teeth together and pushed past him to get out of the truck.

"Liz, be reasonable." He followed her into the house.

"Don't talk to me like I'm an irrational female you're trying to make see sense." She pointed to the

47

back wall of the house. "That man doesn't want children. He's already got one on the way he didn't want to begin with. I'm not about to show up with more bad news for him. Also, I don't want my kid to know her father didn't want her. Jane agrees with me."

Danny clenched his fists. "She does, does she? We'll just see about that. I'll be back." On his way out, he slammed the door.

He broke all traffic laws to get to Jane's. He was angry with her for going behind his back and intended to give her a piece of his mind. At a stop light, he texted to let her know he was on the way.

He pulled into the open garage, and when he got out of his truck, he heard Jane and Breck in the adjoining rec room/home gym. There was a lot of open floor space, which was why he could train with Breck there, but Jane and Breck were dancing together, and his temper flared past the boiling point. How could she be dancing at a time like this?

"I need to speak with you privately," Danny demanded, wondering where the normally nice, calm guy that ruled his brain had gone.

"Yell if you need me." Breck turned to go upstairs.

When the door at the top of the stairs closed, Danny laid into her. "You knew about my sister? *My* sister."

She nodded.

"Answer me dammit. Use your voice."

She crossed her arms over her chest. "Yes."

"Talk to me before I rip your fucking head off," Danny said through clenched teeth.

Jane gave him a half smile and opened her arms. "Take your best shot."

He clenched his fists and wished Breck was back down there because he *would* take a swing at Breck, but there was no way Danny would take a swing at a woman. His mama would roll over in her grave.

It caught him completely off guard when Jane attacked.

***

Even though he was itching for a fight, Jane knew Danny wouldn't come after her, so she made the first move. She centered her mind and went into combat mode.

When she punched him in the stomach, his breath exploded out of his lungs, heating her face. She almost laughed at the shocked expression on his face.

At first, all he could do was back up and block her punches and kicks. It wasn't long before he started giving it back though. In her mind, it played in slow motion like the *Crouching Tiger* movie.

She smiled inside as the adrenaline pumped at an accelerated rate through her system. If he got his hands on her, he could take her down, so she had to use her lighter weight and speed to wear him down. Judging by the sweat on his forehead, it was working.

She ran at him, and at the last moment stepped right, grabbed onto his arm, and vaulted herself up until her legs wrapped around his neck, and she rolled him onto the ground. When she tried to get up, he grabbed her left foot, and she flipped onto her back and kicked him hard in the chest with her right foot. He staggered and landed on his back before he rolled to his feet in a crouch.

Breathing heavy from exertion, Danny's broad chest expanded and collapsed with the effort. Jane knew the hit he'd just taken had effectively knocked the air out of his lungs. She wasn't really trying to hurt him, but she was trying to distract him. If he was thinking about how to survive, to block, to move, to bob and weave, and to keep Jane's fists and feet off of him, then he wouldn't worry about his sister.

She dropped lower in her fighter's stance and rocked side to side. "Have you had enough? Or do you want some more?"

***

Danny's smile spread slowly across his face as he took in her relaxed guard. *Damn, she was hotter than the hinges on the doors of hell.*

His lungs burned, but he licked his lips. "More."

A new respect for Jane bloomed in his heart. Not only because she could hold her own in hand-to-hand, but because she'd known what he needed, even when he hadn't.

He concentrated on the fight. Seeing her in action was a thing of beauty. If he could get his hands on her, he could make her submit, but damn, she was fast. She kept surprising him with drop moves and rolls. Finally, just when he thought his lungs would explode, he was able to grab onto her block and he had her. He pinned her beneath him and propped his elbows on either side of her head.

The rise and fall of her chest against his made him forget why he was there.

Her breathing was labored. "Your sister is going to need you fighting in her corner. You should respect her wishes."

The sound of clapping hands made them turn their heads to find Breck had been watching. "So that's how the pros do it? Impressive."

Danny released her, and she rolled away onto her feet.

"I'm glad you're on my side, Ginger." Breck took the last few stairs and moved to stand beside her.

"Hey, I'm on your side too." Danny feigned offense.

"I know, and I'm grateful for you both, but you have to admit, she's a whole lot prettier than you are, man."

"I can't admit that. Sexual harassment laws and all. You need to watch yourself too, Stanton. You make her mad, she might accuse you of something."

Breck slung his arm over her shoulders. "She's my dance partner. I can say nice things without getting in trouble."

Danny had never been jealous of anyone like he was of Breck. "When you come for dinner tonight, bring your things, Breck. You're bunking with me, and Liz is coming to stay here." He turned to Jane. "I hope that's okay since you seem to be my sister's new confidant."

Her lips pressed into a tight line. "Fine. I'm surprised you parked her next door to the Clarkes and expected her to get over it."

"What are you accusing me of?" Danny wished his voice wasn't so harsh.

"Of being a man. You can't deny it, can you?" She blinked her eyelashes in an exaggerated manner.

Infuriated, Danny spun on his heel and left before he said something he couldn't take back. The woman was going to push him too far.

Chapter Eight

After Danny left, Jane couldn't stop thinking about him. Not only how they'd sparred, but the weight and heat of his body when he'd pinned her. His chest had heaved against her as he'd struggled to catch his breath, and her body had reacted with a surge of heat between her thighs.

She needed to stop having inappropriate thoughts about her boss. That was not part of her plan.

For her own heart's sake, she needed to be angry with Danny. She'd pretended to be, but she wasn't. Seeing how much he cared about his sister touched a place deep inside her that had long been closed off.

Love was a basic human need that came after survival and security in Maslow's hierarchy. She hadn't wanted to love or be loved in so long she'd thought that part of her was dead. Apparently, it had only been sleeping and Danny had awoken it.

Instinct had kicked in when she'd seen him. Judging from what Liz had told Jane while they'd prepared lunch, he was upset about Liz's situation, afraid at the prospect of her raising a baby by herself and keeping it secret from the press and most of all, Ian Clarke. Jane preferred Danny take out his frustrations on her, instead of Liz. Jane could handle it, but she would only put up with it for so long.

She understood Danny's position, but she also knew Liz needed all the support she could get. To Jane's surprise, she wanted to help Liz if she could. Also to her surprise, Breck didn't argue about being moved to Danny's house.

Hoping Breck was as good at keeping secrets as she was, Jane had to trust him to keep theirs. If her bosses ever found out, she doubted the *heat-of-the-battle-lust-theory* would justify her actions in their eyes. She didn't want to lose her job, but she'd made her bed, and she was man enough to face the consequences.

On the way to Danny's house, Breck took her hand. "I'm going to miss you, Ginger. Don't forget, when this is over, we're going dancing."

"It's a date." She squeezed his fingers.

Breck glowed and she liked seeing him happy.

"Does it bother you that I'm famous?"

"You're just Breck to me. Your fame doesn't intimidate me; although, it isn't something I desire for myself."

A tight, closed-lip smile stretched his mouth before he turned to look out the window. Jane thought she'd made him unhappy, but she didn't want to lead him on.

When they arrived, Danny held out a beer to her. "Peace offering. I was an ass."

She took the bottle. "You were upset, but I'm happy to put you in your place anytime."

He tilted his head and gave her a crooked grin. "Well, I guess somebody needs to. I'm also sorry I used the F-word."

Jane felt the corners of her mouth turn up. His contrite grin looked good on him. "Are you kidding me right now? Philly native." She pointed the beer bottle toward her chest. "The founding fathers invented the F-word in my town."

"Still, my mama taught me better." He sipped his beer.

Her heart skittered in her chest before resuming its rhythm. His apology was sincere, and instead of making him look weak in her eyes, it made him look stronger. That low belly thing was happening again. She turned to help Liz with dinner.

Danny's phone rang, and he excused himself to answer. When he returned, he ran his fingers through his hair, making it stand on end. "Incoming."

"What?" Jane asked at the same time Liz asked, "Who?" They laughed together.

"My best friend, Jason, has decided to pay a surprise visit. He's also Liz's ex-husband."

"Twisted," Breck said.

"He's on his way here? Now?" Liz looked distressed.

Danny put his hands on his sister's shoulders. "Relax. He doesn't have to know anything." He looked at Jane. "The quick and dirty of it is that Jason cheated on Liz, they split up, and now's she's forgiven him, but they aren't getting back together."

"Forgiven, not forgotten." Liz's shoulders rose and fell with shallow inhalations.

Jane put her hand on Liz's arm. "Take a deep breath. You're still coming with me tonight. Breck, you'll come with us. We need a cover story."

"I'm training with Danny," Breck said. "Jane, you're my woman. We're taking Liz out tonight to introduce her to a friend. Tommy the Dancer."

The doorbell rang. They were out of time.

***

Danny wanted to punch his best friend in the throat for showing up like this, like he'd wanted to do for years after Jason betrayed Liz. If it weren't for the extenuating circumstances involved, Danny couldn't promise he'd ever let it go. But he had eventually accepted Jason's apology, with coaxing from Liz.

Danny remembered his manners and pasted a smile on his face as he opened the door. "What a surprise?"

Jason was accompanied by his new girlfriend, Roxanne.

"I hope we're not imposing," she said.

"Never. Jason is family and always welcome." Danny helped them with their luggage and showed them to a guest bedroom.

He wished he had a dose of Yankee directness, but he didn't want to be rude to the new girl. He offered them separate bedrooms, but the look Jason shot him let him know they were past that point in their relationship.

They went to the kitchen and Danny made introductions.

Upon meeting the famous Breck Stanton, Jason acted impressed and Roxanne seemed shy.

"Ole' Danny, rubbin' elbows with the big dawgs, huh, Lizabelle?" Jason punched Liz in the arm.

"Nice accent. Where are you guys from again?" Jane asked.

"Georgia," Jason said. "And where are you from?"

Breck answered for her. "Ginger is what you Southern boys might call a *Damn Yankee*. She's from Philly."

"Ginger?" Roxanne asked. "I thought your name was Jane."

"Forgive me for confusing you," Breck said. "I call Jane, Ginger, after Ginger Rogers. She's a dance instructor. That's how we met. She helped me get ready for a movie."

"Roxy and I watched that movie the other day," Jason said. "Not bad for a chick flick. Of course, I like your *shoot 'em ups* better."

Let the BS roll, Danny thought. He also thought about chopping Breck's hands off because he kept putting them on Jane.

Danny's phone rang, and he excused himself again.

Joe was calling with good news, so he texted Jane. *Ballistics came back. Partial print. Arrest made. Stanton can sleep in his own bed tonight.*

Danny went back into the kitchen, wondering

how they could let Breck know without alerting everyone else.

Jane held up her phone. "Look, Breck. Tommy texted to say he might be late tonight."

Letting his acting go when he saw the news, Breck picked Jane up and spun her around. Danny had to look away.

Breck recovered his faux pas. "Don't worry, Liz, he's still coming. Until he gets there, I'll alternate dances between you and Ginger."

"Where are y'all goin'?" Jason asked.

"Dancing." Breck spun Jane around and dipped her.

Danny locked his jaw down, but couldn't not watch the way Breck and Jane moved together.

"We should go, Roxy. It'll be fun," Jason said. "Why don't we go to the bar where Danny's friends play?"

"We're going somewhere else first," Liz said, "but maybe we can meet you guys and Danny there later."

There was a knock at the back door.

Shit. What now? Danny prayed it wasn't Ian Clarke and almost suggested Liz hide.

Jason took a step toward the door and bowed his chest. He must've been thinking the same thing.

Danny opened the door to find Emma Stuart, Ian's new wife, standing there with a hand on her bony-ass hip.

She looked past Danny to Liz. "I knew you'd be here trying to move back in on Ian." She walked toward Liz, pointing a finger at her. "He's mine. We're having a baby together. You stay away."

Jane slid in between them. "Hi, I'm Liz's bodyguard. If you so much as twitch in her direction again, I'll take great pleasure in breaking all fourteen bones in your face."

"Ooh." Jason sounded like a middle school boy. "The fact that she knows how many bones are in your face makes me think she can follow through."

"Besides," Breck moved to put an arm around Liz, "she doesn't want Ian anymore when she can have all this." He gestured the length of his body, and Emma's pupils dilated as she stared, open-mouthed. "Go away, Emma."

Emma stomped her foot and screamed in frustration. "You just stay away from Ian." She turned on her six-inch spike heels and left.

Danny had a brief fantasy about her heel getting caught between the deck boards. He quickly chided himself. Even if she was a she-devil, she was expecting, and he didn't want her or the baby to be harmed.

"I guess you'll have to be my date tonight, Liz," Breck said. "That is, if Jane doesn't mind sharing."

"I'll try to survive." Jane smirked.

Danny thought he saw the beginnings of an eye roll before her features returned to stoic.

The charade was getting out of control, but Danny piled on top of it anyway. "I'll be Jane's date then. Tommy will understand, won't he?"

Considering Tommy hadn't actually been invited, Danny thought it would be okay.

Chapter Nine

Jane laughed at Breck's exuberance as she drove him and Liz back to her house.

"I'm so happy I don't have to lie down in the back seat. We're going to celebrate. I've got two hot babes to dance with. I'm a lucky man."

Later, at Jane's house, she, Liz, and Breck got dressed up for their big night out.

When the ladies entered the living room, Breck let out a low whistle. "You both look beautiful."

Jane appreciated Breck going out of his way to be kind to Liz. She really was a beautiful woman, taller than Jane with a few more curves. But anyone seeing her would be drawn to her deep blue eyes and sweet smile.

Danny arrived to pick them up. Mouthwatering in his dark denim jeans, white button-up, and sport coat, Jane licked her lips. Dark hair was visible at the open collar of his shirt. Heat flared low in her abdomen.

"You're staring," Breck whispered in her ear.

She recovered her expression. "I have to make sure my date is fit to take me out in public. You're not jealous, are you?"

"A little bit." Breck smirked before he helped Liz into the backseat.

Unable to think of anything to say to Danny after he slid behind the wheel, Jane focused on the conversation coming from the backseat.

"I don't know Ian personally," Breck said. "But the fact that you haven't bad mouthed him says a lot about you."

While Liz and Breck chatted, Jane turned in her seat toward Danny, who was driving them in his SUV. "Tell me about the shooter."

He glanced her way. "A man who thought Breck had dallied with his daughter."

"Breck's dallied with a lot of people's daughters. What set this one off?"

"I don't know, but the fingerprint was a match and the man confessed."

She crossed her arms over her chest. "I was sure it was a woman."

"You can't be right all the time, Dillon." The corner of his mouth twitched.

She shrugged and leaned back in her seat, arranging her flared skirt over her legs. Everything she wore, from the braided twist of hair on top of her head to the low-heeled dance shoes with ankle straps, was carefully selected, in case she needed to move. Dance moves or fight moves, either way she was ready.

Breck did his best to conceal Liz when entering

the dance club. It probably made him feel good to be able to protect someone, kind of like Jane protected him. Breck was sure to be recognized, and eventually, even with the blonde hair, Liz might be too. Jane was beginning to wish they'd stayed in.

For a few moments, she watched Breck and Liz on the dance floor, but then she focused her attention on Danny who was sitting next to her at their small table, staring daggers at Breck.

"He's decent you know. And he's trying to help."

He sighed. "I know. I wish I could hate him, but I can't."

"Why do you want to hate him?"

"Jealousy." His eyes cut from Breck to her and then back again. "He's a freaking action hero."

Jane turned in her seat to face him. "You're a real-life hero. And from what I understand, your training is what made him so successful in those roles."

Dark eyebrows lifted just before a small smile graced his lips.

Peeling her gaze away from his mouth as a Latin rhythm boomed, she issued a challenge. "Are you going to sit there all night and be envious of a man who has nothing on you? Or are you going to take me out on the dance floor? Show me what you've got, Baker."

She couldn't read Danny's expression, but he stood and offered her his hand. "I'll try not to step on your toes."

Bachata, baby. Damn. The Latin dance was one of her favorites. Simple, sexy and her partner

could move. With those hips, he must be part
Cuban. It sent shock waves straight to her pleasure
center. If she'd worn stockings, they would've
melted right off her legs. It was more than enough
to get her hot under the thigh holster.

The way he led her around the floor confused
her mind into believing they'd been dancing
together all their lives. Being in his arms made her
tingle, and being close enough to smell his soap
drove her to distraction. In her mind, she kept
seeing them in the privacy of a bedroom, minus
their clothes.

Needing to change the direction of her
thoughts, she asked, "Who taught you?"

"My mama."

Even with the sexy, southern accent, his
admission sucked the libido right out of her.

He continued, "I was young, but I'll never
forget. The way you move reminds me of her. I
guess dancers are more graceful than the rest of us.
Mama always seemed to glide everywhere." He
lifted their hands as she spun under his arm.

Jane smiled as she imagined a mother dancing
with her young son. That must have been very
special for him since Liz had told her his real mom
died when he was a kid. His father had married
Liz's mother and joined their families.

"What about you?" Danny asked. "Who taught
you to dance?"

"My grandfather, sort of," she said. "He put me
in karate and dancing when I started kindergarten.
He didn't know what to do with a little girl. I guess
he tried to find balance for me."

"Thanks to him, you can kick my ass and dance circles around me," he said over his shoulder as he did a merengue step in place, while she literally danced around him. "I'll have to thank him if I ever meet him."

Before she returned to face him, she flared her fingers as she ran her hand across his back, feeling the taught muscles there. She tore her gaze from the fluid movement of his hips to see his eyes twinkling with laughter.

What had he been saying? Oh yeah, Grandfather.

Jane didn't have the heart to tell him her grandfather had passed. Because it reminded her of how alone she was in the world, she didn't like to think about it.

When they left the dance club, the paparazzi were waiting. Danny cleared a path to the car. Jane and Breck sandwiched Liz.

"Great," Liz said once they were in the car. "Now if anyone finds out about me, they'll suspect Breck knocked me up."

"You mean the baby's not mine?" Breck asked with wide eyes.

Once the laughter died down, they decided to go to the country bar because Jason and Roxanne were there waiting on them, and they weren't being followed.

The bar was crowded as Jane led the way inside. Danny had one hand on her waist and the other holding Liz's hand behind him. Breck was behind Liz with his hands on her shoulders.

"I had no idea there was a bar like this in Los

Angeles," Jane said over her shoulder. "Or that it would be so popular."

"Haven't you heard?" Danny said in her ear. "Country's cool."

His voice created a vibration that ran from her ears to her toes. It was a feeling she wanted to get used to, but knew she shouldn't.

They found Jason and Roxanne at a table near the stage. Danny positioned himself so he could survey the crowd, and Jane took a seat next to him. They ordered drinks and listened to the band for a while.

Feeling the weight of someone's eyes, Jane directed her attention to the patrons.

"What's up?" Danny had noticed Jane scanning the bar.

"I don't know, just a feeling." She tried hard to pinpoint what put her on edge.

"Let's dance. Do you know how to two-step?"

Nodding, she took his offered hand.

He two-stepped her around the dance floor, and they both scanned the crowd. "Do you sense danger?"

"It's difficult to explain, but yes." Her gaze darted from female face to female face. "You know when the hair on the back of your neck stands up?"

"That never happens to me."

She looked at him then, brows furrowed.

Squeezing her waist with one hand, he smiled. "I'm teasing." The expression slipped from his face. "Have you ever regretted following your instincts?"

"My biggest regrets have been when I didn't follow them." She swallowed as memories of the worst night of her life swam in her head.

***

Danny was formulating a plan to get them all safely out of the bar. He too sensed something wasn't right. The thing about *feelings* was you could never be sure until later if it was paranoia or real.

Breck and Liz danced past them and said hello.

"Go cut in and dance with Breck," Danny said to Jane. "Send Liz back to the table. I'll keep an eye out and signal you if I see anything."

She did as he asked, and when Liz was safely seated at the table, Danny looked around the room to see who was paying particular attention to Breck. Men and women were both watching Breck and Jane, but no one seemed intent on them.

Focusing more on the men who might cause trouble, he almost missed a petite blonde who walked toward Breck and Jane with a fierce stare, as if no one else was in the room.

Danny moved toward the woman when he saw the pistol in her hand. Sweat broke out on his forehead. He yelled out and shoved people aside as he ran to intercept her.

Jane turned to face the threat and positioned Breck behind her. She grabbed the woman's hand holding the gun and pushed it up to point at the ceiling. A shot split the air and chaos erupted. Jane bent the woman's wrist back, and the gun fell from her grip.

Catching it before it landed, Danny let out a rushed breath. When he looked again, Jane had the lady's arm twisted behind her as she forced her to the ground. Pressing her left knee into the small of the woman's back, Jane slid her hand up her leg and removed a pistol strapped to her right thigh.

Danny didn't know if he was more shocked to see the weapon or Jane's thigh, but the sight would give him sweet dreams for years to come. He'd also drawn his gun, which had been in a shoulder holster under his jacket.

He checked around for another threat and saw none. Then he secured the area as much as possible, considering the large crowd of onlookers.

"Bartender, can we get a cola for Mr. Stanton?" Jane called out from her position on top of the suspect.

Danny guided Breck to a barstool and told Liz to make sure he drank the sugar. Danny knew having a gun pointed at you could cause shock in those unaccustomed to the experience—and in those who were.

After the police left with the woman, Danny spontaneously hugged Jane. She didn't return the hug at first, and when she tried to, he was already pulling away, embarrassed at his display. It was awkward all the way around.

"Nice work, Dillon. I'll take Stanton home after we drop you and Liz."

"I don't want to be alone tonight," Breck said quietly. "One more night at Jane's, okay?"

"Of course." Jane took his hand and squeezed as Liz rubbed his back.

"I'll stay too," Danny said.

"What about your visitors?" Jane asked.

Danny closed his eyes and shook his head.

"They'll understand. Duty calls."

Danny sent Jason and Roxanne to his house, while he drove Jane, Liz, and Breck to Jane's house. He thought about Jane's instincts. She'd been right; the shooter was a woman.

"I remember that girl," Breck said, his voice just above a whisper from the backseat.

"The man who was arrested earlier today is her father," Danny said.

"Did she say anything?" Breck asked. "Like why she wants me dead?"

Glancing at Jane, Danny nodded once.

Jane shifted in her seat to look back at Breck. "She told me you had a one-night stand, and she wasn't that kind of girl. You said you'd call. I guess she took it pretty hard when you didn't."

"She was a little nuts. Acted all freaky to get me in bed, then started planning our wedding before the sun came up. I said I'd call as a parting courtesy." Breck ran his hands through his hair and sighed. "I won't make that mistake again."

Jane shot Danny a smug look. "She was the shooter at the awards ceremony. Used her father's hunting rifle. That's how his fingerprints showed up in the ballistics report."

A surge of anger caught Danny by surprise. Jane could have been killed that night.

Loosening his grip on the steering wheel, Danny hoped Breck was rethinking his approach to women and to life. Danny needed to rethink his own stance on women. Make the wrong one mad, and they could make your life hell.

Jane gave Danny the garage door opener, so he

could let himself in when he returned from getting some clothes from his house.

Entering Jane's house, he set his overnight bag down then went in search of everyone. He found Lizabelle asleep in the first bedroom. In the second bedroom, Breck was asleep under the covers, and Jane was asleep next to him, on top of the covers.

Even if they were on opposite sides of the blanket, Danny didn't like seeing Jane lying next to Breck. He especially didn't like that they were holding hands.

When he nudged Jane's foot, her eyes popped open. She tensed for action, like a coiled snake ready to strike. When she recognized him, she untwined her fingers from Breck's and eased off the bed.

In the hallway, she kept her voice low. "He's afraid to be alone tonight. He was really shaken up."

"I'll bunk on the floor with him. I brought my sleeping bag." Danny held it up.

"I'll get you a pillow." Jane started to move away.

He caught her arm. "You did good tonight, Dillon."

"You already said that, but thank you. Strong work on your part as well. We're a good team."

She was right. He couldn't deny she was qualified for the job. Since they were being respectful of each other, he didn't want to say goodnight, but words failed him. He struggled to think of something, but in his hesitation, she dropped her gaze and turned to go.

Chapter Ten

Jane laid in bed thinking about Danny. If he knew what his touch did to her, he wouldn't do it. He was sleeping right across the hall, and her mind wouldn't let her forget the sound of his voice or the warmth of his presence. But Breck and Liz were also asleep nearby, so she forced thoughts of Danny away. He was her boss, and she was *not* going to risk her job or ruin their working relationship.

After Breck was squared away, she wouldn't have a reason to see Danny much. She was hired for fieldwork, so she didn't have to report to the office. Except, she did like Liz and was beginning to consider her a friend.

Liz could stay with Jane as long as necessary, which would probably only be until Jason and his girlfriend left. Liz seemed to be friends with both of them, but the situation was awkward, especially since she didn't want anyone else to know she was pregnant. Jason had been Danny's best friend since childhood, which was why Liz managed to maintain a friendship with him, even though they were divorced.

That night, as she slept, Jane dreamt of having a baby. When she sat straight up in bed, disturbed by the dream, it was almost dawn. Her heart raced, but she wasn't screaming in terror for a change.

All was quiet and with the shooter in custody, she looked forward to an outdoor run instead of facing another day on the treadmill. Quickly and quietly, she dressed and tiptoed to the door leading downstairs like a cat in a cartoon sneaking away from a big dog. A smile loomed in her heart as she anticipated the freedom and release of the run.

She was in the garage, bending over and touching her toes when the door opened behind her.

"Going somewhere?" Danny stood there, shirtless.

Jane stood up abruptly and swallowed, trying to focus on his eyes, not his impeccably chiseled pecs with the perfect amount of hair dusting them. "I've been restricted to indoor running the last few days and need the fresh air."

"Give me five minutes and I'll join you. I need to talk to you about an assignment."

"All right, try not to wake the baby." She smiled.

He held her gaze for a moment, then turned to go get dressed.

"Both of the babies are still sleeping," Danny said when he rejoined her.

Trying very hard not to be disappointed seeing him wearing a shirt, she opened the exterior door.

Bodies like his shouldn't be covered up.

As they started down the street, she could feel Danny's eyes on her.

"What got you?" He gestured to her thigh.

"Shrapnel. What about this assignment?" A change of subject might keep her from having to answer questions about the white scars on the right side of her body from neck to thigh. When she'd dressed in running shorts and singlet, she hadn't expected anyone to see her up close.

"I want you to guard Liz at my beach house in Georgia. She's building her own house next door, but it's not ready yet, and she sold her condo already. I don't want her to be alone because of the pregnancy, and I want her protected from prying eyes, freeloaders, and reporters."

Jane didn't say anything. Not surprised he would stick her with another babysitting job, she tried to think of the positives. It was unlikely she'd get shot, unless it was with a camera. She'd never been to Georgia, and a house on the beach sounded like a good place to start.

Danny stopped and placed his hand on Jane's arm. "I'm not belittling you by asking you to do this. I know what you're capable of. I trust you to take care of my sister."

His touch sent a chill through her sweat covered body. She hugged herself and rubbed her arms before she started running again. "I know. I was just thinking. My house is here. How much time are we talking about?"

"We can work out a schedule. At least until the baby comes. Maybe a little longer. Ideally, I need to be here the majority of the time. How about three weeks on, one off? I'll relieve you on your off week."

"I think that'll work." Jane was glad she wouldn't be around Danny. With the effect his nearness had on her newly awakened hormones, she needed distance. A couple thousand miles should do it.

***

When they returned to Jane's house, Danny jumped in the shower while she started the coffee. With physical scars like hers, there were definitely emotional ones lurking beneath the surface. He'd take another look at her file later to see what he'd missed.

He'd sensed relief in her posture when she'd accepted the assignment guarding Liz. It was better than the sucker punch he'd been expecting.

The scars didn't do anything to detract from Jane's beauty.

Refusing to have inappropriate thoughts about his employee, despite how much they had in common, he shook his head to clear the image of her tight little body. If only he could remove the picture in his mind of the lacy thigh holster under her raised skirt. That was sexy. It was a good thing he was shipping her across the country.

After his shower, Danny sipped coffee in the kitchen, while watching Jane scramble egg whites. When Liz joined them, she squeezed his shoulder before she took a seat at the kitchen bar.

Danny poured hot water over a decaffeinated tea bag and passed it to Liz. "Good news...Jane has agreed to go stay with you in Quiet Cove."

His sister got up and hugged Jane. "I'm so glad. I'll try not to be too much trouble."

"Yeah, right." Danny winked.

Breck wandered into the kitchen. "Is the nightmare really over?"

"Yep, I spoke to Joe this morning. Your stalker is still in the slammer," Danny said. "When you're ready, I'll take you home."

"I still can't believe she wanted me dead." He sat down hard on a stool.

"You must suck in the sack, Breck." Liz grinned over the rim of her mug.

"I guess." Breck ran his hand through his hair. "I need to find one partner and practice a lot. Like dancing, huh, Ginger?"

It irritated Danny's last nerve when Breck called Jane by a pet name, not to mention insinuating she'd make a good bed partner.

After dancing with her, Danny had no doubts about her ability to move well.

When they'd finished breakfast, Breck dropped his duffle bag on the floor and picked Jane up in a full body hug. "Thank you...for everything." He put her down and kissed her on the cheek. "I'll call you."

Danny didn't realize his fists were clenched until Liz touched his arm and shook her head. He took a second to feel smug, more than happy he was sending Jane away from Breck.

Before he followed Danny out the door, Breck hugged Liz goodbye and kissed her cheek. "Take care of my baby."

Chapter Eleven

Within a week, Jane and Liz were in Georgia. Jane was in awe of Danny's house, which he'd named South Winds. Between the jet and the houses, she decided the security business must be doing very well. She wondered if Liz's wealth had anything to do with Danny's success, but she was hesitant to ask such a personal question.

The exterior of the house seemed to be clapboard, painted seafoam green. With white trim, it had the appearance of a cottage. A big one with three levels. The first floor was a garage and recreation/workout area. They could walk out of the back door, onto the beach, and into the water. It was called the blowout level, in case of a hurricane. The second level had the living, dining, kitchen areas, and the master suite. The third floor had four bedrooms. Jane and Liz took two of the guest rooms and left the master suite for Danny when he visited.

The upper levels of the house had terraces with

beautiful, unobstructed views of the ocean. There was even a hot tub on the lower terrace. Jane shuffled her feet, but didn't breakout into a full blown dance. The water jets would feel amazing after her daily workouts.

A few days after they settled in and Jane had scoped out the area, she and Liz began taking evening walks on the beach to stretch their legs. Jane loved watching the horizon, trying to determine where the sky ended and the water began.

"So, what's the deal with you and Breck?" Liz asked one day.

Jerking her head to see Liz's face, Jane squinted into the setting sun. "No deal."

"He's got it bad for you, and he's hawt."

Jane chuckled at the Southern pronunciations Liz used. "We dance together sometimes. That's it."

"I'm pretty sure he wants more. Are you not interested?"

"I'm his safe place right now. He's a friend, and I care about him, but not that way."

"You're my safe place too." Liz smiled. "You gonna see him when you go back to L.A.?"

"Probably." Jane stopped herself from saying more. She'd always been a steel trap when it came to secrets, and she decided she better lock it down. Confiding was something she saved for the paid professionals.

Later, Jane settled into the hot tub and smiled. Running in the sand every morning revealed muscles long forgotten. Her knee popped when she stretched her legs out, and the click reminded her she wasn't getting any younger. Her career choice could be hard on a body. For the first time, Jane found herself glad to be settling into a less active role.

Resting her head back, her thoughts drifted to her earlier conversation with Liz. Her new friend was more observant than she'd realized, and she and Breck weren't as great at acting as she'd imagined. Jane hoped Danny was oblivious, but her gut told her he was too sharp not to have noticed.

Being around a pregnant Liz had Jane entertaining thoughts she'd never entertained before. Knowing the chances of ever having children of her own were reduced, she assumed these sudden desires could be attributed to her biological clock. At thirty-seven, she was running out of time.

She briefly considered what kind of father Breck would be. He would probably be fantastic because deep down he was the sensitive, artistic type. Kids would love him. As a husband though, she couldn't picture it.

The man she *could* see in that role surprised her.

***

Danny's plane landed at the airstrip near Quiet Cove, Georgia a few days before Thanksgiving to pick Liz up. They'd worked out the schedule to coordinate with the upcoming holiday season. The Bakers were big on family holidays, and Liz had news to share with them.

According to Liz, Jane was going over and above the call of duty. She accompanied Liz to doctor's appointments, prepared healthy meals, cleaned the house, and made sure Liz exercised daily once the doctor said it was all right.

The more he learned about Jane, the more the walls around his heart eroded.

Liz grabbed his arm at the front door. "Danny, ever since we heard the heartbeat, Jane has been talking to the baby every day. It's hilarious. She gives the baby advice—things you would never say to a child."

Later, when Jane came in from her evening run, Danny smirked. "I hear you're giving my future niece or nephew inappropriate advice."

"Just because it's not age appropriate, doesn't mean it's inappropriate, does it?" Jane winked.

Danny couldn't help but smile. It seemed Liz was bringing Jane out of her shell.

Over dinner, Liz told Danny she was going to wait until Christmas to announce her baby news to the family. She would be about sixteen weeks then and would feel safer about not losing the baby to miscarriage. "Plus, I'll be too fat to hide it by then."

Jane refilled her water glass. "Pregnant women aren't fat. Stop saying that, or I'm gonna make you do push-ups again."

"Please no, anything but that." Liz covered her face with her forearm. "Push-ups are the devil."

"Do you have any great advice for the baby, Danny? The more inappropriate the better." Jane grinned.

"Yes." Danny leaned over toward Liz's belly, which was barely a bump at all. "Don't take inappropriate advice from beautiful women. They might lead you astray."

Jane excused herself after dinner. Since she had cooked, he and Liz insisted they'd do the dishes.

When the dishwasher was loaded, Liz yawned so wide her jaw cracked. "I'm so tired all the time. I hate it, brother, but I'm gonna go lay down."

Danny put on his swim trunks and headed for the hot tub, grabbing a cold beer on his way. He opened the screen door to the cool night air and paused when he stepped outside. Jane was relaxing in the tub with her head back and eyes closed.

He started back inside, but decided to let his body rule over his brain for a change "Do you mind company?"

She opened her eyes and sat up, sucking in a breath. "Ah, sure."

"I'm sorry I startled you. I didn't know you'd be out here, and Liz is in a pregnancy-induced coma. Here." He handed her the beer. "Take this, I'll go get another."

Danny felt a little bad for intruding on Jane's privacy, but he did want to get to know her better. The tension between them from when they'd first met was slowly fading.

After grabbing another beer, Danny climbed into the hot tub opposite her. "What are your plans for Thanksgiving?"

"I'm going back to L.A. for a few days." As usual, she didn't elaborate.

"Our crazy family is gathering at Southland. The Bakers are big on holidays." Danny tried to get the conversational ball rolling.

"I've heard all about the Baker's half-dozen. Your family sounds nice." She smiled.

"Yeah, if you like the Brady Bunch on steroids. My dad expects a Baker's dozen of grandchildren. Liz's baby will make eight. They're great, but sometimes *family time* can be overwhelming when we all get together. I can take it for a few days, but then I have to escape." He took a long pull of his beer.

"I wouldn't know about that. It was just my grandfather and me. He died when I was in college. Now, it's just me."

"What happened to your parents?"

"My mom died when I was young, and I never met my dad." Her eyes were focused on the paper she peeled off her bottle.

"Have you always been a loner?"

She nodded.

"I liked my alone time before the military, but rarely got it. After I got out of the Navy, I needed my own space. I had to put some distance between my family and me."

She made eye contact again. "Why did you choose Los Angeles?"

"I knew none of my family would ever follow me there." He grinned and was rewarded with a laugh from her. "What about you? Why L.A.?"

Taking a deep breath, she looked past him out into the darkness. "I needed space too."

"From?"

"Not from the living."

Her emerald green eyes were illuminated by the lights from the tub, and he wanted to remove the pain which flashed in them. Protective instincts tightened the muscles across his upper back.

"Running from the ghosts of your past." He'd had another look at her file and read where she'd lost her team to a crazed killer. "Did it work?"

"Does it ever?"

He wanted to reach across the water separating them and kiss all the bad away. "Not in my experience."

"Mine neither." She examined her fingertips. "Well, I'm nice and pruned. I think I'll call it a night. Can I grab you another beer before I go?"

"Sure, thanks." He was pleased they were making progress, but disappointed she wanted to get away from him.

He wondered what he'd done wrong until she climbed out of the hot tub. Then all coherent thoughts were wiped from his mind as his eyes were drawn to her like a magnet to metal.

The one-piece swimsuit she wore clung to her like a second skin, showing the muscle definition of her abs and rear. As she walked away, he puckered his lips to whistle, but stopped himself just in time.

A moment later, when she handed him a fresh beer, their fingers touched, and when their gazes locked, heat rushed through him, and it had nothing to do with the hot water he was soaking in.

Chapter Twelve

Jane popped a couple of antacids while waiting for her flight to board in Jacksonville, Florida, the nearest big airport to Quiet Cove. For Christmas, Danny had again flown to the coast to get Liz for their family holiday.

Jane was flying to Philly to spend Christmas with friends. For days, she'd suffered from indigestion due to the anxiety of returning to her hometown and the memories she'd tried to escape.

Settling into her seat on the plane, she resolved to think about anything other than her traumatic memories. Danny dancing his way into her dreams from a couple thousand miles away proved a delightful distraction.

An hour into the flight, the captain announced that a blizzard was hitting the Northeast hard, and all flights were being diverted. If she were a singer like Liz, Jane would've burst into the Hallelujah chorus.

She bowed her head and closed her eyes. The delay would just postpone the inevitable. She'd have to go back someday.

When they landed in Atlanta, she checked the weather. The trip to Philly wasn't meant to be.

She decided to go back to L.A., but discovered there were no available flights for two days.

Wandering through the terminal, she thought of Liz and Danny. Their family lived close by, so they could recommend a place to stay while she waited for her next flight.

She texted Danny, knowing Liz would feel obliged to invite her to their home, and the last thing she wanted was to crash their Christmas.

Stuck in Atlanta due to storm. Hotel recommendations?

After a moment, he responded: *Stay put. I'm coming to get you.*

Please don't go to any trouble.

It's no trouble. You can help me through a Southern fried family Christmas.

Yeah, but who's gonna help me?

An hour later, Danny pulled to the curb at the Atlanta International Airport in a truck exactly like his personal vehicle in California—a black Chevy crew cab. He got out and took Jane's suitcase from her.

"Do the Bakers find a truck they like and buy one for every location?"

He opened the front passenger door. "This is Liz's truck. She got it after I told her about mine."

As they pulled away from the curb, she asked, "Are you certain this is all right? I don't want to intrude on your family holiday." Her cheeks were warm.

"My family loves newcomers. You'll be the center of attention."

"Stop the vehicle." She reached for the door handle. "I'll spend Christmas at the airport."

He grabbed her arm to stop her; although, she was only joking. "No such luck, sweet thang. You're expected. They're preparing one of the cottages for you, so you'll have the teeniest bit of privacy."

Looking at the spot where his hand gripped her arm, she knew she needed to get over being nervous around Danny. He was just a man. Men didn't have this effect on her. She hadn't been nervous meeting the great Breck Stanton, but Breck's touch had never made her heart flutter.

"Cottages? Who are you people? The backwoods mafia? I'll have to turn you in if I find anything illegal going on." She narrowed her eyes and fought a grin.

"I'd expect nothing less from you, but I should warn you, my brother Johnny puts out corn for the deer. His son, Nick, likes to watch them, but we don't hunt on the property at Southland. We have a camp for that. The cottage is more like a cabin really." Danny smiled.

God, they were loaded. She returned the expression. "Thank you for this."

"Don't thank me yet. You still haven't met my family. Liz is excited you'll be there when she tells them the big news tomorrow night, after the kids go to bed." With one hand on the wheel, he navigated the Atlanta traffic.

"Oh Danny, I don't think I should be there. That's family business and nothing to do with me."

"Actually, since you've been taking care of Liz and going to the doctor with her, you're in a great position to answer their questions. Liz is going to need you fighting in her corner." Danny turned her words back on her.

"Touché. I'm sorry about that by the way." She looked out the window as they left the city for the suburbs.

"About what? Trying to beat some sense into me? That was exactly what I needed, Jane. You recognized it with your impeccable instincts. I should thank you, but I wouldn't want to encourage you to try it again. The next time, I'll be ready."

She turned a smug look in his direction. "Always looking over your shoulder when I'm around, huh? Just the way I like it. Keeps you on your guard."

***

Danny smiled at the look on Jane's face when they emerged from the long driveway in front of the main house. "Welcome to Southland."

It was late, and Danny had planned to drive her straight to her cottage, even though he knew his family was still up and dying to meet her.

The house was all aglow with tiny white Christmas lights. The formally decorated sixteen foot spruce pine was centered in the front window of the living room. The kids' more colorful tree was in the family room in the back of the house. Mama D also had small table trees in all of the bedrooms of the main house and the cottages.

"This is enormous. It's like a place I saw in a magazine for a mountain retreat."

"Yeah, with six kids growing up here, it needed to be. Dad built the cottages and renovated to accommodate the girls." He pointed to the tree in the front window. "My brother Johnny farms trees in his spare time."

"Is that how your dad made his fortune?"

"Subtle." Danny grinned, wondering how much Liz had shared.

Jane shrugged. "Inquiring minds."

"My dad married well and made his own money in home medical supplies. He's the largest distributor in the Southeast. Mama D and my brothers and sisters all work in the family business."

Danny pointed out the barn, which was covered in white lights as they drove past. "There are a dozen horses, four donkeys, three goats, and two dogs roaming around here somewhere."

He passed the first cottage. "The caretakers, Aunt May and Uncle Ben Hill, stay here. They're spending a few days with relatives."

At the next cottage he pointed. "That's where Johnny's been staying since his divorce. I'll be staying there, and he'll be at the main house with Nick, since that's where Santa is coming tomorrow night."

"And this is you." He stopped in front of the last cabin. It was across the dirt road from his. "I'll see you in and stoke the fire before I go." He smirked at the innuendo in his statement.

He showed her around the small cottage. The

front door opened into the combined sitting, dining, and kitchenette area. A small bedroom and bathroom were off the kitchen, but a two-sided fireplace opened to both spaces.

He put another log on the fire and hoped she'd be comfortable. "Do you want to meet me for a run in the morning?"

"Yes, please." She saw him to the door.

"See you at six. Sweet dreams." He'd certainly have them, knowing she was at Southland for Christmas.

He fell asleep that night with a smile on his face.

**

When he knocked on Jane's door the next morning, Danny could tell she'd been up working out already. He smiled to himself because he had too.

"How'd you sleep?" he asked, closing the door as they stepped onto the stoop.

"Fine, thanks. You?"

"I had trouble getting to sleep, but once I did, I was out." He gestured toward a dirt trail. "I usually run further than usual when I'm here because the food is so good. I eat to excess."

"I've heard about this delicious Southern fare. I could probably stand a preemptive calorie burn too. Remind me of everyone's names again."

They were underway, and Danny would rather talk about his family than tell Jane she'd look good no matter how many calories she ate or burned. He liked that she took care of herself and that he occasionally got to see her and appreciate her efforts.

He focused his eyes on the wooded path in front of him. "There are our parents, Dan and Dixie, whom we usually address as Big Daddy and Mama D, me and Liz, Katie who is married to Robert, Johnny who is divorced and may hit on you, Maddie who is married to Mark, and Paul who is married to Jennifer."

Jane repeated the names back to him.

"The kids are Beth and Bobby, Jenny and Josh, Nick, and Carly and Tyler. It works out because each of them has a cousin close to their age, so they play well together, except for Tyler who's almost three. I guess Liz's kid will be Tyler's playmate when he's a little older."

"Ethan," Jane said. "Liz is naming him Ethan, after yours and your dad's middle name. She told you that, right?"

He nodded once then shook his head. "Yeah, but I'm hesitant to call the baby by his name. That'll make it too real."

"It *is* real. You better get used to it, Uncle Danny." She jumped over a tree stump on the side of the trail. "It might help if you talk to him."

Danny cut his eyes over to her in disbelief.

"I know it sounds ridiculous, but babies can hear in utero. It may be too soon for Ethan to hear us, but I've been giving him some great advice."

Danny laughed. "What was the first advice you gave him when you found out he was a boy?"

"I told him not to piss into the wind."

Danny tripped because he laughed so hard. Jane put her arm out to try to stop his forward fall, and they both went down. After the initial shock of impact, he noticed her body under his.

"Thanks for breaking my fall." He smiled down at her.

She struggled for air. "Anytime."

He moved off of her and helped her to her feet. "Are you hurt?"

"I'll be okay in a minute." She walked around in a circle, hands on her hips.

Angry with himself for hurting her, Danny clenched his fists and paced back and forth. He wasn't hurt at all because she'd taken the force of the impact.

"You ready to run or are you going to sulk all day?" She took off down the trail.

He couldn't ignore the slight hitch in her gait, even though she'd read him like a cereal box.

Chapter Thirteen

After her shower, Jane sat on the sofa to pull on her boots and took a moment to look around the cozy little cottage. The furniture was shabby chic. It was a good mix of rugged and elegant.

She smiled at the small Christmas tree adorning the coffee table. The colored lights twinkled, and she remembered her grandfather. He always let her help decorate their little silver tree. He also bought cookie dough and supervised while she made cookies for Santa.

A tear surprised her and rolled down her cheek. She swiped at it. She always missed him most at Christmas. He wasn't perfect, but he did right by her and raised her the best way he knew how.

To climb out of the melancholy threatening to overtake her, she thought about her morning run and the feel of Danny's body on her as they lay on the ground. She would've enjoyed it more if the wind hadn't been knocked out of her.

A rap on the door got her to her feet as she wiped her face. Thinking was a bad idea.

Danny escorted her to the big house. On the walk, her fingertips glided across her sweaty palms. She was nervous about meeting his family. She almost asked him if she looked all right, but she didn't want him to know she felt inadequate to the task.

Give me a gun and point me toward the bad guy and I'm all over it. But, give me a large, loving family and I might pass out.

Suck it up, Dillon.

It was Christmas Eve day, and she hoped she wouldn't spoil their holiday. There would be a lot of kids, and she hadn't been around many.

What if there was snot? She could handle gunshot wounds, but a snotty kid might send her over the edge.

Stop borrowing trouble.

"Are you okay?" Danny's voice broke into her thoughts as they walked around a huge outdoor pool and spa to reach the back porch.

"Are you certain I won't be intruding?" She wiped her palms on her pants.

"Absolutely certain." He took her hand. "Relax. Take a few deep breaths."

She did, and when she was ready, she nodded. "Okay."

He opened the door and put his hand on her back to usher her into the house. Rather than sending inappropriate thoughts flooding into her mind and body, his touch gave her comfort and courage.

As Danny introduced his family, Jane noted the resemblances. Mr. Baker's sons definitely got their good looks from him. And Mrs. Baker put Jane in mind of an older Julia Roberts. The shared features of Liz and her sisters were remarkable.

Jane's attention was directed to a breakfast buffet of sorts set out on the kitchen island, and everyone was lining up to get food.

"Jane, come on up here, darlin', and get you somethin' to eat. You need to put some meat on those bones," Mrs. Baker said.

"Come on, Jane." Liz handed her a plate. "Guests go first. And Mama, don't pick on Jane about what she eats. She eats for fuel and is all into fitness like Danny."

Jane reluctantly took the plate and stepped up to *the trough* as Mr. Baker called it. She had no idea what some of the food was. Liz explained what grits were, and Mrs. Baker told her the deer sausage was to die for. When Jane finally settled in her seat at the table, she had a little of everything on her plate. She looked around and under the table to see if the dogs she'd seen outside had been allowed in. No such luck.

Liz sat at her left, and five-year-old Carly was on her right.

"I'll be six soon," Carly told Jane. "My birthday is in February like Uncle Danny's. I'm having a party. How old are you gonna be again, Uncle Danny?"

Johnny answered, "Lordy, Lordy, Danny's gonna be forty. You old fart."

Carly giggled and covered her mouth. "We're

not s'posed to say fart."

"I better watch my language then." Jane bit into a link of deer sausage and nearly moaned as delicious flooded her mouth.

"Yeah, if we're bad, Big Daddy might take us to the woodshed. I've never been." Carly drank her juice.

"Well, I'll stick with you. I don't know what a woodshed is, but I don't want to find out."

She looked across the table to see Danny shaking his head. "You definitely don't want to go there."

"Hoo doggies, I've blistered many a backside at the woodshed." Mr. Baker chuckled and winked at Jane.

It wasn't as overwhelming as she'd expected. She was good with names, so remembering everyone was one less thing to worry about.

After breakfast, the adults were seated in the large family room discussing the need for a last minute run to town. Jane hoped the trip wasn't due to her unexpected arrival. She turned to get Liz's attention, but she was deep in conversation with five-year-old Nick.

Danny took the seat next to her on the hearth. "Do you need to do any shopping? You'll be getting gifts, but we don't want you to feel obligated."

She closed her eyes. "Please no." She dropped her head into her hands and then straightened quickly. "I mean, yes."

Danny rubbed her back. "I should've thought to warn you this would happen. I'll help you shop."

"You'd put yourself in harm's way for me?"

She looked into the green depths of his eyes, and her thoughts flew back to a dance floor in L.A.

"Yes." He stared for a second before he continued, "But if you mean last minute shopping on Christmas Eve, I'm a professional, since I do it every year."

"Thanks for the heads-up." Rubbing her forehead, she thought for a moment. "I have some ideas. If I can work it out, I'll just need a ride to a shopping center." She stood. "I need to go back to the cottage."

"Take your time. This crew will take a while to reach a decision about who's going where with whom."

*****

Danny took Jane, Mama D, and Katie in one car, while his brother Paul took the rest of the guys with him in a minivan. Holding his breath and keeping his eye on Jane in the rearview mirror, Danny hoped their trip would be quick and uneventful.

"Leave it to the men to wait until the last minute. No offense, Danny," Katie said. "Do you like to shop Jane?"

"I'd rather get stabbed with a red hot poker."

"Oh, phooey, you're just like Liz and Maddie. They're not shoppers either. Mama and I are the queens when it comes to retail therapy," Katie said.

"Yeah," Danny said. "The store that sells nothing but make-up and beauty products is like Katie's mothership."

"I do most of my shopping online these days," Jane said. "If I find something I like, I just order it in black."

"Honey, that's how men shop," Katie said. "We are females. We need to try things on. Although, you're so skinny, I bet everything looks good on you."

"Kate." Danny shot her a warning look.

"I was raised by my grandfather, so I never learned how to shop like a proper woman. Maybe you can teach me." Jane offered a small smile.

Danny pressed his lips together at the subtle sarcasm in Jane's voice.

"Is your grandfather still living?" Mama D asked.

"No." Jane crossed her arms over her abdomen.

"Do you have any other family?"

"No, Mrs. Baker. It's just me."

"Call me Dixie or Mama D like the kids. I'm so sorry you're all alone in this world."

Before Danny could call a halt to the discussion, Jane said, "I don't feel as though I'm alone in the world Mrs.—Excuse me, Dixie. You've always had your big, happy family, so you'd miss them if you were the last one left. I don't have anyone to miss, except my grandfather…oh, and my lover Karl who was killed in action a few years ago."

Danny almost ran off the road, and when he recovered, he looked at Mama D to be sure she wasn't about to deliver a message from the great beyond. She was kind of like that kid in *Sixth Sense*.

Her eyes were wide, and her mouth hung open. Jane's comment had effectively shut them all up.

He thought about what she'd said. He knew she

wasn't gay, unless Karl was Karla. But Jane wouldn't have bothered to conceal it, since she was clearly trying to shut down the inquisition. That tidbit would've been the cherry on top of the shut-up-and-mind-your-own-business-pie she'd just served up.

When they arrived at the shopping center, Danny told Mama D and Katie to go ahead.

He waited a moment, and then turned to Jane. "I'm sorry about them."

"I shouldn't have said that." She pinched between her brow with her finger and thumb. "It was a bad idea for me to intrude on your holiday, Danny. I'm very sorry." Her hand fell to her side.

"Listen." He put a finger under her chin, so she would look up at him. "Don't you dare apologize. That's why they drive me so crazy sometimes. They've never been anywhere else or met many people who are different from them, so they don't understand not everyone is like them. We owe you the apology."

"I think I shocked them; although, I admit it was my intention." Her eyes fixed on the spot where her fingers tapped on her leg.

"They deserved it." Danny considered warning her about Mama D's gift of supernatural communication with the other side, but decided against it. "It was definitely a shock to hear about Karla."

Her lips twisted, and she looked away. "Karl, not Karla. Breck didn't want to leave my house, so he altered my sexual orientation."

"Sneaky bastard. So you knew he had a thing

for you?"

She shrugged and headed for the store.

Watching her walk away, he wondered how hard Breck had tried to bed her, while he was under her roof. Danny was certainly thinking about it himself.

Chapter Fourteen

When they arrived back at Southland, Jane went straight to her cottage to get her gifts ready and wrapped. She regretted having brought up Karl. Just saying his name had caused a spasm in her soul, which drained her of most every good feeling. But she had to admit the pain was diminishing. The world hadn't stopped turning after all.

I guess time does heal all wounds. Her hand brushed over the large scar on her right side.

Jane also regretted her honesty involving Breck. By revealing that he'd lied, she'd ratted him out. She'd gone along with it so that made her a liar too. They'd be in deep shit if Danny ever found out the whole truth.

She called Breck and left him a voicemail message to let him know the ruse was over.

While thinking she probably wouldn't be getting an invitation back to Southland, a knock sounded at the door.

When she opened it, Liz hugged her. "Danny told me. I'm so sorry. My family means well, but sometimes they misplace their manners. Who's Karl?"

Not wanting to talk about it, Jane turned away and clenched her jaw. She should have kept her mouth shut.

"No one, I said it for the shock value, to take the attention off my *alone in the world* status." Jane tried to brush it off.

"I might believe you if I hadn't heard you scream his name in your sleep." Liz sat on the sofa. "Was he really killed in action?"

Jane nodded and stayed on her feet. She looked out the window, trying not to see the image branded in her memory. "He and most of our team. C4 and a remote detonator. Only two of us survived."

"You loved him?" Liz's eyes were full of concern.

"Yes, but it was a forbidden love." Trying to hold the hurt inside, Jane crossed her arms over her ribs. "We worked together, no fraternization. We had to keep it secret."

Now that she was talking about it, part of her wanted to say more—to share her heartache with someone she didn't have to pay.

Instead, she shut it down before she said too much. "We should go back up to the house. If I'm still welcome?"

"Of course you're still welcome. Oh, and that reminds me, the grown-ups need to get the kids out of the house, so Santa can do some wrapping. You and I are going to take them to the barn, so you can teach them a dance routine."

Jane raised her eyebrows and Liz continued, "I told them you taught Breck to dance, and they went nutso. They want you to teach them too."

She took a deep breath. "I'll try."

A short time later, when Jane saw the kids waiting for her in the barn, she almost panicked. She'd never taught kids to dance, only adults.

She plugged in her MP3 player and put on an old-school dance track. The older boys were reluctant to join in at first, but when she showed them how to move their bodies without moving their feet, they were less intimidated. It also helped that their Aunt Lizabelle was joining in the fun.

Jane nearly fell down laughing when Liz squatted in a wide plié and gyrated her hips, knowing what she hid under that long, bulky sweater. The kids thought it was funny, too.

Jane quickly worked out a routine, so the boys could do simple moves and the girls, who had dance experience, could do the more complicated footwork. After they had most of a hip-hop routine choreographed, she paired them up and taught them some ballroom steps. The boys threatened to revolt until she changed the music and showed them how to spice it up using the same foot patterns in different ways.

They really got into it, and Jane was surprised to find herself connecting with the kids and enjoying teaching them. The footwork practice gave the boys more confidence, so they went back to the hip-hop routine and embellished it.

They were having a good time, and even the

little three-year-old, Tyler, who was standing near Jane's feet, was bouncing around. His dancing was more like a bounce-skip, but she got the idea to send him into the melee for the ending pose of the routine. It was adorable, and the kids were practically rolling on the ground laughing when the barn door opened and the parents filed in to see what the fuss was about.

"Are you guys ready to impress your parents?" Jane asked.

They screamed a loud, "Yeah!"

Tyler ran to her and wrapped himself around her leg laughing. Her heart melted as she peered down at his sweet little face looking up at her with admiration.

Tick-tock, tick-tock.

***

Danny positioned himself on a bale of hay, so he could see the kids and Jane. She started the music, and he was amazed. The kids did an entire routine, including solo parts. Near the end, Jane bent down and whispered to Tyler and gave the boy a push toward his cousins.

He half-skipped, half-ran to where his cousins were meeting in the middle of the makeshift dance floor. He bounced in place a couple of times and plopped down on his knees with his hands in the air just as the music ended. The adults erupted into applause, joining the kids' squeals of delight.

Danny let out a whistle and high-fived as many hands as he could reach. "Way to strut your stuff, kiddos." He turned to Jane. "That was amazing. How did you get those boys to dance like that?"

"I have my ways." She wriggled her eyebrows.

"I bet you do." God, she was sexy with that flush in her cheeks.

They were interrupted when Maddie fist-bumped her. "You're awesome, Jane."

"I told you so." Liz put an arm around Jane.

"My boy's got rhythm," Johnny said.

"Unlike his daddy," Paul said. "And what about my boy? Three years old and already a dancin' fool."

Jen held Tyler. "How did you get him to do that?"

"He was watching his sister and cousins, and he couldn't keep his feet still. Isn't that right, Little?" Jane tweaked his nose.

Tyler reached his arms out to Jane, and Danny laughed as she awkwardly took him and set him on her hip, mimicking the way his mom had held him. It was obvious she hadn't held many kids.

They headed back to the main house. Jane had Tyler on her hip and Carly holding her hand. Carly was talking incessantly, and Danny wondered what he should do, if anything, to help Jane.

Once inside, Carly directed Jane to sit on the floor. She disappeared for a minute and came back with a hairbrush and a box of hair barrettes, clips, and bows.

Oh, God, Danny thought as Jane's eyes widened.

"You don't have to go along with this, you know," Danny said.

"It's fine. What's the use in having all of this hair if no one ever styles it for me?" Jane flipped her hair over her shoulders and sat up straighter.

As Danny settled on an ottoman nearby, Jane shot him a wink which sent a flare off in his core. He bit down on his cheek to rein in the sensation.

Carly talked about her letter to Santa as she brushed and clipped lots of bows in Jane's hair. When she pulled Jane's hair back on the right side, Carly stopped the brush and clipped the hair back. Then she put her finger on Jane's skin. "What happened to your neck?"

"It's a scar." Jane looked over her shoulder at the girl, and saw Danny moving closer to intercept his niece, but Jane shook her head and mouthed, "It's okay."

Danny's racing heart rose into his throat.

"How'd you get it?" Carly asked.

"Well…" Jane hesitated. "I was a police officer, and I was after a bad man. There was an explosion, and some metal hit my neck and cut me."

"Did you get the bad man?" Carly's brow was furrowed.

"Yes, he's in jail." Jane lightened her expression with a small smile.

"Good. He should stay there for making an explosion that hurt you." Carly resumed brushing Jane's hair. "Did you get any more cuts?"

Jane's nostrils flared, and her eyes shone with unshed tears. Danny wanted to take away the hurt, which haunted her.

Jane swallowed before she spoke. "Yes, I had a few more cuts, but they're all better now. How does my hair look?"

***

After Christmas Eve dinner, the Baker family gathered around the Christmas tree to exchange gifts. To make Jane more comfortable, Danny and Liz sat on either side of her to offer moral support.

Danny liked having her there. He liked sitting next to her, feeling her warmth. If he wasn't careful, he might reach out and put his arm around her, and he was trying very hard *not* to do that.

Each family member took turns giving out gifts to the others. Danny hated opening gifts, especially in front of people.

When it was his turn, Jane said, "Don't be shy, Danny. We all want to see what you got."

"Your turn is coming." He shot her a look.

She smiled and raised her eyebrows at him. He couldn't look away for a moment. Captivated, he smiled stupidly back at her until his family started prodding him to open his gifts. He was behaving like a stupid teenager with a crush.

He opened his presents and gave appropriate praise for each thing, and then Mama D said, "Now Jane, we know you wound up here unexpectedly, and we don't expect anything from you, but we just had to get you a little something to open. The kids especially wanted to get you gifts after their dance performance this afternoon."

Danny turned to watch as Jane squirmed in uncomfortable silence. She hadn't known they'd made another trip to town.

Like an elementary school child, he stuck his tongue out at her. "I told you so."

Chapter Fifteen

Jane shifted in her seat as the Bakers watched her open her first present. Once she got into it, she didn't try to conceal her smile. She *had* been missing something by not having a family. She would definitely apologize to Dixie later for her earlier comments.

In all, she received fourteen gifts—seven from the adult couples or singles and seven from the kids. The gifts from the adults were nice, expensive gifts like high-end spa products, sleepwear, and assorted ammunition for her plethora of guns.

"I wrote you a song." Liz handed her a folder.

Jane couldn't read sheet music, but she could read the lyrics. Her eyes stung with tears.

The chorus read:

I've been waiting so long to make a fresh start
To find the perfect partner to Dance With My
Heart

"You'll have to play it for me later. Thank you." Jane leaned in and shoulder bumped Liz, not comfortable enough to hug her like she really wanted to do. Giving and receiving affection from women was a new experience for Jane.

She moved on to Danny's gift—her last present from the adults. She stared, open mouthed for a moment, admiring the bone-handled knife in a sheath on a leg strap. "You got me a knife?"

"Actually, I got you the rig and threw the knife in at the last minute. It's a deer antler."

"Thank you. It's beautiful and practical." She ran her finger down the steel blade as her skin pricked, and a feeling she couldn't name blossomed in her chest.

"You might be at a redneck Christmas if the majority of gifts are weapons," Johnny said.

Jane's smile lifted her cheeks. "If that's true, we had redneck Christmases in Philly. Most of my gun collection is from my grandfather."

Next, Jane opened the kids' gifts as the little ones gathered around close to her feet to help her and see her reaction. *No pressure.*

She opened a nightshirt with the words *Dancing in the Sleep* written across the front. Jane held it up and laughed. It was from Beth, and it was followed by ballet shoe earrings from Bobby, a super soaker water gun from Josh, a pink scarf from Jenny, a coffee cup with a ballerina on it from Nick, a package of pink hair bows from Carly, and a ballet slipper key-chain from Tyler.

"I'm sensing a theme here. Thank you all very much." She tweaked Tyler's nose, since he was closest. "Now, I have gifts for you as well." She enjoyed the surprised expressions on their faces, especially the little ones who bounced in anticipation.

Jane gave instructions. "All of the adults must open their gifts at once, and the children go last." She smiled at the whole party.

The adults opened their gifts with the kids looking on. Silence filled the room as everyone looked at their framed photographs.

Jane leaned closer to Danny. "That was taken from your terrace at South Winds." It was the horizon at sunrise.

"The colors are unreal. Thank you."

"Oh, did I mention that Jane is an amateur photographer?" Liz asked the group as she hugged her photo close to her heart. Hers was of the dock over the lake at Southland, the special place where she thought Ethan might have been conceived.

Jane had only recently gotten a camera and begun playing around with it. Learning new skills kept her from getting bored and from thinking naughty thoughts about her boss.

"This is stunning," Dixie said of the photo of the Southland sign. The pines stood tall to create a green backdrop against the clear blue sky.

"When did you find the time?" Johnny asked of the photo of his son flanked by a pair of bulldogs, sitting on the steps of his cabin.

"This will go perfectly in my house. We have beach cottage decor," Jen said of her and Paul's photo of sea grass, sand, ocean, and blue sky.

"The horses," Maddie said, "are perfect for our

rodeo room."

And lastly, Katie said of her and Robert's photo of her kids dancing together and laughing, "We paid a professional photographer a small fortune for photos, and you've outdone them all, Jane."

Danny put his arm around her. "You done good, Dillon. You're amazing."

At his touch and the sense of belonging she felt, her heart kicked into a higher gear. She was glad she could do something meaningful for each of them.

"Now the kids," Jane said. "I forgot that Beth and Jenny have to go together first."

Jane waited expectantly as the girls opened their pictures.

"Oh, my God!" Beth said.

"It's a signed picture of Breck Stanton. Oh, my God!" Jenny said. "Do you really know him? What's he like?"

Jane thought they were a little young to be so Breck crazy, but he was hot and famous. "He's nice."

"He's so gorgeous. I could just die. You are so lucky," Beth said, and both girls hugged Jane.

Yes, I am. Instead of thinking of Breck, though, her mind favored the man next to her. *Fantasies can't hurt anyone, right?*

Carly opened her gift next—a pair of ballet slippers. She put them on right away and danced around the room.

The boys opened their presents last. Fireworks. Literally. Jane had gotten them all fireworks. She'd tried to think of something the boys would appreciate, and she wasn't disappointed to hear them shouting their admiration.

Even little Tyler, who she had only given sparklers was jumping up and down. "Spawklas! Spawklas!"

Her heart was full from all the love and gratitude in the room. She'd never experienced anything like it.

***

After burning a few sparklers and shooting off a few fireworks, which Danny discovered law-abiding Jane had bought from the back of a pickup truck in the Walmart parking lot, the whole crew went back inside to escape the cool December night. When the kids were sent to bed, the adult beverages came out.

Danny was enjoying a cold beer and a great view of a beautiful woman, when Liz spoke up. "Now that the kids are gone, I have an announcement to make."

Jane moved to stand behind Liz, so Danny mirrored her movements and stood on Liz's other side.

"I want to show you something." Liz pulled the ultrasound photo from her purse and turned it around to show her family. "This is Ethan Clarke Baker. He's due in May. I'm four months pregnant."

Danny studied their faces. Knit brows smoothed into wide-toothed grins.

"Oh, my Lord."

"This is the best news."

"Are you happy about this?"

"Does Ian know?"

The barrage of questions came on suddenly, and Danny felt compelled to speak, but held back to see if he was needed.

"I'm having a healthy pregnancy so far. Ethan and I are doing great. He's a miracle." She stroked her belly. "And, I'm not telling Ian."

That news didn't go over very well. Danny didn't like it either, but Jane put a hand on Liz's shoulder to show her support. He had to speak up after listening to everyone's arguments.

"Hey, guys." He put his hands up to silence them. "Ian is newly married, apparently because his wife is pregnant with a baby he never wanted. He has indicated to Liz *and* me that he has no desire to have children of his own. Personally, I would want to know if I was him, but I stand behind Lizabelle's decision. This is her choice."

"And, I met Ian's new wife," Jane said. "What a bitch. You guys don't want Ethan anywhere near that hag."

The family asked a few more questions, and before too long, Danny thought everyone was on board to support Liz. They agreed not to tell the kids because they didn't want a leak. Innocent words spoken to the wrong person could wind up on the Internet.

Danny wanted to hate Ian, but he tried not to leave a whole lot of room for hate in his heart. Besides being his neighbor and a decent guy, Ian had loved Liz. Danny believed he still did, and that he regretted what had happened. It obviously wasn't their time.

Liz wasn't ready for the celebrity life, and Ian was giving in to the pressures of it. Danny hoped Ian would come to his senses one day. He explained this to Jane as he drove her and their Christmas bounty to their cottages in the golf cart.

Jane brushed his arm. "I hope he wises up soon, too."

After helping her carry her things inside, Danny made sure she had plenty of firewood.

When she walked him out to the small front porch, her attention was drawn to the sky. "It's snowing."

She stepped out into the open air and lifted her arms and face to catch the flakes on her skin.

"Don't get too excited. It won't stick. The ground's too warm."

"I don't care." She smiled at the cloudy night sky. "I got a little white Christmas after all. This place is magic, Danny."

His heart lodged in his throat. With her head tipped back, her arms open, and the delicate move of her feet making her spin, she looked like an angel who might leave the earth at any moment. All he could think about was holding on to keep her on the ground.

She turned and caught him staring. "What is it?"

"You're magic, Jane." He stepped closer and took her hands. "I'm glad you came to Southland for Christmas."

"So am I."

He lowered his mouth to hers as the snowflakes

fell around them. Thoughts of snow faded as he focused on the warmth of his breath mingled with hers and the taste of peppermint on her lips.

His hands were on either side of her face, and her hands were on his chest. She had the power to stop him in her palms, but she didn't, not for a long, wonderful moment.

When she did push lightly against him, he didn't want to stop, but he broke the kiss.

He took a step back and noted a full feeling in his chest. "I'll meet you at five in the morning to run. The kids can't open Santa until six a.m. House rules."

***

Danny's eyes popped open. *What was that?*

He listened to the silence. Had he heard a scream? His thoughts immediately went to Jane as he grabbed his gun off the nightstand and went to peer out the window.

A light in her cottage came on, and he shoved his feet into his boots and ran to see if she was okay. When the cold night air hit his bare chest, he was more awake and alert than he'd been moments before. He was thankful for the long flannel pajama pants protecting his legs from the assault of wintry wind.

Opening the front door, he called out, "Jane?"

With his gun barrel pointed up, he moved into the bedroom. She was sitting up in bed with a dazed look on her face. The covers were thrown off, and she was soaked with sweat.

"Danny?" Wet hair clung to her face.

"Yeah, Jane, I'm here. You're okay." He put

his gun down on the hearth and grabbed the crocheted afghan, which hung on the back of the wingback chair.

She was shivering, and her teeth chattered as she tried to speak. "Bbbbbad ddddream."

He wrapped the blanket around her and scooped her into his arms. Carrying her to the chair by the fireplace, he sat, holding her in his lap, and rocking back and forth. "Shh, you're okay. It was just a dream." In his heart, he knew it was the real nightmare she had survived.

"You're okay, beautiful." He kissed the top of her head and continued stroking her wet hair, pushing it out of her face.

After a few minutes, she stopped shivering and relaxed in his arms. A moment later, she tensed again.

"I'm sorry to have woken you, Danny." She tried to get up, but he held on. "I'm afraid I may have soaked the bed."

"We have waterproof mattress protectors because of the kids. The bed is fine. When you feel like it, go clean up and change, and I'll find some fresh sheets."

Too soon, she made a move to get up. Danny reluctantly let her go, and she headed for the bathroom.

When the shower turned on, he stripped the bed and searched for linens. There were none in her cabin, so he ran to Johnny's cottage to get a clean set.

When he got back to Jane's and was about to make the bed, she exited the bathroom in the new nightshirt one of the kids had given her.

"Nice." He hoped the evidence of his attraction didn't show through his pajamas.

"Thanks. Let me help." She kept her gaze down.

They made the bed together, and after Danny helped her get settled back under the covers, he sat on the bed next to her. "Are you okay? Do you want to talk about it?"

"Sometimes talking about it makes it worse. The dreams, I mean." The covers were bunched in her fists under her chin.

"I'll wait here until you go back to sleep." He gestured to the chair by the fireplace.

"You don't have to." Her body trembled.

He rubbed her arms through the blanket. "I'm going to anyway. Don't argue. Go to sleep. Santa won't stop if you're still awake."

A slow smile spread across her face, and she closed her eyes. He brushed her still damp hair back from her face and kissed her forehead.

"I don't think Santa is coming for me." She yawned. "I'm on the naughty list."

Danny started to ask her what she meant, but he decided he really didn't want to know. Whatever it was, he was sure it had occurred before they met, and it didn't matter now.

Chapter Sixteen

Jane closed her eyes from exhaustion, but her mind refused to settle down. She focused on pleasant thoughts—the kiss in the snow. The one she'd felt down to her toes, and when he broke the kiss at her urging, she'd actually swayed at the shock of his lips not being where they belonged...on hers. When he'd held and rocked her, his body conveyed tenderness and protectiveness. She wanted more, but she couldn't have it, not yet.

The winter storm that brought her to Southland was the same one that prevented her from going to Philly to put a memory to rest. Until she had closure, she'd never be able to fully give herself to a man. She'd learned with Breck that even though she shared her body she never gave him herself, her heart.

When Jane awoke the next morning, she looked down at her sleepwear and hoped it was all part of the bad dream. How could she face Danny if he really had come to hold and comfort her during the night? Her fears were confirmed when she saw him sleeping in the chair at the foot of the bed near the fireplace. He was wrapped in the blanket he'd used to warm her.

She started to go into the bathroom to dress until she checked the time. It was almost five. Since his foot was propped on the end of the bed, she tapped his toes. "Hi. Merry Christmas. If we want to squeeze in a few miles and shower before the Santa frenzy, we better get going."

He peered at her from one open eye and looked sexy as hell doing it. She escaped to the bathroom to change. When she came out, he was gone. She started warming up and opened the front door when he knocked.

"This is going to suck." Jane pulled a beanie down on her head.

Danny was quieter than usual, so she tried to start the conversation. "I'm not going to get any surprise Santa presents this morning, am I?"

"No. Just the kids go this morning." He stifled a yawn.

Her throat felt thick, making the words hard to say. "I'm sorry I woke you last night, Danny."

"Don't mention it."

She was getting the feeling he didn't want to talk, so she shut up and ran off her bad dream and lack of sleep and her desire to feel Danny's arms around her again.

The nightmare had begun with her looking into the night sky at the falling snow. As the snow piled up around her feet, she'd realized it was ash—the ashes of her teammates who'd died in the explosion. She'd tried to run, but the ash turned to cement, holding her feet in place. Karl's head floated beside her, his eyes wild and his mouth open to speak. A blast silenced him and caused her to scream.

She often wondered if she'd screamed in real life when it happened. The detonation had knocked her back, and she'd fallen to the ground unconscious, so the experts said.

It didn't really matter. It was done, and she couldn't change it. Talking the day before about the incident and Karl had triggered her reliving that awful experience during the night.

She sent up a silent *Thank You* to the heavens, glad Danny hadn't come in a few minutes later. Her routine when she awoke from a bad dream, soaked through with sweat, was to strip off her clothes, and roll over to the dry part of the bed. She usually dealt with the aftermath the next morning.

Preferring to come unraveled without an audience, she was embarrassed Danny had seen her like that. She hadn't known Liz had heard her too when they were in Quiet Cove. That was why it was best to be alone, where she could suffer without disturbing anyone.

She needed to get back to L.A., but her flight wasn't until the next day. Maybe tonight she'd get a Christmas blessing and be able to sleep peacefully.

"You're running like something's chasing you," Danny said, sucking wind.

She wasn't surprised her pace had increased with the awful thoughts. Her past *was* chasing her, and she'd never be able to outrun it.

***

Danny left Jane to shower and dress, while he went to do the same. When he got back to her cabin, the hair dryer was on, so he took a seat on the couch.

Jane's phone was on the coffee table, and when it rang, he checked the display to see Breck Stanton calling.

On impulse, he answered. "Hello?"

"Hi…is this Jane's phone?"

"Hi, Breck, it's Danny. Yes, you've reached Jane's phone, but she's indisposed at the moment. I thought you might be in trouble. That's why I picked up."

"Oh, Danny…hello. Merry Christmas."

"Merry Christmas to you, too." Danny leaned back and crossed his ankle onto his opposite thigh.

"Are you in Philly with Jane?"

"No, Jane is with me." He started shaking his foot. "Her trip was cancelled due to the weather, and she was diverted to Atlanta, which is near my family's home. We're showing her Christmas, Southern style."

"I'm sure she loves that." His tone was sarcastic, but then he paused. "To be honest, I'm glad she didn't go back to Philly—too many bad memories. I'm in Maryland with my family. I was calling to see how her friends liked the autographed photos and to confirm our plans for New Year's Eve."

Danny's foot motion ceased. "I'll tell her you called," he assured Breck before he hung up.

He felt like he'd been hit in the gut. He was

already cranky from lack of sleep and trying to sort through his feelings for Jane, and Breck was muddying the waters.

Jane came around the corner. "Were you talking to someone?"

When he saw her, he immediately forgot about Breck. She wore black boots over black jeans and an emerald green sweater that was nearly the same color as her eyes.

He must have stared too long because she said, "I know it'll warm up later, and I'll need to change. I packed for Philly remember? I just wanted to be festive while the kids open their gifts from Santa."

"You certainly look festive." *And drop dead gorgeous.* His heart was racing, and he had no idea where to go from there.

"Who was on the phone?" She returned her gaze to where he held her cell.

"Oh…Breck called to say Merry Christmas. I didn't know you two were so friendly. When I saw him calling, I assumed he had trouble." Danny watched her face for a reaction.

She shrugged. "I'll speak to him later."

Danny's heart sank down to his stomach and tied itself in a knot. How could he compete with Breck Stanton? What was he thinking? He shouldn't even consider vying for her affection.

He was her boss, and he needed to remember that and remain professional, which meant no touching and definitely no kissing. If only he could forget the feel of her soft lips on his and the way their tongues had danced in perfect rhythm.

***

Danny enjoyed seeing the kids open their presents, while he shoved a fat and sugar-laden cinnamon roll down his throat and chased it with black coffee. Sticky buns were a Baker family Christmas tradition.

Jane had a cup of coffee, but passed on the dessert-for-breakfast as she called it.

Liz tossed her a grapefruit.

"Thanks." She began removing the peel.

"We tend to forget about good nutrition around the holidays. I'm sorry we didn't consider your dietary preferences," Liz said.

"Oh, no, Liz, I'm your guest, and I was unexpected at that. I should eat what's offered, but all that sugar before I have something solid in my stomach will make me sick."

"I'll make you some eggs when the kids are finished," Dixie said. "Honestly, it must take Santa weeks to wrap these gifts, and they open them in thirty minutes or less."

Danny moved to the stove and put eggs on to boil. "Good?"

Jane nodded. "Thanks."

The kids got new bicycles, so everyone went outside to watch them ride. Jane took a seat on the steps, and Carly plopped down next to her. Danny sat in the porch swing close by to listen to their conversation.

His dad joined him and pushed them in a slow, rhythmic cadence.

"How are you feeling, Dad?" Danny still worried, even though his dad's bypass surgery the summer before had been a success.

"Grateful to be able to spend another Christmas with my family." He nodded toward Jane. "What about it, son?"

Danny shook his head. "Nothing to it, Dad. Employee, remember?"

"I never let that stop me." His dad let loose with a shit-eating grin.

"No, you didn't. But, I'm not you."

"You can't be afraid to love, Danny. Life's too short not to grab onto it with both hands and all your heart. Especially when it's right in front of you." He stretched out an arm and put it around Danny.

"I don't know what I want." Danny stared at the toe of his boot.

"Holler at me when you figure it out. I've been saving something your mama wanted me to give you when the time was right."

He looked at his father and nodded. Danny was more than curious, but would rather discuss it with his dad privately. Big Daddy got up, and Danny's baby sister Maddie took the vacant seat. They swung in silence for a few minutes.

Danny cleared his throat. "Mad, do you still…you know? See stuff?"

"Not in a long time, brother. Why do you ask?" She turned on the swing to face him and propped her arm along the back.

Glancing at Jane for a second, he shrugged. "Just wondering."

Maddie looked over his shoulder. "Even though I don't 'see'," she made air quotations with her fingers, "doesn't mean I don't know that woman is carrying a heavy load."

"What? Like her aura or something?" Danny furrowed his brow.

Maddie smiled. "No. I can see it in her eyes—the pain she carries. This have something to do with that lover she lost?"

"Mama D's got a big mouth." Danny clamped his jaw shut.

"Actually, Katie told me. Mama hasn't said anything. Maybe you should stop being such a tight-ass and talk to her." Maddie smirked.

"Who?"

"The woman who loved you when you were unlovable. That's who."

Danny swallowed again as heat flooded his face. Sadly, he'd never grown completely comfortable with his step-mom who'd adopted him against his will after his real mom had died. They saw the world very differently. Maddie always had a way of opening his eyes to things he didn't want to see.

He turned his attention back to Jane and Carly's conversation.

"Aren't you going to ride your new bike?" Jane asked.

"Maybe later." Carly leaned to brush some dirt off the wooden step where she sat.

"Is this new bicycle bigger than your bike at home?"

"Yes, ma'am, and my bike at home has training wheels, so I'm not scared to ride it." Carly propped her elbows on her knees and poked her lips out.

"You are almost six, right?" When Carly

nodded, Jane continued. "When I was almost six, I rode the training wheels right off of my bike. I burned up the streets in my neighborhood on that little bicycle. It had pink streamers on the handlebars just like yours." Jane pointed at the new bike.

"One day," Jane moved her arms to mimic the motion of riding, "I was peddling really fast to go meet my friend, and I hit a bump. One of my training wheels shot off to the side and rolled away. I hit another bump, and the other one did the same thing." Jane's arms separated in two different directions.

Carly's eyes widened.

"Do you know what the scariest part was?" Jane asked.

Carly shook her head from side to side.

"The scariest part was that I didn't know how to stop without falling over. I was unprepared."

"What did you do?"

"At first, I didn't stop. I just kept riding in circles outside my friend's house, but I started to get tired, so I had to make a plan. I thought about how the training wheels worked. When the bike was not moving, a training wheel on each side held it up, so it didn't tip over. I needed something on each side to hold the bike upright. Guess what I used?"

Danny smiled as Carly thought through what Jane was telling her. "Your feet?"

"That's right." Jane held her legs out and pointed to her boots. "These puppies right here. I can show you if you want."

"Okay." Carly hopped up with a big smile.

Danny's pulse sprinted into euphoria, and he struggled with what his heart desired and what his head warned. Leaving Maddie on the swing, he followed Jane and Carly to offer his assistance to his niece if she needed it.

As they approached the bicycle, Jane said, "I do have to prepare you for the possibility you might fall over, if you don't get your feet down fast enough."

"Did that happen to you?" Carly asked.

"Yes, a time or two, at first, but once you get used to it, it becomes automatic, and you won't forget. Do you want to practice starting and stopping?" Jane asked.

"We'll stay close by to catch you if you fall," Danny said.

Carly smiled at him, and he bent to kiss her brown curls.

"Yes, we'll be right here, but…if you're ever riding by yourself and you fall, do you know what to do?" Jane asked.

Carly looked up with big eyes and shook her head from side to side.

"You pick yourself up, dust yourself off," Jane mimicked dusting herself off, "and get back on the horse."

Carly giggled. "You mean the bike."

"You know what I mean. Are you ready to ride?" Jane asked.

Danny's heart lightened as Carly squealed, and he laughed with Jane as they ran alongside her bike. None of his family would be able to run along and keep up, but he didn't doubt Jane could.

When Carly was ready to take off unassisted, they hung back and watched her as she joined her cousins to ride on the dirt lanes around the property.

Danny high-fived Jane. "That was a good thing you did."

She shrugged and stepped aside, so Tyler could ride his Big Wheel between them.

"These kids love you." Danny closed the distance between them.

Shrugging her shoulders, she hugged herself. "I haven't spent much time around kids. This could be a fluke."

He resisted the urge to touch her. "I don't think so. You have a way with them."

She smiled and turned to go reclaim her seat on the steps. Danny watched, but didn't follow. He wanted Jane in a bad way...and a good one.

Chapter Seventeen

Jane joined the ladies in the kitchen to help prepare the Christmas Day meal. The smell of turkey baking made her mouth water. Every burner of the industrial sized stove had a pot on it, and Jane could make out peas, potatoes, corn, eggs, squash, and some kind of greens.

Collards, she learned from Dixie.

Jane made it a point to ignore the dessert area, which was full of cakes and pies. There was enough food to feed an army, but then the Bakers were a small army.

The kids played outside, and the guys were in the family room watching sports. Jane tried not to steal glances at Danny, and she especially tried not to think about how he'd helped her with Carly and the bike.

When she realized where her fantasies were taking her, her heart drummed louder than Nick pounding on the full-size drum set Santa had brought him that morning. The dead could've been awakened. Funny how Jane used to think of her heart as dead.

The peaceful atmosphere disintegrated when Beth burst in the back door and yelled, "Help! Tyler fell down the old well."

There was an immediate frenzy of panic and activity. Jane kept her head and saw Danny's back as he ran out the door.

Jane grabbed Liz's arm to stop her from running out. "Wait. We need rope, maybe rappelling gear. Do you have anything like that?"

"The barn. Big Daddy and the boys climb."

"Show me."

In the barn, Jane grabbed rope, harnesses, and carabiners, while Liz pulled out a golf cart on steroids. There were also walkie-talkies. Jane tested two and was relieved the batteries were good.

She hopped on the cart next to Liz. "Stop by my cabin."

She ran in to grab a couple of things and then rejoined Liz who drove them to the site of the abandoned well.

"Did someone call emergency services?" Jane asked as she exited the golf cart with an armload of gear.

"Yes." Danny leaned his head down into the well.

"Talk to me, Danny." She stepped into a harness and started rigging up.

"The well was covered with a wooden lid. Tyler climbed on top and jumped, and the wood gave way. I can hear him crying." Danny ran his hand through his hair before he helped Jane with her harness. "I should go, but I won't fit."

"I've got this." Jane handed him a walkie and clipped the second to the collar of her sweater. She strapped her new knife onto her thigh and tucked her hair inside a ball cap with a side light attached at the brim. She turned the light on and moved to the opening of the well. It was narrower than she'd thought, no more than a yard across. A faint cry made her heart beat faster.

"This is a dry well, correct?"

"Yes, it was dug a long time ago when the water table was higher. It's been dry as long as I can remember." Danny knotted the rope.

She clipped in and handed the lead line to Danny as she sat on the edge of the well. "Don't drop me."

Danny secured the other end of the rope to the base of a sturdy pine tree nearby and got Johnny to help him with it.

Jane turned her attention to Paul and Jen, the boy's parents. They'd been yelling down the well to him, and Jen was crying hysterically.

"Try to speak in a calm voice. I know it's hard, but he'll take his cues from you. If you're hysterical, he might be too. He's already scared, and it'll be easier for me to get him up safely if he's calm."

They nodded and Jen aimed her sobs into her husband's chest as he rubbed her back.

"We're ready," Danny said to Jane, and she scooted off the edge and descended into darkness.

Tyler's wails grew louder as she neared the

bottom of the well. She estimated it was only about thirty-five feet deep as she planted her feet on the solid dirt floor of the space. Tyler was sitting right there, with his arms reaching up to her.

"Let me check you out, Little." She crouched and felt his head, arms, and torso. A cut on his forehead was bleeding down into his face. When she got to his legs, she could see they were both broken, and when she lightly touched his feet, his screech pierced her soul.

She wanted to pick him up, but she was afraid the impact of the fall could have caused a spinal cord injury. The fact that he was moving his arms was a good sign.

It was cold down in the damp, dark space, so she stripped off her sweater and wrapped it around the boy.

She used her knife to cut part of a sleeve off and secured it around his head wound. "There. You look like a festive elf gangster."

"Report." Danny's voice came through the walkie.

She pressed the button on her shoulder. "Do we have an ETA for the EMTs?"

"Inbound, but five to ten minutes out."

She reported her physical findings and her concern about a spinal cord injury. "Do you think we should wait for a straight board or just move him and take our chances?"

"Shit—" Danny's transmission cut out.

Out of the corner of her eye, Jane caught a slow, slithery movement. *Shit is right.*

She unsheathed her knife and turned in the

tight space to block the child from the new danger. The snake was coiling to strike, and all she could think was *don't let it get Tyler*.

The snake sprung and attached itself to her thigh. Its fangs got stuck on the polyester/lycra strap of her thigh rig. She grabbed the back of the snake's head and felt a sting in her leg before she pulled the serpent loose. Forcing it against the wall of the well, she sliced its head off.

She stood terrorized for a moment as she held the lifeless head, but watched the slithery body hit the ground and writhe around. *So much for sweet dreams tonight.*

She cut the other sleeve off the sweater, put the snake's head and now lifeless body inside and tied the ends. She carefully secured the package around the ankle of her boot.

"Come on Tyler, we're getting the hell…sinki out of here." She prayed she wouldn't cause Tyler further damage as she picked him up and turned him, so his back was against her side. His sobs were muffled in the closed space.

She should secure him with the rope, but her gut was telling her to get out *now*. She locked her left arm around the boy's chest, with his arms hanging free over hers.

"Asset secure. Get us the heck out of here." She let go of the walkie button and grabbed the lead line.

When they cleared the top of the well, cries of relief rang in her ears. It was a welcome sound from the eerie quiet of the well. The paramedics were approaching with a pediatric straight board.

"Check him for snakebites." She handed the boy off to them.

Silence descended on the group as Jane swung her feet around and set them on the ground. She opened the sweater sleeve and dumped the snake's remains out for them to see.

The family, which had crowded near, now took several steps back, until they realized the snake's head wasn't attached to its body. Profanity filled her ears.

"That's a rattlesnake."

"It was smart of you to bring it, so we'd know what kind of anti-venom we need," one of the medics said to her.

"Are you bitten?" Danny ran his eyes over her body, followed by his hands.

She removed the sheath from her thigh and handed it to him, but kept the knife. She cut her jeans to expose the area where the snake's fangs got her. There was one small area of broken skin on her thigh, and the area around it was angry red.

***

Danny climbed in the back of the second ambulance, after they'd loaded Jane in on a gurney. Concern burned a hole in his esophagus.

"Our medical covers snakebites, right?" she asked.

He shook his head, unable to believe how calm she was. "It's covered. Is this your worst Christmas ever?"

She let out a small laugh. "It's definitely going to be the most memorable. If Tyler's all right, then I'd say it's a damn good Christmas."

Danny moved closer, and before he could stop himself, he kissed her. She responded to the kiss, and he was reminded of what surviving a dangerous situation could do to the body as desire surged through him.

"Sir." A voice broke into his thoughts.

Danny broke the kiss and looked into Jane's eyes.

"We need to keep her heart rate down until we get her to the hospital and get the anti-venom," the paramedic said. "We keep it on board during the summer, but we don't get many snakebites this time of year."

Jane giggled and bit her lip.

Danny sat back. "Who gets bitten by a freaking rattlesnake on Christmas Day? Hell of a present."

At the hospital, they were told Tyler had *not* been bitten.

"That's good news," Jane said. "He has other injuries to recover from…and not just the physical ones. You should go be with your family."

Danny crossed his arms over his chest, his body aching to hold her. "I'm not leaving you."

The doctor came in with her gaze on the chart in her hands. "Hello, Ms. Dillon, I'm Dr. Cooper. The paramedics tell me you have a snake bite."

She was a pretty, young brunette, and when Danny recognized her, he turned his head, hoping she wouldn't notice him. He backed away from the bed.

"It's more like a small puncture, but I think some venom did break through," Jane said.

The doctor examined the area. "It appears so.

I'm going to give you the normal dose of anti-venom. Too much won't hurt, but too little won't help."

Danny didn't know she'd become a doctor.

She was preparing a syringe when she noticed his presence. "Do you want your husband here for this?" She held up the shot.

"Oh, he's not my husband. He's my—"

Before she could say boss, Danny interrupted, "Fiancé."

Jane tilted her head and narrowed her eyes, but she didn't argue.

Dr. Cooper turned to face him. "Danny? Danny Baker."

The doctor removed her gloves and shook his hand, but she didn't let it go when Danny tried to pull away.

A little smirk landed on Jane's lips.

Amanda Cooper looked into Danny's eyes like a crazy, love-struck teenager. Still crazy.

"No one told me the evasive, rich, and handsome Danny Baker was off the market."

"I'm sorry, have we met?" Danny asked.

Amanda's cheeks turned three shades of pink at not being recognized, but she let go of his hand. "I'm Amanda Cooper. We went to high school and college together. I dated your best friend Jason for a while."

"Oh right, Amanda. How've you been?" Danny asked, crossing his arms again.

"Very well as you can see." She waved a hand in front of herself as if to show off a prize.

Jane cleared her throat. "Can you two catch up

after I get the anti-venom?"

"Of course." Amanda gave her the injection.

She also gave Jane a shot of antibiotics, and Danny worried Dr. Cooper enjoyed sticking the needle in Jane a little too much. The doctor's warm bedside manner had turned icy, and too late, Danny realized his error.

"You're not wearing an engagement ring. If *I* were engaged to Danny Baker, I would *never* take my engagement ring off."

Before Jane could reply, Danny said, "She took it off before she descended thirty feet into an abandoned well to rescue my three-year-old nephew."

"It was thirty-five feet," Jane corrected Danny and added, "The ring would have weighed me down."

Danny pressed his lips in a tight line to conceal his smile.

"Well, now that *you've* been treated, I'll go check on the little guy. I want you to stay here for observation. We won't admit you unless we get overrun with emergencies and need the space. If everything looks good in a few hours, then you can go." Dr. Cooper was all business, and she obviously wanted them to know she too would have a role in helping Tyler.

When Dr. Cooper was gone, Jane said, "You should go and check on Tyler. See if there's an update."

"Not while Dr. Cooper is with him."

One corner of her luscious mouth turned up. "All right, spill it."

Danny groaned and sat on the edge of the bed, so he could speak quietly and not risk being overheard. He took her hand in his and launched into the tale.

"It's not all that exciting really. She stalked me a little in high school. Jason said she was obsessed with me. They went out a few months our senior year.

"Jason said that when they were intimate, she called him *my* name. He cut her loose right after because of it, but she thinks he's an asshole who got what he wanted then dumped her." Danny paused and twisted his lips.

"After they broke up, I started finding girls' panties in my locker. When it got closer to the end of the school year and prom, she kept showing up outside my classes fishing for an invitation. I asked a female friend to go with me. Amanda was pissed and egged my friend's car."

"She was crazy about you." Jane wriggled her eyebrows. "Emphasis on *crazy*."

"That wasn't the worst thing though." Danny tucked a strand of hair behind Jane's ear. "She befriended Katie who was two grades behind me. Katie was nice to everyone, which is why she was Homecoming Queen. I hadn't told anyone in the family, except Liz, about Amanda's antics and that was only because she overheard Jason and me talking about it one day. Katie unwittingly invited Amanda over for a sleepover. I found her naked in my bed that night."

"Wait a minute. Isn't that every teenage boy's dream come true? To find a naked girl in his bed?"

Danny shook his head. "Not *this* teenage boy and not *that* particular girl. I was shy, and I wasn't about to have sex with someone I didn't trust and who was bat-shit crazy."

Jane squeezed his hand. "What did you do?"

"I opened the door, turned on the light, and saw her there. I flipped the light off and said, '*Sorry, wrong room.*' Then I ducked across the hall into Liz's room. She hid me when crazy came knocking. I spent the night on the floor next to Liz's bed."

Jane pressed her lips together, and her chest bounced with stifled laughter.

"Are you laughing at me?"

Apparently struggling to straighten out her smile, she shook her head. "It sounds like you and Liz have had some adventures together through the years."

Danny leaned in and kissed Jane again. The sound of throat clearing behind him caused him to break the kiss.

Dr. Cooper stood there with her fists on her hips.

Chapter Eighteen

Still tasting Danny on her lips, it took Jane a moment to mentally return to her surroundings.

"Ms. Dillon, we're going to have to admit you for observation. We need this area for a multi-car accident that's coming in," Dr. Cooper said.

"Is that necessary?" Jane asked. "I could just sit in the waiting room."

Holding onto Jane's hand, Danny stood and faced the doctor. "Actually, Dr. Cooper, we have multiple nurses and a doctor in the family. I could take Jane home to Southland, and they can monitor her there. I'll bring her back right away if a problem develops."

Jane didn't miss the gleam in Dr. Cooper's eye before she checked her watch. "That will be fine. I work until seven. I'll come out and check on her myself when I get off."

"That won't be necessary," Danny said at the same time Jane said, "We don't want you to go to any trouble."

Dr. Cooper smiled an eerily serene, tight-lipped smile. "If you want me to release you now, Ms. Dillon, that's the condition. I must be permitted to check on you later."

There was no way in hell Jane would let this woman go to Southland to harass Danny or any of his family. "Then you can admit me."

Danny turned to her, his eyes searching. "No, Jane, let's go home."

"Dr. Cooper, would you give us a moment please?" Jane asked.

The doctor stepped out of the room, and Jane lowered her voice. "I'm not letting her go out there. She might be dangerous. I'd rather stay here and have your family remain safe."

"I don't want her at Southland either, but I think she's more of a danger to you. If you stay here, she might try something. I won't let her hurt you, Jane." He covered her hand with his free one. "In high school, she threw eggs, but now she can administer drugs. I don't think it's safe. *I* have a gut feeling about this."

Jane was torn. She trusted Danny's instincts, but she didn't want to endanger his family. If she was the target and she stayed away from Southland, the Bakers would be safe.

"Danny, I think we should tell her we aren't really engaged. Then, she won't be jealous anymore. Maybe she'll just strip down and offer herself to you." Her attempt at humor missed the mark by a long way, judging by his eye roll.

"It won't matter if we're engaged or not. She

saw me kiss you. You're still a threat in her mind. Don't argue, Dillon. Once we get home, we'll put security measures in place for her arrival."

After what seemed like forever, Jane signed the release papers saying she was being released against doctor's orders, but Danny was the one who let out a sigh of relief. He pushed her out of the ER in a wheelchair because she was supposed to stay still for a few more hours.

"Can we go check on Tyler?" Jane asked.

Danny texted Paul and found out they were in the OR waiting room.

When they arrived, Jen leaned down and hugged Jane tightly, crying on her shoulder. "Thank you. Thank you. Thank you. We can never repay you for saving our baby."

Paul patted Jane's back. "They're operating to repair the compound fractures in both of his legs, and they're putting metal plates and screws in his pelvis because of the fractures there too."

Mark, Maddie's husband, the physician in the family, squatted by her chair. "There was no damage to the spinal cord, which I know was a concern for you. It was a judgment call to pick him up, but you did the right thing. A snake bite on top of the other injuries might have been too much."

Danny put his hands on Jane's shoulders and kneaded gently. Some of the tension melted, and she stretched her neck from side to side.

An idea formed and she turned to look up at him. "Danny, we could wait here for a while to make sure everything goes well with Tyler's surgery. Maybe we can be ready to go around 7:00

and swing by the ER to catch Dr. Cooper before she leaves."

He squeezed her upper arms. "Dillon, I knew there was a reason why I keep you around. Smart and beautiful."

His lips were close to her ear, causing little shivers to dance along her spine. The pressure of his kiss on her temple soothed her a moment before she noticed his family looking at them with anticipatory smiles.

Jane put her hand on his. "I think you better explain."

Even though she'd heard it before, Danny telling them about Dr. Cooper, their unstable history, and his fake engagement to Jane had her squirming in her plastic wheelchair seat.

Mama D said, "Jane, honey, since you got snakebit and dragged into a lie that has made an enemy for you, I think you deserve diamonds for real. A pair of two carat diamond stud earrings might do the trick."

"I don't have pierced ears, and I don't wear jewelry, except for a watch." She gestured to her watch and noticed it was dirt caked. She licked her finger and tried to clear the watch face as she wondered about the rest of her.

The dirt was forgotten when the pediatric surgeon came out to tell the family Tyler's surgery was a success, and he was doing great. Jane let out a long breath and smiled at Danny who'd taken the seat next to her.

"Are you the hero of the hour?" the doctor asked.

Jane looked around, not realizing he was speaking to her. "I'm sorry?"

He gestured to her cut jeans and the bandage covering the wound on her thigh. "Is that where the snake bit you?"

"Who told you about that?" Her brow ached from the crease between her eyes.

"Tyler told me when we were getting him prepped for surgery. It was difficult to understand some parts of the story, but I got the gist of it from him and the rest from one of the nurses who heard it from the paramedics. Tyler said the snake jumped and you caught it and cut its head off."

Jane was amazed. "I don't know how he saw any of that. I was between him and the snake."

"I don't think he knows you caught the snake on your leg." The doctor laughed. "You're a very brave woman."

"Anyone would have done it to protect a child." Jane wanted to clear up his false impression that she was a hero. She had a job to do and she did it, no questions asked. She'd been filled with terror when she saw the snake, so *brave* was definitely not the word she would use to describe it. She'd been close to losing bladder control.

A reporter and camera man came into the waiting area, looking for someone to interview about the incident.

"Son of a bitch." Danny moved into a defensive position in front of Jane as did the rest of the family members who were present. They created a wall of bodies to block her from the camera and reporter.

When the surgeon stepped up, she was grateful he thought so highly of her after all. "I'm sorry, gentlemen. This is the OR waiting area. If you don't have a family member in surgery, we'll have to ask you to go. I don't want to call security, but I will if you don't leave."

Jane chuckled to herself. The Baker family was security at its finest. Speaking of finest, her eyes fixed on Danny's backside, which was at her eye level. She admired the curve of muscle there in the just-right fitted jeans.

Stop having inappropriate thoughts about your boss, even if you are his fake fiancé and his kisses curl your toes.

She was just as bad as Dr. Cooper, drooling over the man's finely toned rear.

***

Danny wanted to get Jane out of the hospital and back to the safety of Southland. It was only five in the afternoon, and he knew they couldn't wait for two hours until Dr. Crazy got off work, especially with the press hanging around.

Until he saw Jane's watch, he hadn't noticed, but she had dirt on her face and clothes. He remembered her arms had been dirt covered when she came out of the well in her black tank top, but Danny had wrapped his hoodie around her shoulders, and she still wore it. She hadn't mentioned it or made a fuss about wanting to clean up.

His sisters, including Liz who was low maintenance compared to most women, would be demanding a shower. Instead, Jane wanted to see about Tyler and wait out a lunatic to prevent her from going to his family's home. His heart was swelling, and it hit him that he was falling for Jane Dillon. They needed a new plan, and he had an idea.

"Come on." He grabbed the handles of the wheelchair. "Johnny, we need a lookout."

Johnny scouted the corridors ahead of them and gave them the clear signal until they got back to the ER.

"What are we doing?" Jane asked.

"We need to see Dr. Cooper," he told the nurse at the desk. "Tell her it's Danny Baker."

The nurse picked up the phone to call Dr. Cooper, and Danny leaned down to whisper in Jane's ear. "I'm about to flirt shamelessly. Try not to get jealous, my future wife."

She cut her eyes at him, but her smile betrayed her. "I'll try not to kick her ass when she flirts back."

"Danny, hi." Amanda Cooper stood in the doorway.

Walking toward her, he lowered his head in a conspiratorial way. "I need a favor."

"Of course, anything for you." She put her hand on his arm.

His skin crawled, but he held still. "You may have heard the press is here looking for Jane. They're also at Southland. I need to get her home and secure the gate, so no one can get in. Unfortunately, if you come out later like we planned, you might not be able to get through to the house."

She slid her hand down his arm and took his

hand. "How can I help?"

"Can you go ahead and check her now? And would you mind doing an interview in lieu of Jane? Let's face it, she looks a little worse for the wear." He nodded his head in Jane's direction and watched as the elegant and psychotic Dr. Cooper took in Jane's disheveled appearance with a curled lip.

"You can tell the reporters you treated Jane and are a family friend. They'll put your pretty face on the evening news, instead of her dirty one."

Danny wasn't playing fair, but it was working. Amanda Cooper was feeling very superior to his Jane. *His* Jane who could run circles around this psycho, literally and metaphorically. He was sickened by the very sight of the deluded woman in front of him, but he kept his smile in place and raised his eyebrows in silent question.

"Of course, I'd be happy to be of *service* to you, Danny. Like I've already told you, *anything* for you." Her finger ran down the center of his chest.

Amanda held the door open, so Danny could push Jane through for her final wound and vitals check. Sadly, Danny felt like he was the one getting checked over, like a stud on the auction block. Maybe if he showed her the goods, she'd get scared and run.

Chapter Nineteen

Johnny brought his truck around to the hospital entrance, and surprise danced in Jane's belly when Danny lifted her up into the seat. Even though he didn't need to, he slid her into the center of the bench seat and buckled her in.

Instead of dwelling on the tender way he handled her, and in order to calm her runaway heart, she focused on the music coming from the stereo. She hadn't been in the habit of listening to country radio, until she met Liz. It was growing on her.

"Way to prostitute yourself to get your way, big brother. I didn't think you had it in you," Johnny said after Danny filled him in on what had happened with Dr. Crazy.

"Trust me, I didn't enjoy it."

"Prostitutes don't enjoy it either," Jane said. "They just pretend to, so they can get what they're after."

She got a laugh from Johnny and a more

serious look from Danny. Afraid of what he might be thinking, she added, "That was smart getting her to do the interview. She'll downplay the hero angle they're trying to put on me and maybe boost herself up a bit."

"You *are* a hero." Danny tilted his head to one side.

"Yeah, a super-hot one, even if you are covered in dirt." Johnny winked.

"Please don't say that." She looked back and forth between the brothers.

"Since I met you," Danny said, "you've taken a bullet in the vest protecting Breck, you disarmed his stalker when she was inches away from killing him, you went down an abandoned well to rescue a three-year-old, and you faced down a rattlesnake for God's sake. Anyone with a brain would say that makes you a hero."

"Why do you sound angry about it?" she asked.

"Yeah, bro, chill. I bet Janie thinks she was doing her job. Just like another hero I know who rescued a couple of lost Boy Scouts."

Johnny was obviously speaking about Danny, and she realized she didn't know very much about him, except that women wanted him. That part she got. Physically speaking, he could make the Greek gods ashamed of themselves.

What she did know was she trusted him and he was a good man. He loved his family; although, they drove him a little nuts, but that was normal, right? Her heart squeezed when she allowed herself to admit she wanted to know him better; not just physically, but the man inside. She wanted to know his hopes and dreams, as well as his fears and failures.

She almost reached over to hold his hand, but a little voice in her head made her stop.

He's your boss, not your fiancé.

She couldn't reach out to him. In fact, she should pull back.

***

When they arrived at Southland, Danny cursed under his breath. There were news vans parked at the end of the long driveway, and reporters rushed toward the truck when Johnny slowed to turn.

"Must be a slow news day." Johnny punched the accelerator, and Jane fell over onto Danny before she could brace herself.

He helped her right herself and put a protective arm around her. Her muscles tensed. Something between them had changed in the last few minutes.

He'd been trying to come up with an answer to her question, not wanting to tell her the real reason he had gotten angry, because she wouldn't like it. Not only did he realize he was falling for her, but he should've been protecting her and keeping her out of danger. That's what real men did for their women. The anger had caught him off guard.

Jane was capable of taking care of herself, and the rational part of his brain knew it was true. She'd proven herself over and over. His irrational heart wanted to wrap itself around her and never let anything or anyone dangerous near her.

Jane asked Johnny to drive her straight to the cottage, so she could clean up before going up to the main house.

"Can I help you?" Danny asked as he walked her to the door.

"No, I'll be fine. Thanks." She stepped inside.

"I'll come back for you in an hour."

"Actually," she turned, her gaze on his chest, "if Liz isn't busy, will you ask her to come?"

"Of course." He tried not to show his disappointment. He wanted to be there for her.

At the main house, Danny attempted to focus on the Christmas movie playing, instead of thinking about Jane. He knew she saw her actions as doing her duty, just as he had when he'd rescued the Boy Scouts.

He'd been on hundreds of missions with his SEAL team, but saving those young boys when they got lost exploring caves was particularly rewarding. He didn't feel heroic, but he had the skills necessary to do the job, so he did it, and four boys on the verge of dehydration lived to get lost another day.

When Jane and Liz came in the back door, the kids rushed her, holding up drawings they'd done for her.

"Wow!" Jane admired the artwork. "You guys are so talented. Thank you very much." Kneeling, she gave them hugs.

Danny observed as the new reigning Queen of Southland sat down to get waited on for the first time since she'd arrived. Her bare face revealed dark circles under her eyes.

She had to be exhausted, and she barely ate any of the food Liz fixed for her. If he was right, she hadn't eaten since breakfast.

He nodded at her plate. "Your body will heal

faster with proper nourishment."

"I know, I'm just not very hungry." Her smile was weak.

Danny wanted some alone time with her, but with his family hovering, he didn't think he'd get it.

"Do you want me to call the airline to postpone your flight tomorrow?" Liz asked.

"No, I need to get back," Jane said.

Everyone stopped what they were doing and turned to look at Jane.

"Are you sure it's okay to travel so soon?" Liz asked.

"I'll be fine. I have to rehearse for a dance competition," Jane explained.

"When's the competition?" Liz asked.

"New Year's Eve. We haven't even started the choreography, and my partner needs a lot of practice."

A flash of red burned in Danny's brain. "Breck Stanton is your dance partner."

It wasn't really a question, but everyone thought it was.

"Oh, my God!" Beth and Jenny said in unison.

"Really?" Liz asked.

Jane nodded. "I thought I told you."

Standing abruptly, Danny said, "Jane, I'll take you back to the cottage, so you can pack."

He waited outside and tried to talk some sense into himself, while Jane said her goodbyes to his family.

***

Jane slid onto the seat of the golf cart. Behind the wheel, Danny's jaw ticked. She couldn't understand what he had to be upset about. It was Christmas Day, he had a great family, and his nephew was doing well—all things to celebrate.

She'd been preoccupied since Liz had walked in on her toweling off after her bath. Liz's eyes had fixed on the large scar on Jane's side. Always careful to conceal it, she quickly covered up. People would want to know the details, and she didn't like to share her personal nightmare. She didn't want anyone to know how damaged she was. In fact, besides the doctors, Breck was the only one who'd seen her body, imperfect as it was. He'd called her beautiful, but he was an award winning actor.

Jane sighed and Danny did the same.

When he stopped in front of her cabin, she turned in her seat. "Do you have something to say to me?"

"I have a question for you, Jane." His nonchalant tone was betrayed by his stiff body language. "Are you screwing Breck Stanton?"

She was floored. How did he know? She took a deep breath, ready to come clean. If she lost her job, she'd just have to find something else. "It was only once."

His head dropped as his eyes shut tight. He looked up and gave her a bitter smile. "When?"

She hesitated as a few choice words flashed in her head. "The night before I met you."

Silence filled a tense moment. "So the night of the awards ceremony, after you saved his ass? Maybe instead of calling you a hero, we should call you the hero slut."

"Great idea." She got off the cart and took a

few long strides to reach the porch of her cabin. "Why don't you get me a cape? You can put SS on it for Super Slut. I'll fly around and save all of the eligible men and then fuck them blind." She went into the cottage and slammed the door.

After she leaned against the door with clenched fists for a moment, she locked it and pulled a heavy wooden table in front of it. She wasn't accepting any more visitors. Southland sucked, and she was ready to get far away.

After she packed, she lay down to try to sleep. She wanted to cry, but she didn't have the energy.

The minutes and hours ticked by on the bedside clock. When she gave up and rolled out of bed, it was early the next morning. Her leg looked much better, but she redressed the wound anyway. She moved the table and sat on the sofa, waiting until it was time to leave.

There was a knock at the door, and the speech she'd been rehearsing grew wings and flew from her mind. She had no idea what she'd say to him.

Bracing herself, she opened the door to Liz and Johnny. Veiling her mixed emotions with a stoic mask, she prayed her boss hadn't shared her news.

"Danny went up to see Tyler at the hospital, so Johnny is gonna to take you to the airport," Liz said.

"Great. Thanks, Johnny." She turned to get her luggage.

"I'll take that." Johnny grabbed her suitcase and went to the truck.

Liz hugged Jane tight. "I hope you'll be okay. Are you sure you can't stay?"

"I'll be fine, and I'm pretty sure I've

overstayed my welcome."

"Did something happen?" Liz's brows knitted together.

A long, slow breath escaped Jane's mouth as she pressed her hand against her stomach. "It's best if you leave it alone, Liz. I'll see you in a week, if I'm not fired." Jane tried to walk past her.

Liz put a hand on her arm. "What? Why would you say that? You should get a bonus for rescuing Tyler. I'll talk to Danny."

"Don't do me any favors." Jane turned to go, swallowing the lump forming in her throat. She turned back.

Stomping on the uneasiness it might cause, Jane stepped out of her comfort zone and threw her arms around Liz, hugging her close "Thank you for being my friend."

Chapter Twenty

When she landed in L.A., Jane called Joe to ask for a meeting. He told her to come to the office. She'd already called Breck and left him a message, so he'd know the jig was up.

"You look like something the cat dragged in." Joe directed her to a chair, while he leaned on the edge of his desk.

Sitting, she gripped the chair handles until her knuckles turned white. "I've had a hell of a holiday, Joe. Have you spoken to Danny?"

"No, why do you ask?" Moving to the chair next to her, he sat.

"I think he's going to fire me, and I deserve it." Her lungs deflated once the words were out of her mouth.

"Why would he fire you when you're handling a very sensitive matter for him?"

Taking in a deep breath, she answered, "Because I slept with Breck the night of the awards ceremony." She braced herself for a verbal attack.

His eyebrows shot up just before he pursed his lips. "So?"

"It was a breach of conduct. And it wasn't my first, but I do hope it was my last." She closed her eyes and flared her fingers before gripping the chair arms again.

"You sleeping with someone on staff? Because you haven't had any male clients besides Stanton." His nonchalance was off-putting.

Her gaze landed on his. "No, not here with B&B. My last job. I was intimate with one of my teammates. It was against the rules, so we kept it quiet. It could have endangered everyone. Most of our team, including him, was killed in action, but *not* because of our affair." She looked down at the floor.

"I know what happened to your team, Jane. Your boss from Philly called me. He wants you back. In lieu of that, he wants me to talk you into attending a ceremony to honor your fallen comrades."

She ran a hand through her hair. "He's been calling me too."

Joe squeezed the hand resting on her jean-clad thigh. "I don't want you fired. I think you're an asset to our company. I *do* think we could utilize your skills better if you were here in L.A. full time. Do you want me to talk to Danny about getting you back here?"

"I'm actually enjoying my current assignment." Suspicion made Jane narrow her eyes. "It sounds like you're willing to overlook my indiscretions."

"I know what happened that night. I know what it's like to get shot at. Increased libido after a traumatic event has been scientifically proven. I'd be more surprised if you didn't do it. You're a warrior, Jane. I don't think Danny sees you that way, but that's what you are."

"I used to be a warrior, Joe. I'm changing, and I don't know if it's for the better or not." She rubbed her eyes with the heels of her hands "If you and Danny decide to let me go, can I ask you for a reference?"

"Don't think like that. But yes, you can count on me. I have friends with a similar business to ours in the Big Apple. They'd hire you in a second, and you're accustomed to city living, so it wouldn't be a huge adjustment for you." His comforting smile settled some of her distress.

"Thank you." She rose to leave.

Standing beside her, he said, "Carol wants you to stop by the salon and say hello while you're in town. She has a Christmas gift for you."

"I will. I have something for you guys too." He kissed her cheek and she kissed his.

Joe reminded her so much of her old chief, who had been a good friend of her grandfather. Joe's wife, who was a stylist to the stars, had coached Jane on hair and makeup when she'd first joined B&B. A few times, Jane had gone undercover to clubs and parties, working as muscle for hire for actresses. Joe and Carol were good people, and she was glad someone believed in her.

As she left the office, her phone buzzed with a text: *I need to see you.*

Next stop, Breck's house. They had a competition to get ready for. And possibly an inquisition.

***

Two days after Christmas, Danny left Liz in the protection of their family at Southland, while he flew to L.A. He'd scheduled a meeting with Joe and Breck at Breck's house. It was time to sit down and find out the truth about Breck's relationship with Jane.

Having sensed Danny was too emotional about the situation, Joe had warned him against being irrational. He insisted on being present for the interview because Stanton was one of their best clients and referred everyone he met to B&B. Breck Stanton alone had doubled their client list.

"Do you know why we're here, Breck?" Joe asked.

"Yes." He crossed his arms over his chest.

"Jane called you?" Danny asked.

"Yes. She wanted me to know the ax was about to fall on her ass. Mine too, I guess."

"That's not accurate, Breck," Joe said. "We just want to sort out what happened while she was in charge of your safety. Anything you two do on your own time is your business."

Danny wanted to take issue with that, but he couldn't. He bit back a growl.

Breck gave his abbreviated account of the time he spent in Jane's house, and it matched what Jane had told both Danny and Joe.

"We need to know if you're in a relationship with her, for future reference regarding assignments," Danny said.

"I care about Jane, but she's in love with a ghost. I got lucky that night, pardon the pun, but either way, something…or someone is preventing her from moving forward with me. We're friends and dance partners. And I'd rather have her in my life in a limited way than not at all."

"When I asked you if you had a thing for her, why did you lie and say she was a lesbian?" Danny asked.

"She didn't know about that until after I said it. I panicked. I didn't want her to get in trouble, and I thought if I told you I had a crush on her, you guys would move me. I wanted more time with her. Can you blame me?"

Danny walked away from the meeting with a peace he hadn't expected. Jane wasn't in love with Breck.

He thought back to the night of Jane's bad dream when she'd said she was naughty. At that time, he'd told himself that whatever she'd done before she met him didn't matter.

Her night with Breck had happened "*the night before I met you.*" The words echoed in his mind.

Danny still wasn't sure how he wanted to proceed with Jane, but he'd consider himself lucky if she'd forgive him.

Chapter Twenty-one

On the second day of the New Year, Jane boarded a plane that would return her to the east coast. Apparently, Joe and Danny had ultimately decided not to fire her, since the only thing she'd heard from either of them was a text from Joe telling her *all was well*.

When she arrived at Danny's beach house, she was greeted by Liz who was genuinely glad to see her and gave her an update on how everyone was doing, particularly little Tyler.

"When he opened the package you sent and saw the hat, he was so excited. They can't get him to take it off," Liz said. "It's especially great for nighttime because he's more afraid of the dark now than before the accident. Paul and Jen just remind him to turn on the hat brim light if he gets scared."

Jane smiled at the thought of the little boy sleeping in the hat she'd sent him. She'd almost sent him a stuffed snake, but she was afraid it would scare him. Hell, it scared her. She'd be happy if she never saw another snake in her lifetime, real or fake. It was bad enough on the occasions when they slithered into her dreams.

Liz asked about the dance contest, and Jane showed her the videos online of the two dances she and Breck had performed.

"It was a blast." Jane shifted in her seat as they watched YouTube. "Best New Year's I've had in a few years."

"Amazing," Liz said, "and so glamorous."

The smile which lit up Jane's face was real to her core. "I haven't performed publicly in years, but it was thrilling. I love watching the other dancers as much as I love dancing myself."

"I'm sure dancing with Breck was a bonus."

Jane's exuberance waned a little. "We won first place, but I'm sure it was more about Breck's popularity than our actual talent."

"Y'all are wonderful, Jane. Don't try to downplay how awesome you are just because a little recognition scares you."

"Breck inspires a confidence in me I haven't felt for a while. But, don't misunderstand. I love him, but only as a friend." Jane put on her most serious expression.

When they sat down to eat dinner, Liz asked, "What happened with Danny? I asked him, and he wouldn't talk about it. He said it was work related. I also asked him about your scars, and he wouldn't talk about that either."

Jane sat thoughtfully, trying to decide what and how much she should say. Her gut told her Liz wouldn't talk to anyone else, except for maybe Danny.

"I slept with Breck. It was only once…well, it was only one night. It was before I met Danny, but I was working for B&B and taking care of Breck. I was on duty, so to speak."

"You were on duty, and Breck was on booty. Woot-woot."

"You're making jokes? Don't you think I'm a complete hussy?"

Liz laughed. "I can hardly point fingers." She rubbed her growing belly. "I'm knocked up with a married man's baby, and he doesn't even know. Not to mention, I'm unwed myself."

"Cut it out, Liz. He wasn't married when you dated him. Plus, you loved him, which is more than I can say about Breck. I had a bona fide one-night stand."

"Don't you mean *boner*-fide?" Liz laughed.

"It was bone-a-riffic." Jane slapped the table. "I'm so bad."

"How come you're so hard on yourself?"

Jane shrugged. "I don't know. I do know I regret what I did. When Danny asked me about it, I didn't lie. I wanted to come clean, but he was really upset."

"It's because he has feelings for you."

Jane shook her head. "No, he doesn't. He's too professional for that; although, he doesn't mind faking it when it suits him."

"Sometimes, love sneaks up on you when you aren't looking. How do you feel about my brother?" Liz sipped her water.

"What I feel doesn't matter." She changed the subject. "You asked about my scars. I was in love with a man I worked with, Karl. We were in an explosion. He died and part of me died with him. Can you see the inherent danger in loving someone who works in a job like ours? I can *never* let myself do that again. I don't think I'd ever come back from another loss like that."

"I could never pretend to understand what you've suffered and lost. I'm so sorry." Liz patted her hand. "None of us is promised tomorrow, Jane, and *everything* happens for a reason." She caressed her belly. "I've never met anyone more perfect for Danny than you. I think you two are meant to be together."

"Even if I wanted to quit my job and pursue a relationship with Danny, he'll never forgive me for Breck. Plus, I'm still friends with Breck, which is what prompted Danny to ask me about him. Danny called me a hero slut." The words still stung. She had called herself a slut a million times since the night with Breck, but to hear it from Danny's mouth really was like a slap in the face. Pressure built behind her eyes.

Liz gasped. "He did not call you a slut!"

When Jane nodded, Liz said, "Well, that confirms it. He definitely has feelings for you. Danny rarely loses his temper, and he's never outright rude or insulting to anyone."

"That doesn't confirm he has feelings for me. In fact, it kind of confirms the opposite." Jane put her napkin down next to her plate.

"Uh-uh, I know my brother. I bet he apologizes

the next time he sees you."

"Liz, you're probably the closest thing I will ever have to a sister, but Danny and I...we're not gonna happen."

***

Danny called Liz to tell her what day he'd be arriving and that he might get in late. He didn't want Jane to leave before he got there because he needed a chance to try to apologize for being so hateful to her.

His parents had raised him better than to mistreat people, but with Jane, he had a hard time controlling himself. Whether it was kissing her or yelling at her, he did it involuntarily.

He pulled into the driveway at South Winds and got out to catch a glimpse of the water. A thunderhead floated over the ocean, and the rumble from it mirrored the sensation is his gut. He let his head fall back as a flock of seabirds soared overhead.

Please God, mama, whoever's up there—let her listen.

Not having called ahead, he approached cautiously, in case Jane was armed. He used his key to open the front door and heard the sound of hysterical laughter coming from the living room.

Peering around the corner, he saw Liz in a one-piece maternity swimsuit, rubbing her belly and talking in a funny voice, which Danny recognized as her sexy transvestite voice. Jane was half-lying on the couch in a one piece swimsuit with a sarong tied around her waist, holding her stomach as she laughed out loud.

Danny walked in and put his hands on his hips. "What's going on in here?"

It was a mistake to surprise them after all because within Jane's reach was a pistol, and she was on one knee braced to fire within three seconds.

Damn, she's fast.

He put his hands up. "Don't shoot."

"Danny." Liz hugged her belly and bent over. "Why didn't you call us? You scared the hell out me."

Jane put the gun down and moved to check on Liz by putting a hand on her stomach. "Are you all right? You didn't pull anything, did you?"

Panic went off like a bomb in his gut, and he too moved to check on Liz. "What's wrong? Are you having pain?"

"No, I think I'm fine, y'all. Stop fussin'. I just jumped and felt something pull."

"I'm so sorry, Lizabelle. I didn't mean to scare you." He helped her into a chair. "I just heard y'all cuttin' up, and I wanted to see what was so funny."

"Why didn't you call ahead?" Jane asked, her voice hard like the last time he'd heard it.

"Because I didn't want you to leave before I got here. I need to talk to you."

"If you just want to tell me what a floozy I am, don't bother, I've heard it before." Jane turned to go.

Danny called after her. "I want to apologize to you, Jane."

Halting her retreat, she turned halfway back to him. The muscular lines of her body acted as a momentary distraction. Hope swelled in his chest. If she'd listen, then maybe they could fix what was broken between them.

He stayed kneeling beside Liz, but looked up at Jane. "I behaved very badly when I last saw you. I should've been showing you my gratitude, but instead, I acted demented. I can understand if you find it difficult to forgive me, but I hope in time, we can be friends again."

Jane turned fully toward him. "I'm sorry too. I was stung by what you said, and I reacted badly. I regret my improper conduct."

She appeared to clamp down then, to stop herself from saying more.

"Truce?" he asked.

"Truce." Her phone rang. "Excuse me." She walked out onto the balcony.

"Why does a woman who looks like that wear a one-piece?" Danny asked the air. He was startled when his sister answered because he'd forgotten her for a moment.

"To cover a bad scar," Liz said.

He turned her way. "Are you sure you're okay, Lizabelle?"

"I feel fine. I guess belly laughing could pull something just as easily as getting the pee scared out of me."

"Don't tell me you've lost bladder control already? What was so funny anyway?"

"Jane started it, and I got carried away. A little while ago, we were lying out on the beach to get some Vitamin D. I couldn't get comfortable with this all out front, so Jane suggested we dig a hole in the sand and bury my belly in it."

Danny laughed, but Liz said, "I haven't gotten to the funniest part yet. Anyway, I was real comfortable lying there like that when Jane said, 'horny teen alert'. I started to roll over, but she told me to stay put.

"These two young punks stopped to talk to us. They were hitting on both of us and let me tell you, I was flattered. I haven't had a man look at me like that since, well, since I got knocked up in the first place." She pointed to her belly again.

"Anyway, the boys complimented Jane's toned muscles and my *curves*. Jane signaled for me to roll over, and she said, 'Do you like this curve too?' You should've seen their faces. As they were running away in horror, Jane yelled after them, 'Hey, look at the bright side, you can't get her pregnant.'" Liz laughed again. "I swear, I love her to death."

A much as he wanted to deny it, Danny was pretty sure he did, too.

Chapter Twenty-two

Jane got up early the next morning to run before she had to go to the airport at noon. She'd turned in soon after dinner the night before, to give Liz some time with her brother and to avoid Danny.

Even though they'd declared a truce, Jane wasn't comfortable around him. And she wasn't sure if she'd ever be again.

After she'd packed and put her suitcase by the door, they met her in the kitchen, obviously wanting to talk.

"What's up?" she asked, using the kitchen island to separate herself from them.

"We're going to Southland next month to celebrate Danny's fortieth birthday," Liz said. "We want you to come with us. You can help Danny drive. We're leaving on Thursday and returning on Monday. That Monday is the first day of your next break, so you can fly out of Atlanta if you want. What do you think?"

Trying to place the dates in her mind, Jane blinked. Her heart practically reached out of her chest to say yes, but she wasn't sure she wanted to be in such close quarters with Danny or to return to Southland, where his words probably still lingered. She didn't think it was a good idea. *People call me brave, but I'm too weak to face some fears.*

"I'm not sure." She couldn't look at Danny. "I may be unwelcome."

"Are you kidding? Our family adores you. You're the hero. I know you hate hearing that, but it's true. It's only going to be the grownups because I don't want the kids to see me like this." Liz pointed to her baby bump. "It's too much to ask them to keep it a secret. Plus, it sets a bad example with the whole unwed mother thing."

"And you think I'm hard on myself." Jane shook her head.

"*I'm* the one who made you feel unwelcome before and I'm sorry," Danny said. "The family doesn't know anything about what happened. Only Liz knows and that's because you told her."

Jane did feel better with the knowledge that the Baker clan didn't know she'd had a one-night stand with Breck Stanton, especially since she was his bodyguard.

The urge to apologize to Danny again made her feel weak, but her gut told her he needed to hear it. "I'm sorry for what I did, Danny." Jane looked him in the eyes before her own pricked with tears. Maybe she'd needed to say it, too.

To stave off the waterworks, she looked away. She wasn't a crier, except for in her nightmares or right after she woke up from them, but she was getting better. On the nights it happened, she imagined Danny's arms around her as he rocked and comforted her. Soon, she'd go back to sleep and have sweeter dreams of chasing little girls on bicycles as Danny ran next to her.

She really did wish she could go back in time and undo it, but in life, specifically life and death, there were no do-overs. She could use excuses to justify what she'd done like Joe, Liz, and Breck tried to do for her. She could share the blame with Breck, but ultimately, it had been her decision. She'd known it was wrong, and she'd done it anyway. Danny had taken it hard, and she was sorry she'd disappointed him.

His hand touched her shoulder. "Jane—" A knock at the door interrupted him. "I'll be right back."

***

Danny rushed to beat Liz to the front door as dread settled in his chest. He didn't want her to answer the door in case it was anyone other than Girl Scouts selling cookies.

Opening it to a short, round man holding a pen and pad, Danny stifled a curse. A camera hung from a strap around the man's neck.

Oh, hell.

"Hi, Mr. Baker? My name is Ralph Cunningham. I'm a reporter for the Herald. I'm following up on a story and was told I might find Elizabeth Baker here."

Danny's first idea was to put a bullet in the guy and shut him down, but since lethal force wasn't called for yet, he had to think fast. "Wait here. I'll see if she's available."

He went back to the kitchen and found Jane and Liz hugging.

"We've got a problem. A reporter looking for you." He pointed to Liz.

"Oh no, what do we do?" Liz asked.

"I have an idea, if Jane is willing to play?" He raised his eyebrows.

"I'd be happy to cripple his ass, but I get the impression you have something else in mind."

Sexy and formidable. Damn. Focus, Baker.

"Do you want to be Mrs. Elizabeth Baker for a few minutes? Test your acting skills?"

"I'll do my best, but I'm no—" Her sentence abruptly halted as she headed for the door.

Before he shooed Liz to take cover, Danny narrowed his eyes at Jane's back, certain she'd just stopped herself from mentioning Breck.

Jane opened the door and stepped out onto the porch with Danny on her heels. "May I help you?"

The reporter reintroduced himself. "Are you Elizabeth Baker?"

She nodded once. "What's this regarding?"

"I suppose I'm looking for a different Elizabeth Baker." The man's face fell as he held up a photo of Liz.

"She's very pretty. Why are you looking for her?" Jane crossed her arms over her chest.

"She had five minutes of fame a few months back when she dated television star, Ian Clarke. She dropped out of sight, and no one has been able to get an interview," he said, slipping the picture into his pocket.

"I remember that. That's old news though. Isn't he married to that model? Oh, I forget her name." Jane tapped her chin with her index finger.

Danny fell a little deeper in love with his Jane.

"Emma Stuart. Yes. They were married very quickly after he and Ms. Baker ended their relationship. But no one knows her side of the story. What happened to make it end as quickly as it began?"

"Who cares? There'll be a new celebrity breakup tomorrow. Honestly, I can't keep up," Jane said.

"Where are you folks from?" the reporter asked.

"We're snowbirds from Pennsylvania. We spend most of the winter months here to get away from the snow and ice," Jane said.

Appreciating his fake wife, Danny put his arm around her shoulders. "If there's nothing else, Mr. Cunningham, I was about to drive my wife to the airport. She's flying up to PA for a few days."

"No, that's all. Thank you for your time. I apologize for the interruption."

Danny hugged Jane to his side, while they watched the man leave.

Once they were safely inside, Danny kissed the side of Jane's head before he let out a sigh. "Lizabelle, you're going to have to keep a low profile, sister."

"As if you weren't already." Jane grabbed her phone, dialed, and put it on the kitchen counter.

"Jane, I'm so glad you called. Do you have

good news for me?" A man's voice came through the speaker.

"Actually, Chief, I need a favor." Jane rested her hands on either side of the phone.

Looking to Liz, Danny tilted his head and furrowed his brow. She shrugged and raised an eyebrow.

"Tell me you'll be here for the ceremony and anything you ask is yours."

Jane squeezed her eyes shut, causing Danny's chest to tighten. "I'll be there."

"Great news. What's the favor?"

"I need two people entered into the Pennsylvania DMV yesterday." Jane glanced at Danny.

"I'll need names, photos, the usual info."

"Elizabeth Ann Baker with my photo and Daniel Ethan Baker. I'll send you the photo now." She aimed her camera phone. "Say cheese, Baker."

He stood still and blinked after the flash temporarily blinded him. She told the chief the rest of the information he needed, including an address, which Danny believed to be false.

"Jane, let me know your travel arrangements. I'll pick you up at the airport. You're staying with us, of course. Martha wouldn't hear of anything else."

"Yes, Chief. I'll be in touch. Thanks again."

"I'll see you in a few weeks, Janie."

Jane disconnected and dropped her head in her hands.

"Where are you going?" Liz asked.

She stood up straight. "Philly. I need an extra

day off next month, boss. I'll go with you guys to Southland, but I'll have to fly out on Sunday, instead of Monday."

"Anything you need. Thank you for that by the way." He pointed to her phone. "I wouldn't have thought the reporter might attempt to confirm our identities. Smart move."

"Did you just sell your soul for that favor?" Liz asked.

"I need to go. I just don't want to." Jane put her hands behind her neck and squeezed.

Wanting to do that for her, but knowing he couldn't, Danny fisted his hands. He'd done it at the hospital in Georgia when they'd shared something special, before he'd ruined it. He wanted to get back to the place where they were comfortable with each other again.

Remembering her nightmare at Southland, he'd never wanted to hold and comfort a woman like that before. And he'd wanted to hold her every night since, including the night he found out about her and Breck.

He let go of his reservations as his arms encircled her and pulled her close. Inhaling deeply, he memorized her scent, a mild mint and lavender, which both soothed and enticed.

Her body melted into his for half a second. Then, seeming to remember herself, she pushed away, leaving a need for her Danny had never felt before. He cracked his knuckles to stop reaching out to her.

Having offered to drive Jane to the airport, Danny agreed to let Liz tag along, so she could get out of the house. She laid down in the backseat when they left the house, in case there were any unwanted eyes around.

Jane's phone rang and she answered. "Hi Breck, what's up?"

There he was again, always rearing his head just when Danny managed to put the superstar out of his mind. He wanted an intimate connection with Jane. Breck had taken her to bed and now had the honor of being her friend.

"Yes, Liz is with me. I'll put you on speaker." She held the phone up.

Breck's voice came on the line. "I need advice. The director of this new movie I'm filming wants me to do an all-nude love scene. Not frontal nudity and only the waist up on my co-star. What should I do?"

"Have you done all-nude love scenes before?" Liz asked.

Danny couldn't believe what Breck was asking, and the women were actually going to give him advice.

"No, this would be my first," Breck said.

"I say less is more," Liz said.

"That depends on the context, Liz," Jane said. Liz laughed and Jane added, "What's your gut telling you, Breck?"

"I don't think I'd be comfortable with it. It's one thing if you're alone with a woman and another if you're on a movie set with fifty people, being filmed for an even wider audience."

Danny's mind went down a dark road, where Breck had his hands on Jane. He forced it back to the present.

"I think you have your answer," Jane said.

"Now, I need advice on how to tell the director."

Danny decided to put his two cents in. "Tell him you have a hairy ass."

"Danny? That's good advice man, thanks. Um, do I have a hairy ass?"

"You might if you stopped *man*scaping," Jane said.

"Thanks, guys, I appreciate it. Danny, Lovely Liz, Sweet Ginger, I'll talk to you later."

Danny saw Liz's smile widen in the rearview mirror, and he was pleased with Breck, despite his envy.

"Breck," Jane said. "Stick to your guns. Don't let them talk you into something you might regret."

"Thanks, Ginger. Oh, have you decided about Philly yet? Because I'll arrange my schedule, so I can go with you if you need me to."

"Thanks. I'll see you later this week at Tommy's, and we'll talk then." Jane slid her phone in her pocket.

Danny ground his teeth. It wasn't Breck's place to go with Jane to Philly. And it probably wasn't his either, but Danny wanted to be there for her all the same.

"Jane, I don't know what's waiting for you back home, but I'd go with you if I could," Liz said. "Since I can't, why don't you take Danny? You can fly out of Atlanta in Big Daddy's plane and not have to fly commercial."

Danny wanted to hug his sister. "I'd be glad to

go with you."

"Thanks. I'll think about it." Jane gathered her purse as he stopped at the curb.

"Don't make plans to go with Breck, okay?" Liz cut her eyes at Danny in the rearview mirror.

Jane looked over her shoulder. "I'd *never* take Breck. I'm a low-profile kind of girl. Plus, my husband over here might think I'm stepping out on him." Smiling, she wriggled her eyebrows and got out of the car.

Liz grinned. "She's awesome, Danny."

"I know, Lizabelle." He stared after Jane. It was love.

"I knew it." Liz leaned back in her seat. "You've met your match, Danny Baker."

Chapter Twenty-three

Jane opened the plastic case she kept in a safe at her Los Angeles home. Picking up Karl's gun, she hugged it to her chest as a single tear slid down her cheek. This was the last thing she had tying them together.

When she'd first taken it as her pick of the things his parents offered her, she thought she'd never get rid of it. Now, as she ejected the magazine and removed the slide and recoil spring, preparing to clean it, she thought about its owner. Karl would never have wanted it to sit around in its case. He would want someone to have it who would use it and enjoy it. Someone worthy.

Thankfully, she knew someone like that. And even though they had their differences, her heart had been touched by him. His care. His honesty.

During her week off, she spent two evenings with Breck. She couldn't look at him without thinking of his body double. One evening was spent dancing at Tommy's studio. When she was in Breck's arms, she imagined he was someone else. The second night, he made her dinner at his place.

"What's going on with you and Danny?" Breck asked as he pushed back from the table.

She glanced at him quickly before she stared at her plate. "I'm pretty sure he hates me."

"I'm pretty sure he's in love with you."

"Ha." Jane laughed without humor and looked out at the ocean view. "I can't please him. I want to, but I can't."

"You have feelings for him?"

She didn't respond right away. In her mind, memories flashed of the times Danny's lips had touched hers and the look in his eyes. The look which not only said he wanted her, but he wanted to protect her. Closing her eyes, she remembered the way she felt in his arms when he consoled her. "God help me, but I do."

Breck sighed and she tensed. He'd probably despise her, but she'd never promised him more than she could give. She never promised a man anything. Secret lovers. Forbidden kisses.

She swallowed to force down the emotion threatening to rise up in her. Clearly, she hadn't gotten her priorities right. Proving how tough she could be had only left her alone and wistful. Alone, she was used to. But wistful was a new experience.

Breck changed the subject back to his favorite topic—himself. And easily they were back to being friends. She appreciated him for not pushing.

When Jane left L.A., she was prepared to be away for six or seven weeks, instead of her usual three or four. She didn't know how she would handle going back to Philly, but she agreed with the people closest to her that she shouldn't go alone. Whenever she'd faced danger before, she was part of a team, she had support. She needed it for this, too.

It wasn't danger, but it was a threat—a threat to her sanity if she couldn't let it go and move on. Moving to L.A. was supposed to be her new start, but getting this closure was the only way she could truly move forward with her life. Whatever the future held, whoever was waiting for her when all of her tears for the past finally dried up, she wanted to be ready.

She shared a connection with Danny she hadn't felt since Karl, but she hadn't gotten to know him like she wanted. She hoped their road trip would give them a chance to talk.

***

The weeks passed quickly, and the next thing he knew, Danny was gassing up the SUV, ready to take the four-hour road trip to Southland with his beloved sister and the woman of his dreams.

He hoped they still had the easy camaraderie they'd had when he last saw her.

Jane drove the first leg of the trip with Liz riding shotgun and Danny faux napping in the backseat.

For the first half hour, he stayed alert to chat with them, and then he closed his eyes to rest. He clamped his lips together and listened to the women's conversation. He didn't want to smile or laugh and give away the fact he was eavesdropping.

On occasion, he peered out of the slit of one eye to see them.

"Aunt Jane, do you have any road rules for Ethan?" Liz asked.

"Let me think," Jane said. "Ethan, when traveling with friends, emissions are only allowed to come out of the vehicle's tailpipe."

Liz laughed and pulled a notebook out of her purse. "I'm going to write this down. I should've been doing it all along." She read aloud as she wrote, "Advice from Aunt Jane.

"I know this is off topic, but I think you'll make a fun mom someday. What was the first thing you told him when we found out he was a boy?" Liz asked.

Jane was quiet for a long moment, making Danny wonder if she'd taken Liz's words to heart. "'Don't piss into the wind.' But you might not want to write it that way. When he's at preschool and telling his friends not to piss into the wind, the other mothers might blackball you."

"What can we say instead of piss? Pee doesn't sound right."

"I heard a lady once tell her kids to call number one, whisper and number two, shout. We could say, 'Don't whisper into the wind', and it'll be a super cool double entendre. Ethan's going to be the coolest kid in school."

"Were you cool in school?"

"Oh, heavens, no. I was the last girl in my circle to French kiss. Talk about a late bloomer."

"When was your first French?" The leather squeaked as Liz shifted in her seat.

"I was a sophomore, and he was a really cute senior. I was so nervous, and he kept asking me what was wrong. I finally told him I'd never been kissed, and he was all like, *I'll teach you*." Jane's voice dropped half an octave with the last words. "I think he was trying to see how much spit he could share. It was dripping off my chin when it was over. A little tidbit about me, I hate slobber. I kept trying to wipe the area around my mouth with my free hand, while he was kissing me, and I accidentally stuck my finger up his nose."

Liz laughed hysterically. "I had a kiss like that once. Everybody said the guy was a great kisser, but I felt like he was spitting in my mouth. I started gagging because it grossed me out so much. I kept imagining my gross brothers hocking loogies. Disgusting."

They laughed together, and Danny turned his head to hide his smile, in case either of them looked back at him. He almost defended his sex against the loogie hocking accusation, but there was no defense. They were guilty.

The conversation between the women continued in this manner as Liz tried to write down the advice to Ethan from "Aunt Jane". Danny thought that had a nice ring to it.

"Any sex advice?" Liz asked.

"Oh yeah, I got a whole lot of advice for that. Ethan, if you're going to play in the rain, wear a slicker. If you think she's spunky, cover your monkey."

Danny snorted and laughter erupted from the ladies.

Liz turned in her seat. "You got any sex advice, Uncle Danny?"

He scratched his jaw. "Y'all ain't right, talking to my nephew like that." Unhooking his belt, he scooted forward, leaning toward Liz's baby bump. "Ethan, if you're gonna hump, cover your stump."

Liz wrote it in her book. "Ooh, I've got one. If you go into heat, cover your meat."

"You can't go wrong if you shield your dong," Jane added.

The conversation continued until Liz had to stop for baby bladder.

Danny had made a decision by then. He was going to find a way to spend the rest of his life with Jane Dillon.

***

After the stop, everyone shifted seats. Jane hoped she wouldn't ruin this chance to connect with Danny. He drove, Jane sat up front with him, and Liz planned to nap in the back.

Surprised by sweaty palms, Jane wiped them on her jeans.

"If I haven't told you lately, thanks for taking such good care of my sister." Danny offered Jane one of his rare smiles.

Her heart fluttered for a second, but she wrote it off as anxiety. She thought about the nice things she wanted to say about Liz, but unexpected emotion welled up. She had become one of the dearest friends Jane had ever had. Before the sentiments could take over, she made her mind switch gears.

The other things she needed to tell Danny and

when to tell him filled her mind. She planned to talk to him on their flight to Philly, but she thought he'd appreciate more time to process. He might change his mind about going.

She probably should have called him when she first suspected something was going on in Philly, but she kept telling herself she might be wrong.

When Jane thought Liz was asleep, she cleared her throat. "I need to talk to you about something."

He glanced over at her. "What's on your mind?"

"This trip to Philly, I have a feeling we might be walking into something."

"What do you mean?" He took his eyes off the road to watch her.

She pressed her lips together. "It may be paranoia, but I think there's more to this ceremony than just honoring fallen officers."

With his left hand on the wheel, he rested his other elbow on the console, shifting toward her. "Tell me why you think that."

"Last week, an article ran in the Sunday paper about the ceremony. It mentioned Walenski and I would be in attendance. We were the only two of our team to survive the explosion. Normally, these events don't get *any* press, so it seems a little odd to me. I think it's a flush. Don't know who they're trying to flush, but it feels right." Jane shrugged to show her uncertainty.

"Wouldn't the chief tell you if he was putting you in a dangerous position?"

Jane noted he didn't sound upset, but he most likely thought she was being paranoid. "I think he'll tell me when I see him Sunday. I don't think he'll share the details, until I actually show up. There'd be no need for me to know if I wasn't going to attend."

"So, this is why you agreed to let me go with you." His thumb tapped an unsteady rhythm on the console. "You thought there might be trouble. Thanks for the heads-up. If I'd known sooner, I would've come from L.A. more prepared."

Oh, God. He hated her. Again. It might be a mistake to take him. "I wasn't going to tell you until the flight, so you could enjoy your birthday. But then, I remembered who you are."

"What's that supposed to mean?" The hard edge to his voice took her back to their fight at Southland.

Shoving her pride aside, she chose her words very carefully. "You're protective of the women in your life. I didn't like that about you at first. If you think I might be walking into a dangerous situation, you might try to stop me."

The muscles in his jaw flexed, but he remained silent.

"I may be way off base with this theory, but if I'm right, I can't think of anyone I'd rather have by my side." Jane closed her eyes and waited.

His warm hand covered hers. "Whatever you have to face, we'll do it together."

Jane's heart raced as heat spread from her chest up her neck. She looked out the window and let out a long breath. It'd been so long since she was part of a "we", but the words from Danny's lips felt right. They sealed a crater in her soul.

***

Danny tried to wrap his head around what Jane had said, but his heart was too busy dancing in his chest.

I can't think of anyone I'd rather have by my side.

He lifted her hand to his lips and smiled when she looked at him with something akin to affection.

His thoughts shifted, considering all possible scenarios they could face in Philly. He was glad he'd be there to protect Jane, if there was really a threat. His logical brain hoped she was overreacting, but in the few months he'd known her, he'd learned to trust her instincts. If she thought something was amiss, it probably was.

His dad and brothers were gun enthusiasts, so he could choose his arms from among their supply. He wanted to stop worrying. He'd hoped he and Jane could get to know each other better on this road trip, and he was missing his opportunity by thinking too much.

He blinked to clear his head.

"Liz tells me your playing guitar now. How's that going?" he asked.

Apparently, Jane needed to keep busy so she wouldn't grow bored. Danny knew the feeling.

She seemed glad for the change of subject because with a relieved smile, she said, "I suck."

"It takes a while to get the muscle memory. Are you practicing every day?"

"Yes, look at my fingertips."

Turning the hand he was already holding, he looked closely. "Nice callouses."

He stopped himself from kissing each one. His body and mind tended to act outside of his control when he was close to Jane. Not letting her have her hand back, he put it back on his thigh.

She wiggled her fingers, rubbing the back of his hand which was twined with hers. "It feels so weird. I'm a tactile person, but touching anything with the tips of these fingers feels odd. This hand, no problem." She mimicked holding a guitar pick with her right hand.

"You'll get used to it. Do you sing?"

She chuckled. "Not in public."

"Me either. Liz and Maddie are the singers in our family. At least, they're the good singers. Everyone else makes a joyful noise." He gave her the stink-eye.

Her smile widened. "Do you play anything besides guitar?"

"Bass. I tinker with the mandolin, and I have a banjo that's collecting dust. I'm not a big bluegrass fan, but I admire the skill of the musicians."

"That's amazing. You guys are so talented." She angled her body toward him.

Progress. Thank you, Lord. His heart tried to pound through his chest cavity. "You might not think so after you hear us jam. No escaping to your cottage. If I have to endure it, so do you." He winked.

"You're very lucky to have your family, Danny."

He nodded and smiled. "I know."

They talked until Liz woke up and said, "I need to whisper."

Chapter Twenty-four

After almost five hours on the road, they arrived at Southland in time for dinner. Jane wasn't content with the few hours she'd had with Danny. She wanted more, and now she had to share him with his wonderful family. She'd try to endure.

Jane helped Liz get settled in her room at the main house, while Danny took Jane's things to the guest cottage.

Overwhelmed by the welcome she received from Dan and Dixie Baker, Jane tried to camouflage herself into the background. Of course, they fussed over Liz too, especially now that she was clearly pregnant. When they'd been there for Christmas, she'd barely been showing and had hidden it well under bulky sweaters.

It was Thursday night, and the rest of the siblings and spouses would arrive the next day, except for Johnny who still lived on the estate. They told Jane he was packing a few things to move into the main house, so Danny could stay in his cottage.

She focused on looking relaxed and containing the giddiness that made her foot tap. It was clear Danny wanted to be close to her.

Jane was introduced to the elderly couple who occupied the third cottage. They'd been with the Bakers since Danny was little and helped take care of the grounds and buildings.

Miss May hugged Jane. "We thank you for saving our baby from that well. You're a brave one. Ain't she, BH? Brave and perty."

Jane was reminded of hugging a body pillow. Aunt May, as she insisted Jane call her, was soft and cozy and smelled of sweet almond oil.

"Sho is." Uncle Ben Hill shook her hand.

"Let's hope no one will need rescuing this trip," Jane said.

Danny and Johnny came in, talking about a new horse. Jane knew the Bakers had a lot of money because of their estates, cars, toys, private planes, and horses. The interesting thing was they seemed like ordinary people. They were unpretentious, kind, and very generous, not just with money, but with their affection.

Jane realized Dixie was speaking to her. "If it warms up tomorrow, Jane, maybe you'd like to ride horses with the boys?"

She felt her eyebrows climb higher. "I've never ridden a horse."

"City girl," Johnny said.

She shot a playful warning glare at Johnny who towered over her. He reminded her of a big kid.

"If you want to try, I'll help you," Danny said.

"It's easier than playing guitar."

"All right." She smiled and shrugged. Aunt May was right about one thing. Jane never backed down from a challenge. Some people called it brave. Some called it stupid.

She trusted Danny would be sure she was as safe as possible.

***

The next morning, Danny whistled the University of Georgia fight song as he saddled a horse for Jane. When she came into the barn wearing a B&B sweatshirt, black leggings, and combat boots, the warmth in his heart dropped down about eighteen inches.

He shifted his feet. "Mornin'. How'd you sleep?"

"Like a log." She said the last word like she'd lived in the South all her life.

"Careful. I might think you're teasing me about the way I talk." He lifted his brow.

"Liz is teaching me to fit in."

Danny stepped close enough to feel her body heat. "I like that you're unique."

Her gaze bore into his, and she licked her lips. He needed to think fast or a certain body part of his might reach out and poke her. "Come meet Pez."

Taking her hand, he pulled her to the head of the horse.

She rubbed the horse's neck. "He's so big."

Danny saw the hesitancy in her eyes. "He's very gentle."

"Even after someone named him Pez?"

Danny grinned. "You'll be fine. I won't let

anything happen to you."

"I know you won't." She looked right into his eyes.

He explained the saddle, stirrups, bridle, and reins and told her how to lead the horse. "Like dancing with a partner, gentle pressure to indicate which way you want to go."

She smiled. "A simile I can relate to. Thank you."

He stared at her, caught in the moment. "I love when you smile at me that way."

Johnny walked into the stable, interrupting their moment. "Hey, the city girl's gonna mount up."

Danny turned his attention back to the horse as his dad and brother got their own mounts ready.

"Do you want us to wait for you, son?" Big Daddy asked.

"No, sir. Go ahead. I want to be sure Jane's comfortable, not rushed."

"We'll see you out there, Philly," Johnny said as he and his dad starting out slowly.

"You better be calling me by my city, because if you're calling me a kind of horse, I might take offense." Jane raised her voice after them.

"I'd never call you a horse," Johnny said, looking over his shoulder. "Mama didn't raise no fool."

They rode away.

Jane took a deep breath. "All right, let's do this."

Danny gave her a boost onto her horse, then mounted his own. They practiced starts, stops, and turns for a few minutes before heading down one of the wide dirt lanes.

There were single track trails, but Danny wanted to stay by her side in case she needed him. He took them around familiar places she would recognize from their morning runs, like the lake and the shooting range. He also took her to the abandoned well to show her the new, more secure cover.

She shivered.

"Are you okay?" The leather of the saddle groaned as he reached over to rub her back.

"It wouldn't have been so bad if it weren't for the snake. If I never see another one, it'll be too soon."

"They put a picture of the snake in the local paper," he said. "You have to admit it makes a great story."

She nodded thoughtfully. "If I was the type of person to tell my stories, then yeah, it'd be a good one."

"Why do you suppose we're the way we are?" He furrowed his brow.

She shrugged. "It's probably a combination of personality type and life experience. In our chosen careers, we were trained to keep secrets, but we were probably already good at it. I bet your friends growing up always told you their most intimate secrets and trusted you not to tell."

Danny thought back and realized she was right. "Did your friends tell you their secrets too?"

She nodded.

"Who did you tell your secrets to?" He guided

his horse along the path beside the creek.

"Most of my secrets growing up were other peoples', not my own. My grandfather was a cop, so I was a rule follower. I didn't do anything worth telling."

"What about now? Who do you tell your secrets to now?"

"I try not to tell, but sometimes people pester me to death until I do, your sister, for instance…and Breck."

Danny bit back a groan. "I know why you trust Liz, but why Breck? He knew you were thinking about going to Philly before you decided to go."

"He's actually a very good friend to me. He asked about my scars, and I told him how I got them. Then, he saw a text on my phone from Walenski about this memorial thing. I guess he realized my scars aren't just physical, so he offered to go with me if I needed him."

But you picked me. Danny tipped his chin up ever so slightly. "I got the basics from Joe and Liz and my own research. One day, when you're ready, I'd like you to tell me what happened. You can trust me, Jane."

"I already trust you. I just don't like to talk about it. The nightmares are always worse afterward. My shrink says I haven't buried the dead yet."

"*That's* who you talk to," he said with a new understanding.

"Chief made it mandatory after the incident. When I relocated to Los Angeles, I tried to go for a while without seeing someone, but keeping it in had me anxious all the time and paranoid. I found a doctor there, and I've been seeing him once a month ever since. The official diagnosis is Post Traumatic Stress Disorder. I don't take medication for it since all they have to offer are anti-depressants and sleep aids."

"Who else knows about this?" Danny asked.

"Just you, me, and the shrink."

"Now, you've told me one of your secrets." He smiled.

"It's a rare, but wonderful thing—your smile." Her gaze lingered on his mouth as her cheeks took on a slight blush.

His heart might have stopped for a second. He took a mental snapshot, noting the contrast of the cool air to the heat burning in him for Jane. When his pants grew tighter, he clicked his tongue and rode on to distract himself.

***

When they caught up to Big Dan and Johnny, Jane finally felt like she was getting the hang of riding horseback.

I like having a big, strong stud between my thighs.

She laughed inside at her own ridiculousness and thought of Liz. If she were here, she'd laugh right along with her. They'd become such good friends, and Jane hoped they would remain so after Ethan was born.

The four horsemen—make that three horsemen and one horsewoman—were riding along together and talking.

"I have some news," Johnny said. "I've been

seeing Dr. Amanda Cooper."

Jane's hackles went up.

"What? Why? Didn't I tell you she used to be obsessed with me?" Danny's serious voice was intimidating.

"Well, since you're engaged and all," Johnny looked pointedly at Jane, "and are off the market, I thought, why not? She's hot and she's a doctor. I invited her over for your party tomorrow, but she's going out of town."

"Thank God for small favors," Danny said.

"Instead, she's going to stop by tonight after she gets off work at seven," Johnny added.

Danny started cursing, but Jane calmly asked Johnny, "Did you forget about Liz and her secret?"

"Frog balls, yes, I did forget about that. But Amanda's a doctor, she has to keep secrets, right?" Johnny asked.

Jane couldn't believe Danny and Johnny were from the same gene pool. "Only if Liz was *her* patient."

"Well, I don't see how I can un-invite her," Johnny said. "What are we going to do?"

"You have to un-invite her, you little…" Danny's voice trailed off as he cursed under his breath.

From an arm's length away, Jane reached out to Danny, putting her hand on his shoulder. "Calm down. He made a mistake. We see Liz more than he does, so it's easy to forget about her pregnancy. Out of sight, out of mind, you know? We can come up with a solution. This is what we do." *Troubleshoot, stupid.* She added the last part silently, not wanting to insult anyone.

"You're right." Danny's anger dissolved into laughter. "I'm sorry, brother. I hope you find happiness with Dr. Cooper if she's the one you want. Maybe we can sit Liz in the corner and put her guitar in her hands. Amanda won't be able to see her belly then."

"When Liz has to whisper, we can distract Cooper, so she doesn't see Liz come and go," Jane said.

"The distraction will be Johnny, of course," Big Daddy said. "Maybe lay a kiss on her, son, if you two are at the kissing stage."

"Oh, we're way past that," Johnny said.

Jane didn't even blink at the overt sexual reference. Working in close proximity with men, she'd heard it all.

Danny leaned over to Jane. "You can shoot him if you want."

"I don't think deadly force is necessary, but I could…how does Liz say it? *Put a hurtin' on him.*"

A slow smile spread across Danny's face. Jane liked that she was the one who put it there.

"As if," Johnny said, having overheard their exchange.

Danny looked smug. "Brother, she'd have you begging for mercy in five minutes or less."

"Bullshit," Johnny said.

"Boys," their dad warned.

"The difference between you and Jane, little brother, is that while you got a black belt when you were fourteen and haven't sparred since, Jane's been trained in many styles of martial arts and continues to use her skills in *actual* combat. I'd bet money on her."

Johnny looked a little sheepish. "What if I went back to karate and re-honed my skills? Then I would accept your challenge." He hit his chest with his fist and moved his lips out of time with his words, like the old voice-dubbed movies.

Jane couldn't help but laugh. She liked Johnny, despite his lack of taste in women. "What style of karate?"

"Tae kwon do," Johnny answered.

Jane grinned. "Tae kwon girly? You're on, big boy."

"What? Are you calling me fat?" Johnny grabbed a fist full of gut. "But seriously, I could never fight a woman. That's not right. Let's just say you bested me."

"You're smarter than you look, Johnny," Danny said. "The only way I beat her in a fight was because she let me."

That got the men's attention and made Jane squirm in her saddle.

Later, when Danny helped her off her horse, she said, "I didn't let you beat me. You got me fair and square."

When he winked and smiled, she realized his hands were on her hips. She remembered the feel of his body on hers, their chests heaving, and a furnace blast of heat surged through her. She'd like to get there again, maybe take a different route this time.

Chapter Twenty-five

After dinner, everyone prepared for a family jam session and the arrival of Johnny's new girlfriend. Danny still couldn't believe his brother could be so dense. He admitted to himself he'd seen the darker side of humanity in his military days and not everyone was as suspicious and jaded as him, but come on.

Jane was seated between him and Liz. The women were going to pretend to share a beer when in fact Jane would be the only one drinking it. Mama D had given Jane one of her biggest diamonds to wear as a *fake* engagement ring.

When Danny saw the ring on her left hand, though it didn't suit her, he wanted the engagement to be real. Finally, he knew what he wanted. The woman who'd stolen his heart had no equal in his eyes. As his perfect match, he wanted Jane to wear his ring and be his wife.

The upcoming trip to Philly would be an

important step for her. Maybe, after she had closure and said goodbye to the ghosts, she'd be able to move forward with him.

Danny was actually glad when Amanda Cooper arrived because he had an excuse to touch Jane in front of everyone. He already had trouble keeping his hands to himself when they were alone.

Among the family musicians, they had three guitars, a bass, a mandolin, a fiddle, a harmonica, a tambourine, and a hand drum. Almost everyone in his family played at least one instrument, most played two or more. Johnny opted to play bass, so he could show off for his woman. Danny took the mandolin, so he could sit closer to Jane. She hadn't been playing guitar long enough to feel comfortable playing with them, so she just looked pretty and listened.

He looked over at her sometimes to find her smiling at him and his heart beat double-time. Danny noticed Amanda Cooper's eyes were frequently on him. When he caught her looking, she would quickly turn her gaze to Johnny. It happened enough to make Danny uneasy.

Jane must've noticed it, too, because her touches, laughs, and whispers became more frequent. It was the easy intimacy he needed from her. Now that she was close, he planned to keep her there.

***

The *good* doctor had her eye on the wrong brother more often than not. It was starting to piss Jane off. It was clear Amanda had wormed her way into Johnny's life, and his bed, to get closer to

Danny. Jane felt sorry for Johnny and hoped he didn't have real feelings for Dr. Cooper.

A revelation struck Jane. Johnny emulated his older brother. She would bet he had spent his life trying to compete with Danny, but Danny, who never viewed his little brother as competition, just went on his merry way and left Johnny in his shadow.

Jane's thoughts were interrupted when the song ended and Dr. Cooper asked, "So, have you two lovebirds set a date?"

Jane gave Danny a frustrated look. "We still can't agree on that."

"If you can't agree on *that*," Amanda said, "maybe you're not a good match."

Danny put his arm around Jane and pulled her closer. Her heart rate increased as his touch made her warm and tingly.

"We're perfect together, even when we disagree. Aren't we, beautiful?" Danny touched his forehead to hers.

His long, dark lashes nearly collided with hers as he looked into her eyes, a sexy smile gracing his gorgeous mouth. She didn't have to fake the desire she felt for him. All she could do was grin as she nodded her head. And try to remember to breathe.

Their breaths mingled. Speaking would have been too difficult in that moment.

Then, Danny did exactly what she willed him to. He kissed her with the purest mix of gentleness and passion. Yearning coiled low in her belly and she was a goner.

He broke the kiss. "We should dance."

She blinked. "Right now?"

Setting the mandolin aside, he stood and held his hand out. They moved to the other end of the recreation room, where there was empty floor space. The family played a slow song. He placed one hand on her waist, and she placed one hand on his shoulder. They clasped their other hands together. With ease, he led and she followed. He knew how to move, but he might not know how much he moved her, inside and out.

They never broke eye contact, and soon she forgot she was dancing. She never wanted to stop floating in his arms. In all her years of dancing, Jane had never had a partner with whom she had more natural chemistry. The urge to explore this thing between them was increasing with every moment.

When the song ended, Jane brushed Danny's cheek gently with the back of her fingers. If they hadn't had an audience, she would have had a hard time letting go of him.

"Thanks for the dance," she said.

"I could dance with you for the rest of my life." His lips covered hers.

***

It was close to midnight when Dr. Cooper decided she was ready to leave. Danny was sure everyone else had passed that point about two hours before. Johnny walked his date out to her car, and Liz made a mad dash for the bathroom.

Danny shook his head and said to Jane, "I can't believe how often she has to whisper."

"If you had a sack of amniotic fluid and a roughly three pound baby boy sitting on your bladder, you'd have to whisper a lot, too." Jane winked.

He smiled. "Three pounds is good, right? I mean, it's healthy for how far along she is?"

"Yes, Ethan is healthy." She put her hand on his. "Try not to worry. I have a good feeling about this. More importantly, so does Liz."

Danny pulled her into a hug, even though Dr. Cooper wasn't there to see it. "Have I told you lately how much I appreciate what you're doing for Liz? You're an angel from heaven."

"Just doing my job, boss." Her rosy, pink lips turned up at the corners.

"Liz is more than a job for you and you know it."

"Yes, she is, and I feel guilty for getting paid for something I would do for free if I could. I hope you don't think I'm taking advantage of you or Liz."

He stroked her cheek. "I absolutely do *not* think that. Jane, you're the person Liz needed in her life. There are no coincidences." He leaned back and intertwined their fingers. "I think *you* needed her too."

"You're right. That's why I feel like I may be taking advantage. I pay a shrink to give me the assurance Liz gives me just by being herself." Her eyes watered, and she tried to look away.

He took her face in his hands and gave her a light kiss. "I know she's special and so are you. I'm in love with you, Jane Dillon."

***

Jane jerked a little at Danny's words. She put

her hand over her heart and opened her mouth to speak.

"You guys can stop pretending," Liz said.

Jane's heart tried to leap out of her chest. Had he just said...? No. She must have misheard. It was too soon. Wasn't it?

Thrill and trepidation competed for top emotion. She glanced to Liz who'd turned away to help clear the after dinner drinks.

Her mouth attempted to form words, but her brain was noncompliant.

"You don't have to say anything, Jane." Danny's gaze bore into her soul. "I just needed to tell you."

Jane looked away, certain all eyes were on them. *Wrong.* She'd just had a real intimate moment with Danny in a room full of Bakers, and no one had noticed. Everyone acted as if nothing had changed; although, his confession had sent her into a tailspin.

Dampness on her cheeks caught her off guard, and she wiped her face with her hands. "I'm sorry. I didn't mean to get so emotional. I must have had too much to drink."

"Don't worry about it." His thumb gently rubbed under her eye. "No one is paying attention to us anyway now that Dr. Crazy is gone."

Thank God, he offered a new subject. "You noticed it too?" Jane leaned against the back of the sofa. "I feel bad for Johnny."

"So do I. But he was probably just in it for the sex, if that makes you feel any better."

"Yeah, I'll remind you of that when you're

standing up for him at their wedding."

"No way in hell," Danny said. "Come on, I bet you're as tired as I am."

They said goodnight to everyone and walked hand in hand in the direction of the cottages.

"What time do you want to run in the morning?" she asked.

"You're gonna make me run on my birthday? Damn, you're hardcore."

She laughed. "Now that we're getting older, we have to be more disciplined, so Father Time doesn't kick our asses."

"I'm glad you said *we,* so I wouldn't be insulted by the age crack."

As they approached Johnny's cottage, where Danny would be spending the night, Jane got a strange feeling. The hair on the back of her neck stood up. She yanked his arm and pushed him against a tree.

"Did you notice if Amanda's car was still here?" Jane whispered.

"No, I didn't. Johnny was up at the house, right?" His hand landed on her hip.

She nodded as she peered around the tree. A light went out in the cottage.

Danny tensed and pulled Jane closer before he reversed their positions.

"We have two choices," she said. "We can go to my cottage and wait for her to come to us, or we can go to Johnny's place now and confront her."

"How about we go to your cottage to get armed and then confront her?" Danny asked.

Knowing Danny took her seriously made her

heart swell. Before she could stop herself, she kissed him.

"Forget her." Danny pressed himself into her. "Let's just go to your place and lock ourselves in."

His excitement sent a flare straight between her legs.

"You're going with the…*if we ignore her…she'll go away* theory?" Jane asked between kisses.

He sighed. "Why are you always right?"

"Maybe I'm psychic?" She grinned.

They turned to go to her cottage. He held her hand, and she followed closely as they stuck to the shadows.

Chapter Twenty-six

Danny slid a Beretta into his holster. "I'm going in first."

"Nonsense," she said, strapping her thigh rig over her jeans. "If she jumps out naked, I can either shame her or beat her."

Danny took a step toward her. "If she feels threatened, she may try to hurt you. Johnny has guns and knives all over that cottage. She'll be less likely to harm me, if she is in fact still obsessed with me."

"But if she's upset with you, feeling jilted, then she might retaliate and try to hurt you. Remember Breck's stalker." She chambered a round before she slid her 380 into its holster.

"There's no way I'm letting you go into a potentially dangerous situation, where you could get hurt."

"Aha!" Jane said, throwing her hands in the air. "I knew it. I knew you didn't have any confidence in my abilities. Why do I always have to prove myself to you? Why do I even want to? I should march over there and show you once again what I'm capable of, so you'll let me out from under your thumb. Damn men! Chauvinistic macho bullshit!" She stomped over to her jacket.

Danny got the feeling she'd stopped talking to him and started talking to herself a few sentences back. Pacing and mumbling under breath, she clenched and opened her fists.

He stood in front of her and put his hands on her upper arms to get her attention. "Jane, I do have confidence in your abilities. You've proven yourself many times over. I would never want you to feel like I'm holding you back, or putting you under my thumb. I want a partner in life, not a doormat. Don't get mad at what I am about to say, but my father taught me that as a man it's my duty to protect the weaker sex."

Her jaw tightened, but he plodded on. "When I say weaker sex, I don't mean that women are weak. In fact, the women I know have more inner strength than any man I've met. *You* are definitely not weak, Jane. But as men, we're physically stronger, and when possible, we should use our strength to protect women and children and those who can't protect themselves. I *know* you can protect yourself, and if you want to go over there now, I won't stop you. It's just, now that I've found you, I don't want to lose you. I don't want to see you hurt…ever."

***

Okay. Yeah. That was a good speech. The kind of speech that could make a woman fall in love.

Jane let out a breath, and as it left her lungs, so did her anger. The desire she had minutes ago to kick some ass dissolved into melancholy. She dropped her head and rested it on Danny's chest.

She remembered telling Joe she used to be a warrior, but she was changing. With the current situation at Southland and the unresolved one in Philly, she couldn't let go of her warrior yet. She needed to stay strong to see this through.

Looking up into his dark green eyes, her thoughts scrambled. "Danny, if we're doing *this* now, I'm not sure about Philly. I wanted you by my side, but if you're going to try to be a step in front of me, I'm not sure if I can take you with me."

His shoulders preceded the drop of his chin.

"That was a great speech by the way," she said. "I think I could be willing to let you be my protector, but not yet. I have unfinished business. You can either walk beside me or stay out of my way." She turned toward the door, but paused and looked back. "I'm going to have to quit my job. It's too dangerous to work like this with someone you care about."

Danny was about to speak, but she felt like the conversation needed to end. It was late, and if she got cranky, she might say more regretful things or kill a crazy doctor with her bare hands.

She snapped her fingers. "I just thought of something. Text Johnny and tell him to come down to his cottage. We can wait outside and see what happens. If Dr. Crazy is in there waiting for you, he can be the one to catch her. She won't hurt him because he's her lifeline to you. She'll probably just say she was trying to surprise *him* anyway."

Danny blinked at her. "That might work."

He texted Johnny who replied: *On the way.*

They eased out the back door and moved toward Johnny's cottage. Danny covered the front and Jane went to the back.

She sought to put physical distance between them, but as she did, the night felt colder.

***

As Johnny walked through the front door of the cottage, Danny made his way onto the porch and stood out of sight, just outside the door his brother had left open.

He closed his eyes in disbelief when Amanda said, "Happy birthday, Danny." Jane must really be freaking psychic.

He entered the cottage to see Johnny standing just inside the door to his bedroom and a naked Dr. Crazy Cooper stretched out on the bed. It was high school all over again.

Scurrying to get up and cover herself, she was a streak of bare white ass.

"Wanted to give my brother a birthday present, did you? Get dressed and get out. You're no longer welcome here," Johnny said.

Danny gave his brother points for remaining calm. Johnny was normally more reactive than that. Danny moved inside so she could see him.

Once she tied the robe around her waist, Amanda's face took on a menacing appearance as she pulled a small revolver out of the pocket and pointed it at Johnny.

"I have wanted Danny Baker for as long as I

can remember. If I have to kill you and that undeserving bitch who calls herself his fiancée to get him, I will. Now go away, Johnny. I'm going to make Danny forget every other woman. He's mine, and he wants me just as much as I want him." Her tight-lipped smile did nothing to make her more appealing.

Danny's skin felt like a thousand spiders were crawling on him, and he held his breath.

"You're right, Amanda." Johnny backed away. "I saw the looks you two were giving each other tonight. I'm not as dumb as I seem. I'll just leave you alone, so you can celebrate."

Johnny turned and walked past Danny with a pale face. When the door closed behind him, Amanda lowered her gun and smiled.

Danny had drawn his pistol when he'd first entered the cottage, but in order to get close enough to Amanda to disarm her, he'd need to holster it again. He did so slowly and watched as her smile broadened. He took a step toward her and forced his lips apart in a teeth-baring grin.

"I'm sorry Johnny spoiled the surprise," he said as he moved deeper into the bedroom.

She put her gun down on the night stand, unbelted her robe, and held it open. "Happy birthday."

The robe fell to the floor.

***

From Jane's vantage point outside the bedroom window, she could see what was happening, but she couldn't hear. The moment Dr. Cooper raised her gun, Jane's own sites had been trained on the

208

disturbed woman. Shooting through the window glass would alter the trajectory of the rounds, but Jane would aim three center mass, knowing one would hit its target. She prayed Johnny wouldn't be hurt.

It'd been a mistake to send him in. If something happened to him, Danny would never forgive her.

Johnny was a bit of a wild card and didn't seem like the type of person who would remain cool under pressure. Fear must have been a big motivator for him because after a brief verbal exchange, he calmly turned and walked out.

Jane hoped he would call local law enforcement. Relief coursed through her when Dr. Cooper lowered her weapon, then set it down to show Danny her goods.

Damn, now that she's naked and unarmed, I can't justify shooting her. I should have done it when I had the chance.

Dr. Cooper being unarmed didn't mean she wasn't a threat. The gun was still within easy reach.

Jane shifted her weight as Danny entered the room and walked toward the doctor. His sidearm was holstered, which explained why the crazy lady put hers down.

If Danny got too close to Amanda, Jane wouldn't be able to shoot without endangering him.

A sound in the darkness behind her caught her attention. She strained to listen and heard a loud whisper.

"Pssst, Jane, where are you?"

She slowly backed away from the window. She

didn't want to lose sight of Danny, but if Johnny exposed her position, it might create more problems for the man she was falling in love with.

She lowered her gun and stepped to the side of the house. "Johnny, over here." Her voice was barely a whisper.

She heard him before she saw him as him as he walked in a low crouch to rest beside her.

"I called the cops. That bitch is 5150 crazy," Johnny said.

"I know. I'm sorry we sent you in there. I had a line on her when she was aiming at you. I should've taken my shot, but she could have fired and hit you."

"If Danny can get his hands on her, he can take away her gun and hold her down or something, until the cops get here," Johnny said.

"She already laid down her arms. Now she's probably trying to get into Danny's pants," Jane said.

Johnny grinned. "I should've listened. I'm so damned hard-headed sometimes. Next time, I'll give heed to the warnings."

Jane put a hand on his arm. "I'm going in to pitch a fit over my cheating fiancé. Go watch through the window, but stay off to the side. We might need an eyewitness if something goes wrong."

Johnny hugged her. "Be careful."

***

Danny could reach out and put his hands around Amanda Cooper's throat, but he resisted the urge. She was still close enough to the revolver on the night stand that a threatening move from him might cause her to go for it. He could draw and shoot faster than she could, but he would prefer not to use deadly force if he could get around it.

He heard the door open behind him followed by Jane's voice. "Danny, are you in here?"

He didn't take his eyes off Amanda, and when she lunged for the gun, he grabbed her arm and twisted it behind her, forcing her face down on the bed.

Jane stood in the bedroom doorway with her piece by her side and a smirk on her pretty face. "So you like the rough stuff, huh?"

He cocked his head. "Get your ass over here and help me."

Holstering her gun, she sauntered to the opposite side of the bed.

Danny watched Jane's expression and followed her gaze as Amanda's free hand inched under the pillow. Jane extracted her knife and placed the blade solidly, but gently across Amanda's wrist.

"Uh-uh-uh." Jane lifted the pillow.

There was a machete under it, and she moved it out of reach as Danny secured both of Amanda's arms. Jane gave him a couple of zip ties she pulled from her boot, and he cuffed Amanda's hands behind her back.

She squirmed. "At least let me get dressed."

"You should've considered that before you threatened this family," Jane said. "I bet county has a nice orange jumper you can wear when you get there."

Danny liked how protective Jane was of his

family. He raised an eyebrow. "What else are you hiding in those boots?"

"Toe jam," Johnny answered from the doorway.

Jane laughed and Danny's smile grew.

"That's the little brother I know and love," he said.

"I love you too, bro, and I'm sorry I invited Dr. Cuckoo into our lives," Johnny said.

Danny put an arm around his brother. "Don't mention it. This'll be a great story for us to tell our grandkids." He winked at Jane and her eyes widened.

Danny hadn't told her yet, but she was gonna be the mother of his children.

Chapter Twenty-seven

It was after three in the morning when the cops left, so Jane decided they should skip the birthday run after all.

Danny insisted on sleeping in Jane's cottage. "I'll never be able to sleep over there again. It's like you and your snake."

Jane shivered at the memory and understood how he felt. "You take the bed. I'll take the sofa. Don't try to pull any weaker sex needs a soft bed bullshit, I will cut you." She tapped her knife.

He laughed. "It's not that, it's guest rights. You're the guest, so you get the bed."

"Why are we arguing about this? Aren't there like fifteen bedrooms up at the main house? Go pick one. Or sleep in this one with me." She removed her weapons.

Exhaustion made her speech garbled. She didn't wait for him to respond. She crawled into bed fully clothed.

A moment later, he slid into bed next to her. His hands gripped her arms, and he pulled her so her cheek rested on his bare chest.

God, he was warm. Part of her wanted to wake up and make more heat. The other part just wanted to be held.

It was good to be loved. It was better to love.

When Jane opened her eyes the next morning, she groaned and stretched. Rolling over, she poked her lower lip out. She had the bed to herself. That's when she saw Danny sitting in the wingback chair by the fireplace.

A shy smile crept across her face, and she sat up. "What are you doing?"

"Watching you."

"That's not creepy at all." She threw a pillow at him. "Why are you watching me?"

"Because you're beautiful...and, today is my birthday, and I get to do what I want on my birthday."

It was then she noticed the wrapped gift on his lap. A bead of sweat on her upper lip preceded the thudding in her chest.

"What's this?" He held it up.

Her throat constricted. "It's your birthday present."

"Can I open it?"

"If you open it now, you won't have anything to open from me at the party later." She was stalling.

She thought giving it to him in front of his family would make it less emotional for her. She had also played out the scenario where he opened it privately and she explained its value, but she always cried in that scene, and she didn't want to do that.

"I'd rather open it now. It's my birthday, and I get to do what I want today, remember?"

She pressed her lips into a tight line to suppress a grin. "Are you going to be like this all day? Let me wake up first." She threw back the covers. "You're such a pain in my ass."

She closed the bathroom door behind her and leaned against it. Shaking out her hands, she struggled for air. It was time to let it go.

***

Danny waited while Jane got dressed. He'd seen the gift the night before, prior to the incident with Dr. Cooper. He knew it was meant for him, whatever it was. It had a nice weight to it. He shook it gently and listened, but heard nothing.

He thought about his mama. She was the one who used to say, "Today is your birthday and you get to do whatever you want on your birthday…within reason." She'd smile when she added the caveat.

He missed her most on his birthday. She'd always given him gifts of great sentimental value, rather than buying him a disposable toy. On his twelfth birthday, the last one before she lost her battle with breast cancer, she'd given him her father's pocket knife. He still carried it with him. It wasn't fancy, but he knew how special it was to her and that gave it value in his eyes.

He looked up to see Jane watching him.

"Can we go in there?" She pointed to the small sitting room.

"Why can't we stay right here?"

"Are you going to be disagreeable all day? If this is how you behave on your birthday, I vote no more birthdays."

He leaned forward and caught her hand, smiling as he pulled her closer. She didn't resist and took a seat on the end of the bed in front of him. He let go of her hand and ran his fingers along the sides of the present. For a moment, he considered putting it aside and pulling Jane into his lap. She'd be the best present.

He tore the paper off to reveal a plastic case. He opened the latches holding the lid in place and slowly lifted it. Inside the foam lined case, rested an automatic handgun. One he'd always thought would be fun to have. He picked it up and gripped the receiver. It was set for his hand size. Custom. He examined it and finally looked up to see Jane's eyes shining; although, her beautiful smile lit up her face.

"I knew you were the one," she said.

"The one?"

"The one that piece belongs with. I couldn't let it go to just anyone."

His heart pounded louder, and he knew his mama was smiling down from heaven.

"Tell me." He caressed the metal slide.

She reached out and lightly ran her fingers along the barrel and swallowed. "It belonged to someone I loved. When he died, this was my pick of the things he left behind. It was his favorite, and for a while, having it and holding on so tightly seemed like the only thing that kept me going. I have to let it go now, but I couldn't let it go to anyone

216

undeserving. I can see it belongs with you by the way you handle it with such care, the way you handle everything you love."

She placed her hand on his cheek. "It's yours now. Happy birthday."

Her lips brushed his, soft as feathers, and his spirit soared to new heights.

***

Jane's heart was racing by the time she broke the kiss. She had to get out of the bedroom or else she might try to give Danny the present he'd missed out on with Dr. Crazy. She almost told him she was in love with him, too.

She sprinted for the door before he could stop her. Once she was outside, she took in a deep calming breath and let it out slowly. Her lifeline to Karl was gone. She hoped when she got to Philly, she could finally say goodbye and let him rest in peace.

Walking nowhere in particular, she was surprised when Danny stepped up beside her and took her hand. "Come on. I want to go shoot my birthday present."

They walked past the barn and out to the shooting range. While he loaded rounds into magazines, she set up targets. All the while, she laughed to herself.

You might be a redneck if you have your own gun range. Johnny had told her a bunch of Jeff Foxworthy jokes the day before.

Nodding to Danny when she was clear, he aimed and fired.

"I want to tell you about my mama." He talked

during the relative silences of changing magazines.

Jane hung onto his every word. When he told her about the birthday gifts his mom had given him, the way he looked at her made her chest tightened. The love would bubble out eventually.

"I really think you're an angel from heaven," he said.

"I'm no angel, Danny. I had to run away so I wouldn't molest you back at the cottage. I'm sure you don't want another repeat of last night."

He stepped close to stand in front of her, and heat rushed through her.

"Don't be so sure, my angel." His voice was low and husky and sexy as hell. If he kissed her, they would wind up naked in the woods on a cold winter's day.

A slow smile spread across his face, and his green eyes sparkled. "Thank you for my birthday present."

He hadn't moved away from her. There was an inch of space between them. Her belly tightened as he held his mouth millimeters from hers. She could feel his heat. He was holding himself back, and it only made her want him more.

***

Danny could cut the sexual tension with a knife. He knew why she'd run out of the cottage. It wasn't safe for them to be in close proximity to a bed right now. He was determined not to rush her, while she was making huge strides to let her past go. It was one reason her gift meant so much to him.

He wanted her like he'd never wanted a woman

before.

Just as his lips touched hers, the buzz of an electric motor approached, and he pulled back. They turned to see a golf cart with Liz at the wheel.

"It's your birthday." Jane took a step back. "You should be spending it with your family." She turned her attention to the arriving family members.

Danny put his arm around her. Her face lit up when she realized who else was on the cart. Paul got out with Tyler in his arms.

His nephew reached out to her. "Aunt Jane! Aunt Jane!"

She took him from his father, and Danny's heart thumped against his ribs as she hugged the boy close.

"Hi, Little! I've missed you." She kissed his cheek.

"Do you have a hug for your Uncle Danny?" he asked.

Tyler reached for Danny then, and he took him into his arms.

"I like those space boots, Little," Jane said. "Where can I get some?"

Tyler held up one leg and pointed to his walking casts. He had graduated from the hard plaster casts he'd worn after his surgery. He was already going to physical therapy and could now walk clumsily.

Danny held his nephew and slid onto the backseat of the cart next to Jane. Paul sat in the front next to Liz, and they made their way back to the main house.

Paul turned in his seat. "Tyler wasn't doing

well being separated from us. He's been a little spoiled with all he's been through, and Jen's mom couldn't settle him down. Carly stayed with Grandma, but we brought him back here with us. We think he's too little to tell secrets." Paul squeezed Liz's shoulder, then looked back to Jane. "Carly thinks you're a guardian angel. She's got Tyler saying it."

The little boy said something Danny couldn't quite make out, but it sounded a little like "golf and angle."

Jane shook her head. If there was one thing Danny knew about her, she didn't like being called out as a hero.

Tyler reached for Jane, and she took him. He wanted to be in her arms the rest of the day.

Danny could relate. He wanted to be in her arms, too.

Chapter Twenty-eight

Danny grabbed his guitar, sat next to Jane, and willed his heart to stop slamming against his ribs. She had Tyler on her lap and a piece of birthday cake in her hand. In his mind, happy fantasies of a not so distant future repeated like an animated film clip.

Danny wiped icing from her lip. "Do you want me to take him? You've had him all day, your arms might fall off."

She dipped her chin. "It's a good upper body workout. Plus, he's the sweetest." She squeezed Tyler with her free arm.

Liz came over and sat with them. "Who has my big boy?"

Tyler's response was unintelligible, but they all understood it.

"Aunt Jane's your guardian angel?" Liz asked.

"She's mine too, buddy." Johnny winked.

Jane pointed at Johnny. "Stop saying that.

Danny's your guardian angel. I was his backup."

Jason and Roxanne showed up, and Danny passed his guitar to Liz, so she could hide her belly. Then he moved out of the crowded family room to talk to his friend, away from his ex-wife.

But Danny's attention kept moving back to Jane.

"Dude, what's going on there?" Jason asked. "Doesn't she work for you?"

Danny tensed. How had he managed to forget Jane was technically his employee? And, she had strong opinions about work relationships due to her past experience.

Hadn't she said something about that this morning? Or was it last night? Her words rushed back to him. *I'm going to have to quit my job. It's too dangerous to work like this with someone you care about.*

He had something to say about that, but he hadn't had the chance to say it because of the crazy naked lady harassing them.

"Jase, you're never gonna believe what happened last night." Danny told his best friend the sordid story.

"Damn man, you have all the fun," Jason said.

"Believe me, it was no fun at all." Danny puffed his cheeks out.

"So, G.I. Jane saved the day again? Is that giving you a complex? Being outdone by a woman?" Jason asked.

"Not really." He glanced her way. "We work well together. I might have to fire her, so I can marry her."

"Congratulations!" Jason slapped him on the back. "I never thought I'd hear those words from your mouth. She must be special."

They both looked over at Jane who rocked a sleeping Tyler in her arms.

"That kid looks good on her, too. If you're planning to have any of your own, you better get busy. Your swimmers are old, dude." Jason laughed and landed a playful punch on Danny's bicep.

It occurred to him again, that he would love to have kids. He'd never thought it was in the cards for him. Not knowing how Jane felt about the topic, he was hesitant to ask because he hadn't even proposed yet. *Too much, too fast.*

"I'm going to see about putting Tyler down," Danny said. "Don't go anywhere. I want you and Roxanne to sing a song, so I can dance with my woman."

Danny crossed the room, enjoying the way Jane's gaze started at his feet and worked its way up to his eyes. The heat in her expression drew him like a magnet.

"Come on. Let's get him to bed." Danny helped Jane stand.

"My feet fell asleep." She passed Tyler to him and shook her legs out.

Danny laid his nephew on his bed, and Jane pulled the covers up. "I hope you haven't given your heart away today." He gestured to the sleeping little boy.

"I didn't have a choice. You Bakers are difficult to resist."

He smiled and pulled her into a tight embrace.

After kissing her soundly, he led her back into the family room. He was scared to death, but once he knew what he wanted, he went after it.

***

Jane was still catching her breath when she and Danny returned to the family room. All eyes were on them, and she froze, missing the camouflage Tyler had provided.

"What?" she asked.

Dixie stood. "We want to thank you for everything you've done for our family."

Jane tried to shrink behind Danny, hating to be called out in front of an audience.

Danny must have sensed her unease because he put a protective arm around her. "Y'all are making her uncomfortable."

Dixie ignored him. "We know you don't like attention, but if you're going to be a part of this family, you have to get used to it."

Huh? Part of this family? Me? She wanted to look at Danny to see if he was about to propose or something, but she couldn't. *Not yet. I'm not ready yet*, she pleaded silently.

"You've rescued Tyler and Johnny and Liz and Danny, and we are eternally grateful to you. We all think you're an angel sent from above." Dixie gestured skyward.

Jane did look up at Danny then, smacking him on the chest. "See what you started?"

"I didn't say anything about it." He held up three fingers on his right hand. "I swear."

Jane strengthened her resolve and let out a rushed breath. "You each have expressed your gratitude to me. I'm very glad I was able to help, but I can't take credit for the events in my life that led me here."

She paused and made eye contact with several of them. "Things happen for a reason. Many of you have said those words to me at some point since I've met you. I'm not the only hero here. You saved me, too."

Danny squeezed her shoulder, but she wasn't finished.

"I've never had a family. I really *was* all alone in the world. On my job, we were a team with a common objective. It was the only to be successful. I never translated the idea of a team objective to life. I was trying to do life on my own, but that's not how it's supposed to be. You guys are a tactical team for life. You support, stand up for, protect, and teach each other."

Danny's smile widened just before his lips pressed against her temple.

Jane looked to Liz and took her hand. "I'm grateful to all of you for welcoming me into this big, crazy family. There's so much love here it overwhelms me. I don't know where life will take me next, but I know I don't have to face it alone."

Liz had tears in her eyes, and she stood, putting her guitar down. "I have to whisper."

"Holy shit," Jason said.

Jane started laughing and buried her face in Danny's chest as his arms encircled her.

"Oh, by the way, Jason, Roxanne," Danny said, "Liz is pregnant, and if you tell anyone, I'll have to kill you."

Chapter Twenty-nine

The next day, Danny and Jane boarded Big Daddy's plane for Philly. Danny packed his new gun, as well as a few other things he might need, in case there turned out to be a threat.

Rather than have Frank, also known as Chief, pick Jane up from the airport, Danny rented an SUV and Jane drove. They were in her hometown, and he listened with interest as she pointed out places and things that had been important to her.

They pulled up to the curb in front of a little red brick house. Danny unloaded the luggage, while Jane greeted their hosts, Frank and Martha Lombardi. Danny had offered to get them hotel rooms, but after Jane spoke with Frank about it, Martha insisted they both come. Their kids were grown, and there were two guest beds waiting to be used.

Before they went inside, Jane made the introductions. Danny found the couple to be pleasant, even welcoming, but he was always reserved around strangers, never wanting to give too much away.

"So Danny, Jane works for you in Los Angeles?" Martha asked over dinner.

"Yes, ma'am. My partner and I run a security business for Hollywood clientele, mostly bodyguards for big events."

"How exciting!" Her hands fluttered to her chest.

"We also train actors in hand to hand combat and weaponry for action movies," Jane added with a pointed look at Danny.

"Have you worked with anyone we've heard of?"

Danny tore his gaze away from Jane's, and cleared his throat. "I'm not permitted to say, ma'am, but if you've seen any movies recently, you may have seen some of the actors we've worked with." That sounded just ambiguous enough to include anyone in Hollywood.

"How about you, dear?" Martha directed her question to Jane. "Are you permitted to tell us any names of stars you've worked with?"

"I can't disclose anything associated with my work for B&B," Jane leaned in, "but I can tell you when I first moved to L.A., I met someone famous in a dance class." Her hushed tone conveyed she was revealing a great secret.

Danny stifled a chuckle.

"I'm thrilled to hear you're still dancing. Frank still takes me out, you know? He's a good little dancer, especially since you worked with us." She patted his hand. "You and Karl made good dance partners. I'm so glad you came back for the ceremony."

Taken aback, Danny hadn't realized *dancing* had been how she'd fallen for Karl in the first place.

Danny was disappointed he'd been deprived of his dance with her the previous night because of Liz's baby news and Jason's near meltdown.

After the commotion, Jane had fallen asleep in bed with Liz. Danny had stayed up and talked to Jason and Roxanne for a while to be sure they understood the situation and all of the ramifications. Danny had considered carrying Jane back to the cottage, so he could have her for himself, but he couldn't bring himself to disturb her.

***

It was inevitable Jane wouldn't get through the evening without Martha mentioning dancing and Karl. Jane hadn't told Danny or Liz or even Breck about dancing with Karl. She *had* told Tommy she'd lost her best friend and dance partner back in Philly. She didn't want to make a big deal out of it in front of Danny.

There was understanding in his expression, and he squeezed her knee under the table.

After the dinner dishes were put away, Martha excused herself. It was time for their talk with the chief.

Jane braced herself as she sat on the sofa next to Danny. His presence was a comfort she hadn't expected, and it was hard not to reach for him.

"I need to brief you on tomorrow's events." The chief settled into his chair across from them.

"We ran articles about the event in the last two Sunday papers. The serial killer, Ray Walters, who killed your team, may be working with someone on the outside.

"We believe the new perp is a fan of Walter's and continues his work to try to impress him. There's a chance he might try to take you and Walenski out before, after, or during the ceremony tomorrow."

Jane looked at Danny, whose eyes filled with concern. He dipped his chin once.

"How did you know?" The chief asked.

Jane shrugged. "A feeling."

"That's why we need you back here, Jane. You have great instincts. You were born for this. This memorial thing—it's a flush—plain and simple. I couldn't tell you until your feet were on the ground here. Walenski is in, and I hope, if you're still the same warrior you used to be, that you're in too."

Shivering inside at his word choice, she put on her metaphorical armor. "Chief, Ray Walters killed the warrior in me two years ago. Ever since I woke up from that explosion, I've been trying to reconcile Jane the warrior with Jane the woman. I can't be both anymore. I'm making a choice…"

Long moments passed as both men waited for her to finish speaking.

"I'll be Jane the warrior *one* more time to catch this guy. Then, I'm out."

Danny closed his eyes. It was her turn to offer him some reassurance.

She pressed her elbow into his arm. "We're going to take him down."

"No doubt." Danny slid to the edge of his seat and regarded the chief. "What do you have in place?"

They spent an hour going over the details and logistics. Frank agreed to give Danny special permits and position because he was Jane's "bodyguard" as far as the rest of the world was concerned.

Before they went to bed, Danny and Jane stood in the hallway outside their rooms. He hugged her and she held on, memorizing the hard lines of his body.

"I'm not going to let anything happen to you," he whispered in her ear.

She pulled back to look into his eyes. "I know. Thank you for being here with me. I'm not going to let anything happen to you either." She winked. "I love you."

His mouth fell open, and she stifled a laugh. His grin turned predatory as he lowered his lips to hers. Her heart stopped, then started again and sped up. Fire ran through her veins, and she clung to him, knowing from his slow smolder they'd reach full combustion any moment.

"Jane." He broke the kiss and caught his breath. "When this is over, I'm going to marry you."

Chapter Thirty

The morning of the ceremony, Danny dressed for a winter's day in Philly—layers. He wore a black wool suit, which had been tailored so body armor and weapons wouldn't be so obvious.

He waited for Jane in the living room and ran over some details of the case in his head. The usual MO for victims was a knife across the throat. The chief's concern was that since Walters had used explosives to kill the SWAT members, his copycat/protégé might do the same.

The Philadelphia Police Department had taken measures to prevent anyone from getting into the venue to plant explosives by choosing a secure location. They hoped to force the copycat into other action instead. The profilers were sure it would work.

Danny looked up and stood when Jane joined him. God, she was beautiful. She wore black boots and a long black skirt. A figure flattering wrap sweater in dark green made him suspicious. He reached out and patted her down, where he discovered her other layers. They included Kevlar and her weapons.

With nothing but naughty thoughts, he reached beneath her skirt and skimmed along her tights toward heaven. One hand gripped her outer thigh and the other one rested on the gun between her legs, he cut his eyes up at her.

"Satisfied?" Her raised eyebrows held the right touch of sass.

Not nearly. His smile came on gradually as he stood and adjusted himself in his pants. "That color brings out your eyes."

"I didn't think it was my eyes you were interested in." She straightened his tie and kissed him. "I'm not going to be overly affectionate with you, starting now. Game face on."

Thrill and pride lifted his chest. She had what it took to take down a killer and still melt his heart with one sizzling kiss. A well-rounded woman.

Mine.

His gaze fixed on the deepest part of her V-neck top where what he'd thought was a camisole turned out to be Kevlar. How could that be so damn sexy? With effort, he turned off the emotive, lust-filled side of his brain, so he could focus. He shifted into combat mode as they left the chief's house.

Walking into the venue at Jane's side, his eyes scanned every item in the room, excluding the faces. There were a lot of guns. He felt better knowing he was close enough to jump in front of a bullet if one was aimed at her.

Jane smiled and moved forward to hug a plain-clothes officer. She introduced Walenski, and Danny shook his hand.

"Do you still have nightmares?" Walenski asked her.

Danny looked at her, wondering the same.

"Not as often as I used to." The corners of her mouth turned up.

"You'll have to tell me your secret."

She glanced at Danny. "Love."

Even though he didn't let it show, Danny's heart took flight. Reminding himself he couldn't afford to get distracted, he directed his attention to the faces around him. He was looking for someone suspicious or out of place, but no one stood out. It would make his job easier if people with evil intentions had it tattooed on their foreheads.

Cops were everywhere, and the idea struck him that the guy they were after would blend in nicely if he were in a uniform. He shifted his focus to the officers. Still standing next to Jane, who introduced him to several people, he greeted them politely, but didn't give them his full attention.

An older couple approached Jane. The woman was well dressed and attractive with graying hair, sparkling eyes, and a kind smile. She hugged Jane tightly and held on for a moment. The man was tall with salt and pepper hair and a strong jaw. Danny didn't often think of men as attractive or not, but he would bet money this man had been considered a heartthrob in his day.

Leaning in with one hand on her back, the man kissed Jane's cheek.

"Mr. and Mrs. Rhodes, I'd like to introduce you to Danny Baker. Danny, meet Pat and Jean Rhodes, Karl's parents."

His attention caught, Danny shook their hands in greeting.

"We're so glad you're here, Jane," Mrs. Rhodes said. "Seeing you, knowing what you meant to our son, you give us a connection to him."

Danny wanted to put an arm around Jane to help absorb any pain those words might cause, but he decided it was more important to exhibit a professional relationship.

Mr. Rhodes pulled a small velvet box out of his coat pocket and handed it to Jane. "Happy belated birthday."

When was her birthday? It was in her file, but Danny had only looked at the year, not the date.

"Thank you. You shouldn't have." She opened the box. Inside was a bullet fragment suspended in clear glass.

"This is the bullet they took out of Karl's shoulder, the one that got him on his last overseas tour. We want you to have it," Mr. Rhodes said.

Danny had his own bullet fragment in a box at home. Thankfully, his right quadriceps muscle had healed nicely despite the bacterial infection that accompanied his wound. South American water could be as dangerous as some of its criminals.

The main reason he'd kept the souvenir, though, was in remembrance of the man they'd lost that day. Stoic people could often be sentimental when it came to the heroes they fought beside, loved, and lost.

Jane's nostrils flared, even as she recovered
with a small smile for the Rhodes. They were being
directed to take their seats, so she closed the box.

Danny pulled her to his side. "I'll hold onto
that for you."

Her eyes glistened as she placed the box in his
hands. She held onto him a moment before she gave
a quick squeeze and then let go.

The ceremony was uneventful. The fallen men
were appropriately honored. Jane and Walenski did
their part in the program by each taking a corner of
a hanging cloth and unveiling the bronze plaque,
which would be displayed at the precinct. The press
took photos and it was over.

Refreshments were being served in the back of
the room, and Danny went to get a drink for Jane.
When he turned back, he saw her exiting through a
side door with Walenski and another officer. His
muscles bunched as a single bead of sweat trickled
down his back.

***

Apprehension crawled up Jane's spine the
moment Danny left her side. She almost called out
to him, but refrained, self-doubt creeping in. She
and Walenski had been speaking to the local crime
reporter, and Jane had learned more about the
unsolved cases piling up.

When the reporter stepped away, a uniformed
officer approached and said, "I need you to come
this way please."

Though he concealed it, Jane saw the remote
detonator in his hand. Attempting to disarm him
would probably cause the charge to go off, and

since she didn't know where it was and who might get hurt, her only option was to do as he said. She looked to Walenski, whose face had blanched.

She walked in the direction the faux officer indicated, which was to a side door exiting outside. There was a van parked there. The man tossed her a set of handcuffs and told her to cuff Walenski. When she started to cuff him in front, the man rebuked her and waved the remote. She was forced to cuff Walenski's hands behind him.

"Now you." The man tossed her a zip tie.

His first mistake was to assume she was a lesser threat than Walenski.

She put the zip tie around one wrist and fed the zipper through leaving the opening wide enough, so she could get her other hand in. By pulling the end with her teeth, she tightened it.

She stalled as much as possible, knowing Danny would come looking for her as soon as he noticed she was missing.

The man opened the back doors. "Get in."

Jane stepped up into the back of the van and crouch walked toward the metal grate, which separated the front seats from the back. That was good and bad. Good because she could see the driver and where they were going. Bad because he might also see her.

She turned to face the back door and sat on the floor of the vehicle with her legs out in front of her. Facing the opposite way, Walenski seated himself cross-legged next to her. The man climbed into the driver's seat and pulled away.

Jane raised the alert by activating the

transmitter in her boot.

She hoped the bomb wasn't inside the venue and that he wouldn't detonate it now that he had them. Her heart clenched at the thought of Danny being in the building.

Choosing to focus instead on survival, she dragged her mind away from the dark thoughts.

Walenski nudged her and nodded toward the front, where the man had removed his uniform cap and placed it on the passenger seat next to the detonator. That's when she saw the bomb.

More adrenaline flooded her system, and sweat beaded on her lip and hairline.

She set her jaw when the man started talking. She knew he would. Certain serial killers liked to explain to their victims how smart they were for killing so many people and not getting caught. When she'd seen the smug look on his face, she'd known he was a talker.

"Ray Walters will be so pleased when he hears I got you two. People in our line of work don't like unfinished business. Of course, you aren't the typical victims we go for, but every once in a while, it's thrilling to deviate from the normal routine."

"Are you good friends with Ray Walters?" Walenski asked.

"Oh, I've never met him, but I've admired his work for years. I've heard he keeps clippings of my deeds." The pride in his voice made Jane grind her teeth.

How many psychotic people am I going to have to deal with this week?

The man continued to talk while Jane eased up

the end of her skirt and extracted her knife. The blade was very sharp. Even still, cutting through the thick plastic of the zip tie would require effort.

Walenski must've seen what she was doing in his peripheral vision, but he never looked her way. Instead, he drew attention to himself by asking the killer probing questions about his victims.

Good. If we survive this, we can give testimony to help put his ass away.

Several pulls of the blade across the plastic did the trick, and the tie fell onto her lap. She also managed to cut her sleeve and the skin underneath, but that was the least of her worries.

The van slowed to make a turn, and Jane acted on impulse. She pulled her gun, turned around, and put two rounds in the driver's head. His foot went heavy on the accelerator, and the wheel jerked hard left, causing the van to tip.

Jane fell against the side wall, and Walenski landed on top of her. When the van impacted against something and stopped abruptly, her head slammed against the metal frame. She didn't know how long she lay there dazed and unmoving.

Walenski's voice sounded far away. There was pounding, and she wondered if it was inside her head.

Someone was pounding on her skull. She squeezed her eyes shut to stop the assault.

Danny. His name was written on her heart.

Cold air swirled around her, and then she floated away.

***

Danny and Frank followed the van in an

unmarked car. They worried that if the perpetrator felt them closing in, he may forego his original plan and kill his victims.

Swallowing against the lump in his throat, Danny's heart went from zero to tachycardia. It was strange how the nurses in his family had influenced him with technical talk over the years.

Frank drove, hanging farther back when they reached a desolate part of town.

The air was frigid and snow blanketed the ground. In other areas, people were still out and about, but here, in this old industrial section, the streets were abandoned like the empty warehouses.

Their killer was probably using one of the buildings as his base of operations.

If he hurt Jane, Danny would make sure no one ever found his body or recognized it if they did.

There was a dead end ahead, and the van slowed to turn. Suddenly, it jerked and tipped over.

Shit.

He imagined Jane getting bounced around inside. The van continued its forward momentum, sliding off the road and down an incline out of sight.

Frank sped up and called for backup. Before the car was in park, Danny drew his gun and bolted for Jane.

A concrete barrier at the bottom of the drainage ditch had stopped the downhill slide of the vehicle. Frank moved several feet away with his gun aimed at the wreckage.

As they got nearer, they heard pounding. Someone in the back was kicking the doors.

Jane.

Danny's shoulders sagged as he forced the air out of his lungs. The doors were probably locked, and he bet the driver had the key. He hoped the bastard was unconscious or preferably dead.

Danny banged his fist on the back door and yelled, "Jane?"

The voice that replied was not hers.

Walenski shouted, "There's a bomb in here. We're locked in."

At the B-word, Danny's heart dropped to his stomach and dread rose in his throat, tasting like bile.

The doors didn't budge.

"Is the perp moving?" Frank asked.

"Dead. Jane shot him in the head." The muffled reply came through.

"Jane," Danny called. "I'm going to get you out of there."

Another muffled response from Walenski. "She's unconscious."

God, please, no. Panic rolled like a wave over Danny, and his muscles jumped under his skin.

He holstered his gun and climbed on top of the overturned van. Through the passenger window, he could see the dead driver with two holes in his head.

That's my girl.

The keys dangled from the ignition. A bomb with a timer rested against the console and seemed to have its own heartbeat. Danny couldn't see the display or if it had been activated.

He put two rounds through the glass, and then stomped with his foot to break through. Avoiding the shards as much as possible, he lowered his upper body into the van through the broken window and reached for the keys. It was the longest reach of his life. He pulled them out of the ignition and prayed the one he needed was among them. He tossed the keys to Frank then climbed down.

When the door closest to the ground opened, Walenski tried to scoot out on his butt. From the strange angle of his arm and the way he cradled it, Danny knew it was broken. He lifted the top door and held it open, so Frank could help Walenski out.

Jane was lying inside, not moving, and Danny's heart lurched.

In an instant, he darted into the back of the van and scooped her into his arms.

Frank held the upper door, so Danny could carry her out, and they all moved toward the road. Sirens grew louder, and he hoped there was an ambulance among them.

As they neared the road, an explosion behind him knocked him to his knees. Danny cradled Jane to his chest and kissed the top of her head. Before his ears could stop ringing, Frank helped him up, and they took cover behind the car.

Danny rocked her in his arms. "Jane, angel, stay with me," he said in her ear and kissed her there. "I love you, please don't leave me alone."

Chapter Thirty-one

Jane opened her eyes. She regretted it and closed them again. Moving her head, a wave of nausea swept over her. She'd been here before—coming to after losing consciousness. Her thoughts were a jumble of images and sounds amid the throbbing in her skull.

She decided it would be better to go back to sleep, but questions kept invading her mind.

Where am I? How did I get here? Is this a hospital? The last time I woke up like this, I was in a hospital.

She took an intentional breath, testing the air. She wiggled her nose to confirm the pressure on her cheeks was from nasal oxygen tubes.

Where's the doctor? She tried to think of what caused her to lose consciousness. *What's the last thing I remember?* His face was clear in her mind and her lips twitched. *Danny. Had he been hurt?*

The thought of losing him tore through her

soul. Certain the wound was physical, it threatened to break her spirit once and for all. She made herself breathe.

Holding very still, she opened one eye, then the other and allowed them to adjust to the light. She swallowed, but her throat was so dry she choked out a weak cough. Everything ached.

God, I'm going to have to stop living so dangerously. Maybe I'll get a job teaching kids to dance.

She looked around with her eyeballs, trying not to move her head. Something was on the very edge of her peripheral vision, and she turned her head less than an inch.

She clenched her jaw as the dizziness threatened to overtake her. When it passed, she focused her vision on Danny's dark hair. An involuntary smile spread across her face. He was sitting in a chair but leaning forward onto the edge of the bed with his head resting on his folded arms.

He was close enough to touch, so she stretched her fingers and stroked his hair. The slight movement of her arm sent pain radiating to her shoulder and back. He lifted his head, and after a moment, relief softened the lines of his face. He leaned over her to kiss her.

She sunk her head into the pillow and clamped her lips together.

"What is it?" he asked. "Are you okay? Did I hurt you?"

She squeezed her eyes shut and waved him back with a slight movement of her other hand. Not nearly as painful.

He called for the nurse.

Jane braved a glance a few minutes later when someone came in.

"Jane, I'm glad to see you're awake. I'm sorry we keep meeting like this. Can I recommend a change of profession?" Dr. McVey smiled at her.

He'd taken care of her the last time she'd been a patient. While he checked her vitals and performed a physical exam, checking her pupils and reflexes, she fought the roller coaster in her stomach.

"Your fiancé tells me he's going to talk you into a safer career." The doctor probed the side of her head.

She winced, but forced her teeth together, trying to be still.

"You had a pretty good bump of your head the last time you were here, too," Dr. McVey said. "Too much head trauma is never a good thing. Can you speak?"

Blinking slowly, she pried her lips apart. They skin peeled away in a strip, and a warm, coppery taste touched her tongue. "Water," she whispered.

Danny held a straw to her lips and let a few drops of water fall into her mouth. With dark stubble shadowing his face, he looked more handsome than ever. She probably looked like hell because that's how she felt.

Still playing that fiancé game, are we? Her thoughts were becoming less hazy.

He gave her more water and some dripped onto her chin. He used his thumb to wipe away the spill, and she blinked a long time, focusing on the way his touch made her tingle.

This was much better than when she'd nearly puked on him a minute before.

"How are you feeling?" Dr. McVey asked.

"Like someone put me in a big metal box and flipped it over," Jane said, finding her voice.

The doctor laughed. "You did get a little beat up, but nothing is broken. No internal injuries this time. Your biggest problem is that bump on your head. You probably recall that nausea and dizziness will come and go. Don't operate heavy machinery until those symptoms subside. If things still look good tomorrow morning, we'll get you released so you can get home to recuperate."

"How long I have I been here?"

He checked his watch. "About eight and a half hours. They brought you in around noon today."

She closed her eyes and let out a long breath. *I didn't lose two weeks and the love of my life this time.*

When the doctor left them, Jane pitched her body toward Danny and grunted at the twinge in her shoulder.

He sat on the edge of the bed and brushed her hair back. "Can I get you anything?"

"More water." As he turned to get the cup, she asked, "Are you hurt?"

He shook his head. "I'm fine."

Her mind was fuzzy on the details of the accident. "What happened?"

He filled her in. "Frank told me to call him when you wake up, but not so he can get your statement. He wants to know you're okay. He was shaken up. The killer had a hideout close to where you ended him."

She winced at his blunt words.

"Sorry, I shouldn't have said it like that." He dripped water into her mouth. "Why did you take him out when you did?"

She returned in her mind. "I'd just gotten my hands free when we started to slow. I didn't really think it through, I just acted." She gave a small shake of her head and squeezed her eyes closed. "I'm done with crazy people. Do you think that argument will hold up in court?"

He cupped her chin. "Don't even worry about that. I'm so glad you're okay. I really do think we should talk about getting you in a safer line of work."

"You don't have to convince me. I quit."

"Good, then you don't have a reason not to marry me." He lifted her left hand.

When she was unconscious, he'd slipped the ring on her finger. She used her thumb to test the fit. Perfect.

"This was my grandmother's ring. My mama used to wear it on a chain around her neck. Dad gave it to me before we left Southland with a letter she left me." He paused and pressed his quivering lips together.

She gripped his hand tighter. "What did the letter say? If you don't mind sharing."

"Mama had instincts about things, just like you. She said I'd know it was right when I saw it." He kissed the ring on her finger. "Somehow, it looks like you."

Jane couldn't argue. In a whole world of rings, she'd never seen one that looked like it'd been made with her in mind.

He pressed her hand in between his. "I know you came here to put the past to rest, so I was going to wait on this, but I almost lost you today. I don't want to spend another day without you. I love you like I've never loved anyone. Please put me out of my misery and say yes."

A slow smile spread across her face. "I want to say yes, but…" She ran her tongue around the inside of her mouth. "I can't just yet."

"Why not?" he asked.

"Because I'd like a kiss, but my teeth are wearing fur coats." She locked her lips together.

He chuckled and leaned toward her. "I'll get you a toothbrush."

With the little strength she had in her arms, she pushed him away when he tried to kiss her. "Seriously, I can't celebrate just now, Baker, or I might vomit on you."

He kissed the tip of her nose. "That's okay, Dillon. We'll celebrate for the rest of our lives."

**

Tired and dizzy after Danny helped her to the bathroom, Jane rested on the toilet long after she'd emptied her bladder. She kept staring at her finger, admiring her ring. His mom had been right. The emeralds and diamonds were oddly unobtrusive and appeared sturdy set deep in white gold. It reminded her of Danny too—beautiful and solid.

She loved him so much her heart threatened to spring out of her chest and dance. She managed to get to her feet and gave her teeth a quick brush. Again, she noted soreness in her right shoulder.

When she opened the bathroom door, he picked her up. "You were supposed to call for me, stubborn woman."

Her head started spinning. When he set her down on the bed, his hand hit the grapefruit size bruise on her right hip, and she sucked air through clenched teeth.

"I'm so sorry. Are you okay?"

"Yes, just a little...or maybe a lot bruised."

"Can I see?" he asked.

She pulled at the hospital gown, and he helped her get it lifted. He ran his finger lightly around the bruise and bent to kiss her hip. A shiver ran over her skin and a fire lit deep inside.

"You can't do that," she said.

"Do what?" He straightened.

"My head is already spinning from the concussion. You make my head spin on a good day when you touch me and kiss me."

"Do I?" One side of his mouth lifted. "You never let on."

"I'm good at keeping secrets." She cut her eyes up at him.

"I want to know *all* of your secrets."

"Can I tell you later? My head might explode from this throbbing." She pressed her fingertips to her forehead.

"Of course. I'll be right here if you need anything." He gave her another light kiss. "I'm so glad you're safe, my angel."

Chapter Thirty-two

The next morning, Danny exited the bathroom freshly showered and shaved to find Jane awake. Even banged up, she radiated beauty and confidence.

"I'm jealous. I need a shower."

Just as he leaned in for a kiss, there was a knock at the door, and Frank stuck his head in. Martha came in behind him with a bouquet of flowers.

"Oh, Jane," she said. "I'm glad to see you're so much better than before."

Frank gripped Jane's hand. "I'm sorry to have gotten you mixed up in this. I never dreamed it would go that far."

"Calm down, Chief. The witch is dead. Walenski and I crawled away or got carried away in my case. I knew the risk and went in with my eyes open." She paused and looked at Danny. "I won't be coming back to work here."

"I figured that much when Danny told me you're getting married," Frank said.

"Yes, congratulations. This is beautiful." Martha held onto Jane's ringed hand. "Why didn't you tell us before?"

"Jane wanted to wait until after the ceremony." Danny looked at her, hoping she would back him up.

She smiled and nodded once as she looked at her hand.

"This ring must have been designed for you." Martha squeezed her fingers.

"The emeralds match her eyes," Frank said, looking at Danny. "Very nice. Her grandfather would approve."

Danny hoped he meant the ring and the man.

Another knock preceded Dr. McVey. "How's our patient this morning?"

Jane fidgeted with the blanket. "I haven't thrown up yet, but I also haven't tried to get up."

"We'll go," Frank said. "I'll need to get your statement later."

Danny shook Frank's hand before he and Martha left. The doctor started checking Jane again.

"Will you look at my shoulder? It's probably just sprained, but it hurts to move." Jane lifted her elbow to the side.

The doctor slipped her right arm out of the hospital gown. Danny's gut clenched when he saw the dark purple bruising on her shoulder and back.

Dr. McVey poked around. "I don't think it's a tear. We can do an MRI to check it or you can give it a few days."

"I'm sure it's fine." She looked over at it. "No wonder, I didn't know it was so gnarly looking." She rolled it backward and forward, a little crease between her eyes. "When can I shower?"

"I'll start your discharge paperwork. You can shower now. I'll send someone to assist you?"

"I've got it," Danny said.

When the doctor left them, Danny helped her up. "I hope it's okay for me to do this for you. I mean, you did agree to be my wife, and I'll have to see you naked eventually."

"I'm not sure how attractive I am covered in bruises." She limped as she took a step.

He leaned in close, supporting her weight. "I've been attracted to you since the first day I met you. I thought I might take Breck's head off when he waltzed into your living room wearing nothing but a towel."

"Technically, he didn't waltz, he swaggered." She winked. "How good are you at washing long hair?"

As usual, her smile had his heart racing. *Easy, Danny, she's still hurt. You're going to have to be extra careful with her.*

"Swagger, my ass," he said. "I need to start practicing with the hair washing. Shall we?"

At her nod, Danny scooped her up and carried her into the bathroom. He started the water and waited until it was warm, but not too hot. Cooler water would be better for her bruises and swelling, but taking a cold shower sucked, unless you were overheated.

"I'm gonna put some shorts on real quick. I

can't be naked in the shower with you because…I just can't."

He kept his gaze locked on hers as she slid out of the hospital gown and let it fall to the floor. He held her arm as she stepped into the stream of water.

"How's the temperature?"

"It's fine, Danny. Don't worry. I'm all right."

After changing, he stepped into the shower with her. She faced away from him and her wet hair hung down her muscled back. Her lats made a V-shape that ended at her narrow waist. Her ass was like sculpted marble.

"Those are the most well developed hamstrings I've ever seen," he said.

She turned to look at him over her shoulder. "Dancing gave me those bad boys."

He chuckled. "Where do we start?"

"I've already done the important parts. I need help with the hair though."

She handed him a tiny bottle of two-in-one shampoo plus conditioner. He put a small amount into his palm.

"More," she said.

He dispensed more, rubbed his hands together, and placed them on top of her head. To give him better access, she leaned her head back toward him.

Using light pressure, he massaged her scalp to work the shampoo into lather. On the right side, he could feel the goose egg. Not wanting to hurt her, he worked the lather down to the ends.

Smiling like a jackass, he enjoyed washing his future wife's hair. It was fun and sexy as hell. She was naked, and she was beautiful.

When they were ready to rinse, she turned to face him, so she could lean back into the shower stream. Her eyes were closed against the soap and water, and it gave Danny a chance to marvel at her body.

Her breasts were perfection like the rest of her. He hardened, and it took all of his will not to push his erection into her abdomen and let her know how arousing she was. To tamp down his libido, he shifted his eyes to her right shoulder and then hip, since they were discolored and swollen.

He studied the long, jagged scar that ran along her right side. It started a few inches inside her pelvic bone and fanned out to her right waist. He reached to touch it, but his thoughts were interrupted.

"Can I get a little help?"

"Sure, I'm just…I can't get too close." He put his hands back in her hair to help her rinse.

"Why not?"

"Because you're beautiful and I'm very turned on."

She smiled. "Danny, I trust you not to take advantage of me in my weakened condition."

"I'm not sure I trust me." His voice was nearly as tight as his shorts.

She wiped her eyes and opened them. "You love me. You won't hurt me."

He hugged her close, no longer caring that she would feel his excitement. Memories of every time they had spoken or touched or kissed danced into his mind. She must have at least cared about him the day she went in the well to rescue Tyler, maybe even before.

"When? When did you first know it was me?" he asked.

"You'll think I'm crazy." Her hands found his and their fingers twined.

"No, I won't."

"If I'm completely honest, it was the first time I met you. When we touched, I tingled all over. And the way you looked into me... You really saw me. I'm not sure you liked what you saw, but everything I was trying to hide felt exposed."

"I didn't know what you were hiding then. I knew you had secrets, and soon I wanted to be the one you shared them with. I was so busy keeping my guard up around you I ignored my instincts, which were pushing me toward you in the beginning."

"I did the same thing, but the timing had to be right for us. I still had to deal with what happened here. Thank you for being patient with me."

He kissed her long and deep until he was ready to push her against the shower wall. He lightened the kiss and pulled back. "We should get you dried and dressed, before I get carried away, and before the doctor comes back."

***

After Jane signed her statement and said her farewells, she had one last stop to make before they left Philly. Danny waited in the car as she walked to the grave. A brisk wind blew through her, and she tightened the scarf around her neck. Light snow was falling and her boots crunched with each step.

She dusted the flakes from the headstone and squatted beside it, groaning at the pain in her hips.

"I'm getting too old for this, Karl. I know it's silly for me to come here to talk to you. You've been with me every day since…" She swallowed. "I guess, you'll always be with me." She put her hand over her heart.

"You were the first man I ever loved. Thank you for loving me." When the warm tear hit her cheek, it cooled quickly and she wiped it away. "I have to say goodbye now. Someone very special has come into my life. And for the first time in a very long time, I have hope for a future, not just an existence."

She closed her eyes and imagined that future with Danny by her side. There was a beach, and Liz, and children, and Southland. It was a family. Her family.

The wind whistled around the headstones, bringing her back to the present.

"I know you have better things to do in heaven than listen to me, but if you see my grandfather and Mrs. Baker, give them hugs for me. All of you taught us how to love, and we'll never forget you."

She pressed two gloved fingers to her lips, kissed them and touched the letters of his name on the grave stone. With a final look, she turned from her past and toward her future with Danny.

***

Danny had his pilot pick them up in Philadelphia. Jane slept most of the trip with her head on his lap or his shoulder. As Danny played with her hair, the strands were like silk between his fingers. He'd done the same to his mama's hair when she was sick, before it fell out.

The night before the ceremony, when he went to bed, he'd read the letter she'd left him. Then, he'd laid there and cried like he had when she'd died. He'd been twelve, and he'd thought life was over. No woman would ever love him unconditionally like his mama.

How wrong he'd been.

Mama D loved him, despite the fact he always pushed her away. His baby sister, Maddie, had been right. He'd been unlovable and ungrateful, but they loved him anyway.

When Danny and Jane arrived at Southland later that afternoon, he gave Mama D an extra long hug and thanked her for everything.

She patted his cheek. "Honey, you've showed your love for me and our girls, whether you wanted to or not. I'd do anything in the world for you, don't cha know?"

He grinned at her familiar phrase.

Mama D and the rest of the family were concerned about Jane and her injuries. They spent two nights at the main house, where Danny kissed Jane goodnight at the door to her bedroom each night.

As much as Danny didn't want to, he had to get back to work. After arriving at South Winds, they started working on a plan.

"I want to stay to help Liz," Jane said.

"I'll hire her myself," Liz said. "Skip the middle man."

"I need to go back to L.A. for a few weeks. I

don't want to leave you…either of you." Danny looked from Jane to Liz.

"It's okay, brother. I know it's your future bride you'll miss the most. Did I tell you how thrilled I am?" Liz asked.

"Only every time you dance Ethan around in circles." Danny couldn't contain his joy either.

"Jane, who I already love like a sister, will be my sister-in-law, and my big brother is happier than I've ever seen him. I knew you were perfect for each other."

"I think you should remain employed by B&B, Jane," Danny said. "I know you're concerned about workplace romances, but your current assignment isn't too risky, except that my sister may drive you up the wall."

"She will not. Be nice to Liz, Ethan can hear you." Jane reached out and stroked Liz's swollen belly with a gentle hand.

Touched by Jane's action, Danny envisioned her in a similar condition. He shook himself to get back on track.

"I'll talk to Joe," Danny said. "He'll be disappointed. I guess when you get back to L.A., you can train actresses in combat techniques and choreograph fight scenes, but no bodyguard duty, nothing with the potential to get you shot or hurt."

"What do you think Joe will say? About us?" Jane squinted one eye shut.

"He'll say it's about damn time." Danny grinned.

"I trust your judgment," Jane said. "There was a time when I would have bristled at you calling the shots for me, but now, I'll do whatever you ask."

"Whatever I ask, huh?" He pulled her close and kissed her.

When it was time for Danny to leave, he hugged his sister then Jane. "How am I going to stand being away from you?"

"It's just a couple weeks. When you get back, my injuries will be healed. Then you can have your wicked way with me. I'll miss you every day." Jane kissed him like tomorrow might never come.

When she broke the kiss, he had to catch his breath. "Damn woman, I do believe I've met my match."

"It's high time you admitted it." She raised her eyebrows flirtatiously.

He wondered if she'd always been sassy or if the South was bringing it out in her.

Chapter Thirty-three

The weeks passed, but not quickly enough for Danny. When they finally reunited in the middle of March, the two weeks they'd been apart had seemed like an eternity.

They were getting hot and heavy in the foyer when Liz interrupted. "Um, Jane, Danny, I think my water just broke."

"Oh, my God," Jane and Danny said in unison and went to her.

"It's too early for that, isn't it?" Danny asked.

"Let's get her in the car." Jane put an arm around Liz.

Please God, let them be okay. Danny prayed on the drive to the hospital as Jane sat in the back holding Liz's hand.

When they arrived at the hospital, Jane volunteered to call his parents so Danny could stay with Liz.

Pacing, he wrung his hands. She was only

seven months pregnant and premature babies sometimes had problems. He forced down his worst fear that the baby wouldn't make it.

"The cord is prolapsed," the doctor said. "We have to take the baby now."

Danny squeezed Liz's hand. "Hang in there, Lizabelle. Ethan is gonna be fine. You can do this, stay strong."

Many things happened in quick succession, and the next thing Danny knew, the doctor held up a wrinkled, red-faced baby and handed him off.

"He's not breathing," someone said.

The moments spent waiting to hear the baby cry were the longest of Danny's life. The sensation of his ribs vibrating with every heartbeat rattled him.

A wail pierced the silence. "You hear that, Lizabelle? That's your son hollering."

Liz laughed and cried at the same time. "I can't believe I'm a mom. How did this happen?"

"Did Mama D forget to tell you about the birds and bees?" He blinked and a tear slid down his cheek. He wiped his face and turned his focus to the baby.

Liz didn't get to see Ethan before they took him to the Neo-natal unit. They already had him on oxygen. Danny was told he could see him there later.

When Liz was asleep from the meds, he walked to the waiting area where he found Jane wearing a path in the hospital grade linoleum.

"Well, Aunt Jane, Ethan can't wait to meet you."

Jumping into his arms, she hugged him tight. "And Liz is okay?"

He put her feet on the ground but didn't let her go. "Fine. She's resting. You can see her and the baby in a little while. They had to do a C-section, so she'll need our help for a few weeks." Danny took a deep breath before he asked something he'd been wanting to know. "Do you want kids, Jane?"

That little crease he loved formed between her brows. "I...I...I don't know. I'm down an ovary, so it might be a problem."

He rubbed his thumb over her scarred side. "Hey, there's no pressure, we just never talked about it. You aren't opposed then?"

"Are you sure you aren't opposed to marrying a woman who may not be able to give you kids?" she asked.

"Are you kidding? I'm in love with you, and if we have kids, great. If not, we have eight nieces and nephews we can spoil." He forced his eyes wide to show his excitement.

"Maybe we can get married first, make sure the wedding tackle works, and see what happens," she said.

Danny raised an eyebrow and pressed his hips into her. "Now who's the one who has to prove himself? Maybe we should run down to the courthouse real quick."

She stood on her tiptoes and laid one on him. It was a good thing his buddy was a Justice of the Peace, and he had him on speed dial.

***

When she realized people were staring, Jane

broke the kiss and took Danny's hand. They needed to go see Ethan, and she wanted to not strip Danny's clothes off in the hospital waiting room. She didn't need a piece of paper to show him she loved him.

Arriving at the NICU, they stopped to look in the window. Incubators were lined up in a row, and they struggled to locate a name.

A nurse came through the door. "Are you the father of Ethan Baker?"

"I'm his uncle," Danny said.

"You can come in. We'll scrub you in and give you a gown to cover your clothes. He's a good weight, but he needs to grow. He's going to be okay."

"I'll wait here, Danny," Jane said. "Tell Ethan hello from Aunt Jane."

"You can come in too, hon. You're both on the list."

They followed her into a room where they washed up, put on disposable gowns, and went into the unit.

Jane stared, awestruck. Ethan was so tiny.

Her heart stuttered at his cries. She didn't know what to say or do. After sanitizing, Danny put his arm in the opening and rubbed the baby's tiny fingers. His hand was big next to Jane's, but next to the four pound baby, it was enormous.

"Hey, little man, I'm your favorite uncle. I'm so glad you're safe." He looked over his shoulder at Jane. "Aren't you going to talk to him? Give him some inappropriate advice?"

Emotion made speech difficult, but she cleared

her throat. "Hi, Ethan." She put her hand in the incubator and lightly brushed her fingertip along his arm. "It's Aunt Jane, and I'm so happy to meet you. Welcome to the world."

The baby settled down to a whimper and Jane smiled.

Danny's eyes widened and he cocked his head. "I think he recognizes your voice."

"He ought to by now." She blinked back tears. "He's amazing."

"So are you."

She looked into the eyes of her future husband and struggled to breathe.

Whole again. It was the only way to explain how the dark empty space in her soul no longer ached.

***

Fear of humiliating himself was the only thing that kept Danny's feet from dancing the hoedown right there in the hospital room. He slid one arm around Jane and held Liz's hand with the other. "You did good, sister."

"Ethan is beautiful." Jane squeezed Liz's leg.

Liz's smile was shaky. "Thank you. And thank you both for getting us here so quickly. It could've been bad."

"Hey." Danny narrowed his eyes at her. "None of that, shoulda, coulda, woulda crap. He's fine. You're fine."

She nodded. "They're going to keep me a couple of days, and Ethan will have to stay for a few weeks."

"Is there anything you need?" Jane asked.

"I need you and Danny to stop fussing over me and go enjoy your reunion. You haven't seen each other in weeks, and the minute he walked in the door, Ethan decided he was ready to be born."

"Couldn't wait to get out and meet his Uncle Danny, could he?" Danny winked. "We're not leaving you here by yourself."

"Fine, stay and watch me sleep. See if I care." Liz nestled her head back on the pillow.

Danny was hesitant to leave Liz. She looked pale and tired, but he supposed that was normal after childbirth.

His phone rang. After talking briefly to Mama D, he said to his sister, "Grandparents are dying to know the score. Do you feel like talking, Lizabelle?"

She took the phone and spoke to her mom, while he and Jane discussed their plans.

When Liz hung up, she said, "You guys need to go home and get the house ready for the Baker invasion. I'll be fine here overnight. Maybe tomorrow, I'll feel more like having company. Jane, will you bring me a few things?"

They talked about what she needed, and before Danny knew it, Liz had convinced them to go.

When they exited the hospital, Jane stopped him. "Are you sure you want to leave? I can handle the house stuff."

"They'll be fine. Let's go home and move your things in with me and get the guest rooms ready for everyone."

"What will your family think of me if I'm sharing your room?"

"You're kidding, right? We can't get married fast enough to suit them. They love you more than they love me." He kissed her cheek. "Plus, we're stopping to get our marriage license on the way to South Winds."

"Really?" She bounced on her toes once. "It's not true that they love me more. They love seeing you happy. I intend to do my best to make sure you always are."

He kissed her again. "Let's go."

Chapter Thirty-four

Danny drove them to the courthouse, where they ran into his friend from college, Judge Harrison.

"Marriage license, huh?" He rocked back on his heels. "Care to step into my chambers and make this official?"

Danny looked at Jane and silently pleaded for her to say yes.

"Your family will be here tomorrow, and they'll be pissed we didn't wait on them," Jane said.

"They'll turn it into a circus. And it'll take attention away from Liz and Ethan. Do you really want to steal their thunder?"

She tilted her head to the side. "You know I don't, but look at me. I'm not dressed to get married."

With one arm, he drew her closer. "You've never looked more beautiful. We can do it again, a real ceremony... Or if you want to wait—"

"No, let's do it."

Danny owned that the small office was not the most romantic setting to commit his life to Jane, but he knew his family. They would do it again and do it big, unless he could rein them in.

As far as a honeymoon, they had the night. But when Liz and Ethan were home, he'd make it up to Jane and take her anywhere in the world she wanted to go.

When they got to South Winds, Danny had his hands on Jane before they got in the door. They left a trail of clothes all the way to their bedroom.

Danny couldn't think of anything but claiming his wife. His angel. And giving her pleasure in every way. He tried to slow down his response to her, but the sensations flooding him with every touch of her lips and hands and body threatened to break him. She knew exactly how to bring him to his knees. Every cell in his body reached out to her.

He pulled back from kissing her to see her heavy-lidded eyes open and the smile she wore grew wider. If he could get harder, he did it then.

When they were completely naked, he set her on the bed. "I've dreamed of you like this."

She put her hand on his chest and pushed him away a little.

"You've seen me, but I haven't seen you." She gestured with her finger for him to turn around in a circle.

Obliging, he tried to calm his racing heart. This delay tactic could give him the moment he needed to regroup. He drew his shoulders back and turned slowly.

She licked her lips as her gaze travelled down his body and paused below where his belt had been. He'd never fidgeted under the scrutiny of a woman, but Jane was intense. He willed himself to hold still.

Heat flickered in her eyes followed by a softening as her examination focused on the scar on his left thigh. The soft caress of her fingertips on the raised skin where the bullet had hit him made every muscle contract.

Sliding her hand up, she gripped his hip. "Perfection. You're better than any dream I've ever had."

She ran her fingertips lightly up his chest and ended with them behind his neck as she pulled him in for a kiss. The gesture reminded him of dancing, and he instinctively knew how to make love to her.

He took over their dance, and she responded just like he'd known she would. Their bodies moved and synced perfectly as she whispered his name again and again.

Mine, he thought as his release came with more intensity than he'd ever known. *My wife*.

***

When Jane awoke early the next morning, she was sore in all the right places. They hadn't slept much, but she didn't regret a moment. Danny was the partner she'd waited for her entire life. She couldn't believe they were actually married.

He was wrapped around her and his heat fueled her desire. She checked the clock to be sure they had time for a morning tussle before they left for the hospital. He moved against her, and she had no doubt they'd make the time.

"I love you, husband."

He kissed her neck. "I love you, too, Mrs. Baker."

"That has a nice ring to it."

"Speaking of rings," he lifted his head. "We need to pick up bands."

"We'll get to it. We should get to the hospital."

Danny followed her into the shower, and once again they briefly put Liz and Ethan out of their minds to concentrate on each other. Realistically, Jane knew they would have to spend a little time apart while he went back and forth to L.A. and she stayed to help Liz. She didn't want to think about being apart from him, so she pushed those thoughts aside and took the shampoo bottle from him.

They washed each other and that led to the best shower of her life. The first one had been tender and a little sensual, but she was hurt then. This time, she was crying out his name as he buried his face in her neck and moaned her name right back. She was clinging tightly to him as he set her feet on the floor.

"I'm sorry. I lose myself with you." He gripped her head with his hands. "I didn't hurt you, did I?"

"Uh-uh. Your wife's a badass. Or didn't you know?" She grinned.

"Oh yeah," he cupped her butt. "I know. The most beautiful badass on the planet."

"We *are* going to do this forever, aren't we?" She rested her hands on his chest.

"Forever and a day, my angel."

On the drive to the hospital, Jane was

contemplating transportation for the Baker family when Danny interrupted her thoughts.

"I wish she didn't have to raise him alone. It's not fair. Ian may never know he has a son. I couldn't imagine missing out on a life I helped create."

"He's a different man than you are, Danny." Jane squeezed his arm. "Your family is more important to you than your career. You're right that Ian will miss out. He's already missing out on Liz, and I bet she's the best thing that ever happened to him."

"If I could just convince Liz to tell him about Ethan, maybe he'd change his mind about not wanting kids."

"I know you want Liz and Ethan to be happy, but you have to respect her wishes. She's his mother, and she wants to protect him. Can you imagine what it would feel like to have a parent who didn't want you? Who wished you were never born? I know what it's like. And let me tell you, it shapes your life in a way you couldn't imagine."

Danny took his eyes off the road and looked at her.

"Don't get me wrong, I think those things had to happen to make me the person I am. If I hadn't become G.I. Jane, I might not have met you. But if there's a way to save a child a little heartache, don't you think we should trust Liz and help her protect Ethan?"

"Angel, tell me who rejected you." The concern in his eyes melted her heart.

Jane swallowed before the lump in her throat

had a chance to form.

***

Danny parked at the hospital and opened Jane's car door for her. When he intertwined their fingers, he prayed she'd let him in.

She let out a long slow breath. "There's still a lot we don't know about each other. Damaged goods, but you knew that. I hope you don't regret the impulsive decision to marry me so quickly."

"Don't be silly. I'm in love with you, and I am committed to you for the rest of my natural life. Whatever happened in your past, it didn't damage you, it made you stronger. I love your strength and your gentleness. I love everything about you."

"I didn't mean to alarm you about my past. I shouldn't have let it get to me like that, but I want to tell you about it when we have a moment."

"Tell me now." He squeezed their fingers together.

She glanced down before she looked into his eyes. "My mother had an affair with her boss, who was a married man. When she told him she was pregnant with me, he fired her and gave her a severance package, so she could 'take care of it'." She did air quotations with her fingers on the last few words.

"She went to my grandfather and asked for advice. He told her if she kept me, he'd help support us, but if she aborted me, he wouldn't have anything to do with her. My grandfather put her up in a little apartment and bought my crib and everything to get us set up."

Pausing, she took a deep breath. Danny ran his

hands up and down her arms, encouraging her, even as his heart dreaded hearing more.

"After I was born, my mother resented me. When she saw me, she saw everything I'd taken from her, a man she loved and a job that paid her well. She was depressed and started using.

"My grandfather came by every few days to check on us, and he could tell she was behaving oddly, but she told him she had post-partum depression. He didn't question her then, but nearly two years later, he was on to her. Our neighbors called him. They could hear me crying through the door because my mother was ignoring me again."

She shivered, and he wrapped his arms more tightly around her.

"When he got there, he found me sitting on the floor with a box of cereal turned upside down. My mother had been dead for two days. Overdose."

She huffed out a short breath. "I was malnourished because I hadn't been fed properly. My grandfather told me I hoarded food until I went to kindergarten. He would find it under my pillow or under my bed. I stole other kids' food at daycare. When I said that some things shape your life, I meant subconsciously. My cupboards are never bare. It's a control thing. It was thirty-six years ago, and I still have to beat it."

Danny pressed his lips to her forehead. "Angel, stick with me, and you'll never be hungry again. I'm sorry that happened to you, but I'm glad you told me. I love you even more." He leaned back to see her face. "By the way, when was your birthday?"

She tried to stop her smile. "The same day as yours."

"What? Why didn't you tell me? My family will be horrified they didn't have gifts for you."

"It was your big day. You only turn forty once. Plus, I haven't celebrated birthdays in a long time."

"That ends now. You're a Baker, we celebrate the day you were born, even if your parents didn't." He hugged her close and squeezed his eyes shut.

She'd had scars before she had scars, and all he wanted was to make it right. To make her happy for the rest of their lives.

Chapter Thirty-five

Baby and mother were doing fine, and after visiting for a little while, Jane went to the airport to pick up the Bakers and their rental cars.

It made her excited to be one of them, but she and Danny agreed to wait and tell them later. She wasn't so sure he'd be able to keep quiet though, since he'd spilled the beans to Liz within five minutes.

Mrs. Jane Baker. She felt like a high school girl trying on her boyfriend's name, but this wasn't high school and the ring on her finger spoke to the reality.

Her ringing phone brought her out of her reverie. When she looked at the display, her heart fell. This would be a delicate situation.

"When are you coming home?" Breck asked. "I miss you like crazy."

"Ah, there's a situation here, and I'm not sure I'll be able to get away anytime soon." She was deliberately vague.

"Are you in trouble? Do you need me to come? Does this have anything to do with you getting hurt in Philly?"

"No, no, and no. Calm down, Breck. Some things have happened, but they're very good things. I'm sworn to secrecy about some of them."

"What can you tell me?"

She wanted to shout from the rooftops that she was in love and married to Danny, but Breck was going to need a little TLC. He was B&B's biggest client, and he sent them a lot of business. She didn't want to anger him and risk severing the connection—business or personal.

After Philly, she'd told him about the accident, but not the engagement. The timing wasn't right then. Her happiness would hurt Breck. Although she considered him a good friend, she knew he wanted more.

The joy in her heart started to deflate a little as she struggled with how to break the news to him. If Danny were here, she would get his advice, but he wasn't, so she had to face this on her own.

"Actually, Breck, I might try to get away for a day or two. I need to see you." She hoped she wasn't making a huge mistake.

Danny would not like it, but Breck deserved to hear it from her face to face.

*   *   *

Danny sensed Jane was preoccupied when she returned to the hospital with his family in tow. He hoped they hadn't said or done something to upset her. They had the best of intentions, but sometimes they made Jane uncomfortable without being aware of it.

They took turns seeing Liz and the baby. Danny was as proud for Liz as if the baby had been his. He held onto Jane's hand, but he positioned her in front of him and wrapped his arms around her, so they could see Ethan through the glass window.

He leaned down to her ear. "Would you prefer a boy or a girl?"

She leaned her head against his chest. "I think I would be more suited to raising a boy, but I guess I could figure the girl stuff out."

"I don't think I could handle a girl, especially if she looked like her mom with strawberry blonde hair and big green eyes. I'd shoot every boy who glanced her way."

"True. If we had a boy, we'd only have to worry about *one* penis. If we had a girl, we'd have to worry about hundreds of them."

Danny laughed against her ear and kissed her sweet spot just beneath it, enjoying how she shuddered in his arms.

"Don't you two look cozy?" Johnny said.

"Did you miss the memo, little brother? Jane's my wife," Danny said.

"I thought she might have agreed in Philly because of the bump on her head," Johnny said. "It's not too late, Jane. I can help you make a run for it if you change your mind… Hold on—did you say…wife?"

"Okay, so there wasn't a memo." Danny shrugged.

Jane just shook her head as her chest convulsed

with laughter.

"Holy shit. I didn't think you'd ever do it, bro. Congratulations." Johnny wrapped his arms around both of them, making a Jane sandwich. "I have a new sister."

A squeak came from Jane. "Can't breathe."

"Whew, everybody," Johnny shouted as he released them, "I have a new nephew and a sister."

The family closed in with questions and plans. In a matter of minutes, there was a beach wedding in the making.

***

At the house that night, Jane's wedding had been planned while she sat back and laughed at her new sisters and mother-in-law. It wasn't important to her, but she could see in Danny's eyes how much he wanted it. Celebrating with his family was something she could do.

What she couldn't do was wait much longer to discuss her plans with Danny regarding Breck. Part of her wanted to sneak away and handle it, then tell him after the fact.

Wasn't it better to ask for forgiveness, rather than permission? She wanted to be honest with Danny though, and she didn't plan to start her life with him by keeping secrets.

After everyone went to bed, Danny took her hand. "Come with me."

With a blanket under his arm, they walked out onto the sand. The moon was almost full, so they had enough light to see by as they strolled down the secluded shore, putting distance between them and the house.

This end of the beach had been privately owned for a long time. Only recently had the family begun to sell off the land furthest from their home on the point.

Jane tensed with anticipation at what her future husband was planning to do to her on that blanket.

Breck's face invaded her thoughts, and she knew she couldn't proceed with their lovemaking until she got him off of her chest.

"Danny, I need to go to Los Angeles for a couple of days."

"I know you haven't been there in two months, but can you wait, so I can go with you? I don't want to go back to being two ships passing in the night. Mama D can stay and help Liz for a little while, so we can go to L.A. Maybe we can take a honeymoon trip afterward." Danny spread out the blanket and laid her down.

The last coherent thought she had was an image of Danny's perfect naked body as he lay beside her in the moonlight.

***

After a gritty roll on the beach with his wife, Danny had sand in places that never saw the light of day.

He traced his fingers along the muscles in Jane's back, memorizing every line.

"Danny, I have to go see Breck. I have to tell him about us in person."

That was a dash of cold water on the old scrotum. He ground his teeth. "No, hell, you don't."

He sounded unreasonable even to his own ears, but he didn't want Jane anywhere near Breck

Stanton and his Hollywood good looks, especially knowing Breck had the hots for Jane.

"See," she said. "This response is why you can't come with me."

"What do you mean I can't come with you? If you think I'm going to give Stanton the slightest chance of taking you away from me, you can forget it." His voice had a hard edge to it.

"Green isn't a good color for you, figuratively speaking. You can cut the possessive macho bull for a minute and let me remind you of a few things." She propped up on her elbow.

"First of all, no one can take me away from you. I chose you. We're married 'til death do us part. Secondly, you still own a little security company, and Breck is one of your best clients. You can't afford to alienate him. I'm afraid if you go with me, as hard as you'll try not to, you're still going to piss all over me to mark your territory."

Danny tried to interrupt, but she put a finger over his lips.

"Lastly, Breck is my friend. Yes, I know he has feelings for me. I care about him too, as a friend. He's a good man. I want to tell him face to face, so he can see how happy I am. If I tell him by phone, he'll doubt my sincerity. If I see him in the flesh, then he'll know how much I love you."

Danny sighed. "Why did I have to marry such a smart, level-headed woman? You can't know what it's like to feel like you're in competition with Breck Stanton. He is the most sought after man in Hollywood. Women go wild for him. I'm jealous, and I'm angry that he had you before me."

"That happened before I met you, Danny, or did you miss that detail in your anger the night I told you about it?"

"I remember, but I don't understand it." He tried to settle down.

"The day I met you, things started to change for me. I started to change. I wanted to deny it had anything to do with you, but from that first moment when you looked into me, you started breaking down my walls. Plus, there's no contest between you and Breck, not in my eyes. I love the fact that you have chest hair." Her pointer finger started at the hollow of his neck and trailed down.

"I love that you don't wax your eyebrows." She ran a thumb along his brow.

"I love that your touch makes me tingle down to my toes and your kisses light a fire deep inside of me and that your love pours into me and surrounds and protects me.

"And if you haven't looked in the mirror lately, you're a beautiful man and I'm completely taken with you. Breck's got nothing on you, Danny Baker. I'm in love with you, not him."

He hadn't known how much he needed to hear those words from her. He let all thoughts of Breck fade away, and he made love to Jane again with only the night sky as a blanket.

Chapter Thirty-six

When they boarded Danny's jet for L.A., Jane's cheeks cramped from smiling so much. It had been six weeks since they'd legally tied the knot, but they had just left their beach wedding and reception. Typical little girls grew up planning their weddings and dreaming of their big day, but she was atypical. She'd never envisioned it, but somehow the Bakers had made it a day she'd never forget. Of course, marrying the man of her dreams for the second time was like getting a big, fat love bonus. Getting another wedding night made her want to sing, and Lord knew, nobody wanted to hear that.

She'd chosen an emerald green dress, which highlighted her eyes. Danny wore khaki pants, a white shirt, and a green tie that accentuated his eyes and dark coloring. Together, they'd chosen simple white gold bands, which complimented the emerald and diamond ring that had once belonged to

Danny's mother.

Jane had never been happier than when Danny held her hands and promised to love, honor, and cherish her always, again. She spoke her vows to him, and when he kissed her, she swooned. She was so in love she'd felt lightheaded.

Once they were on board the plane, Danny turned on some music. "I can't wait to get you home, my beautiful wife."

They hadn't even really discussed the logistics of cohabitation. Jane supposed they'd figure it out later.

"Mrs. Baker, may I have this dance?" He held out his hand.

She put her hand in his, and he whirled her around the tight space in the rear of the jet. It was a good thing the Gulfstream had a couch in the back because the dance turned into more. They consummated their marriage, again, at twenty thousand feet somewhere between Georgia and California.

They laughed about never telling that story to their kids as they shared a bottle of champagne.

When they landed and were about to disembark, Jane lost her balance, and Danny caught her.

"Must be the booze." She laughed and shook her head to clear the fuzzy-brained feeling.

***

Jane arrived at Tommy the Dancer's Thursday night mixer. It was a weekly event where his students could practice and show off their dance moves. It was where she and Breck usually met

282

when she was in town, and she'd arranged to meet him here tonight.

As per his usual greeting, Breck picked her up in a full body hug and spun her around. It was strange being back in his arms after she'd spent so much time in her new husband's. It had never felt exactly right with Breck like it did with Danny. She supposed her subconscious knew all along that Danny was her perfect mate.

"Let's dance," Breck said.

That was what he'd said to her the night of the awards ceremony just before they'd danced the horizontal mambo. The scene came rushing back to her, and she felt woozy when her feet hit the floor. She fought a wave of nausea as Breck put a hand on her waist and led her in the waltz.

She talked as they danced. "Breck, I have some news."

"I have some, too. I met someone. She'll be here later. I want to introduce you."

"That's great, Breck. I'm so happy for you." She beamed. "And to think I was worried about telling you my news. Danny and I got married."

He stopped dancing and took her left hand in his to inspect the rings. "Are you pregnant? Jane, you didn't have to marry him. I'm here for you."

"No, Breck, I'm not pregnant. I'm in love."

This wasn't going like she'd planned. A pretty, petite blonde approached them, and Breck dropped Jane's hand to put his arm around the woman.

Breck stared at Jane a moment before he schooled his face into a mask of indifference, which must've mirrored her own.

"Anna, I'd like you to meet my friend Jane."

"It's so nice to meet Breck's savior," Anna said. "I've heard so much about you."

"I'm pleased to meet you, Anna." Jane shook her hand. "I need to go say hello to Tommy. Excuse me."

Jane turned and walked away, but she could feel Breck's eyes burning a hole in her back. While she danced with Tommy, she tried to ignore Breck, but once when their eyes met, he offered a small smile with a single nod.

She and Tommy were spinning and because her attention was on Breck, she didn't spot to keep herself from getting dizzy. The last thing she remembered was her field of vision narrowing and fading to black.

**

A worry niggled at the back of Danny's mind as he tried to brush off Jane's misstep on the plane. She was the most surefooted, graceful person he'd ever met. He pushed the thought aside and focused on the story breaking online: *Celebrity Couple Divorces after Six Month Marriage.*

He couldn't believe his eyes. Actually, he could believe it, this was Hollywood. People did drive-by weddings and divorces as a rule.

Ethan was almost six weeks old and had gained enough weight to finally leave the hospital, but they were keeping him due to jaundice. Now, his father was divorcing his model wife.

Danny picked up his cell to call Liz and give her the news. While he was talking to her, his phone beeped. He checked the display to see it was Breck calling. He couldn't imagine why Breck would call him unless it was to cuss him out for marrying Jane. He hit ignore and continued talking with his sister.

When he disconnected the call, frustrated with Liz's adamant refusal to tell Ian Clarke he was a daddy, he noticed he had a voicemail.

His heart bottomed out, and he headed for the door before he heard the end of Breck's message.

On his drive to the hospital, he kept imagining different problems, which might have caused Jane to faint. The most obvious was the head trauma she'd suffered a few months before. It seemed like such a long time ago, and the realization that it had only been a short time made him angry at himself.

He should've taken more care with her and made sure she was fully recovered before she resumed her active workout regimen. He sent a prayer up for her to be okay as his lead foot stomped the accelerator.

When he arrived at the hospital, he double parked and ran into the Emergency Room. At the desk, he was told Jane was having tests run and a staff member would come get him soon. He didn't want to wait, but he clenched his fists and clamped down on his teeth, so he wouldn't say something he'd regret.

"Danny, I'm glad you got my message. I called Joe too, in case…and there he is," Breck said.

"Danny, what's going on?" Joe asked.

"I don't know. I just got here. Breck, what happened?" Danny asked.

"Jane was dancing with Tommy when she fainted. I rode in the ambulance with her. She woke up before we got here, and she was really embarrassed. Is she pregnant, Danny? I asked her when she told me you got married, and she denied it," Breck said.

Tightening his fists, Danny lunged for Breck, but Joe stepped in between them and struggled to hold him back. If Danny had been serious about hurting Breck, Joe couldn't have stopped him.

"Calm down, Danny. You're upset. Don't take it out on Breck." Joe paused to make sure Danny had control of himself and turned to Breck. "Breck, you might be the only person on the planet to not realize that Danny and Jane belong together."

Breck ran his hand through his hair and let out a long sigh. "I can see how well matched they are. It doesn't change the fact that I've been crazy about Jane for more than a year, and Baker knows her for four months and marries her. It was a shock." He turned and took a few steps away, shook his head and turned back to them. "I just want her to be happy. I want you both to be happy."

He extended his hand, and Danny looked at it with suspicion a moment before clasping it.

"Congratul—"

A voice interrupted Breck. "Mr. Baker?"

The three men turned to see a doctor standing with clipboard in hand.

"That's me." Danny patted Breck on the back and followed the guy in green scrubs.

"We'll wait here, Danny," Joe said. "Let us know how she is."

***

Jane was slightly panicked as she waited for

Danny to get to the hospital. When she'd awoken in the ambulance with Breck, she knew her plan to break the news gently had failed.

Now, she had bigger problems than Breck. She would try to smooth things over with him, if she could, for the sake of B&B. He would come around eventually. She hoped Danny and Breck weren't duking it out in the waiting room.

Danny came in and immediately sat next to her and pulled her to his chest. "I was scared to death. Are you okay?"

"Your wife is fine, Mr. Baker," the doctor said from behind him. "She made us aware of her recent injuries, so we were about to do a CT scan when I opted to run a different test. When she told me she was newly married, I thought we better check, and we found the reason why your wife fainted."

"Why? If it isn't her head injury, what is it?" Danny asked the doctor.

"She's pregnant," the doctor told him.

Jane loved how he just talked about her like she wasn't there, but did he just say…? She must have heard wrong.

Danny started to ask the doctor a question when Jane spoke up. "I'm sitting right here. If you'd prefer to take this conversation *about me* outside, then please, don't let the door hit you in the ass. Did you just say I'm pregnant?"

"It's very early judging by the date of your last cycle. Once you see your obstetrician, you'll have a more accurate due date, but my guess is December or January."

Her reaction was a mixture of joy and terror as

she took several shallow breaths. The fact that Danny hadn't responded yet made her twitchy.

He blinked as the news sunk in. Then, he squeezed her so tight she could barely breathe. "We're having a baby."

When he pulled back, his smile eased some of the fear simmering in her chest.

"You work fast, Baker. I just said *I do* yesterday." She widened her eyes.

"Ha-ha." He pumped his fist. "Well, this is sooner than we thought, but I'm so freaking excited I'm gonna go buy cigars and actually smoke them."

She grinned before she frowned. "Maybe, we should keep this quiet for a while. I'm nervous. Oh God, I've never even held a baby."

"You can practice on Ethan," he said. "Jane, there's nothing to be afraid of. We're gonna do this together. We're a team. This is going to be the most loved baby in the world."

He put his hand on her belly, and she rested hers on top of his. His smile was intimate, loving, and reassuring.

She nodded. "Yes, it will be."

He kissed her until they were both breathless.

Epilogue

"You've never been more beautiful than you are at this moment." Danny kissed Jane deeply.

She grabbed his shirt and twisted. "If I ever have to go through pain like that again, I will castrate you while you sleep."

"Vasectomy it is then." He grinned.

She would do it a hundred more times if she could, just to see the joy on his face. The nurse approached and placed a pink bundle in her arms.

Another nurse handed Danny a blue bundle. "This is your firstborn, Mr. Baker. What will you name him?"

"This is Davis, after my mama. And our little girl," he leaned over to kiss the baby Jane held, "is Dillon, after my beautiful wife."

Jane could only smile as love overflowed from her. She hadn't known a human heart could hold so much joy, and she'd never dared to dream she could be so blessed in her life. And it was all because she'd found the perfect partner to dance with her heart.

ABOUT THE AUTHOR

Meda White is an award-winning author who writes sweet, sultry, and southern contemporary and new adult romance. Born with Georgia clay running through her veins, she continues to enjoy the Southern lifestyle with her husband, a very spoiled Collie, and a stray cat who adopted the family. When not writing, you might find her making music, shooting zombie targets, teaching yoga, or explaining the meaning of her unusual first name.

A Note to Readers

Dear Reader,

Thank you for reading *Dance With My Heart*. I hope you enjoyed Danny and Jane's love story. I had fun taking couples dance classes with Hubba-luv and pretending we never missed a step. There was a lot of laughter and bruised toes.

If you're interested in the other Southland Romances, stay tuned for a sneak peek at *Ride With My Heart*.

If you have a moment to leave an honest review, I'd really appreciate it. Not only do reviews let authors know how they're doing, they help readers find new books.

I love to hear from readers. Please look for me on my Website, Facebook, Twitter, and my Dirt Road Darlings street team. If you sign up for my Newsletter, which contains bonus material and sometimes prizes, it'll make sure you never miss a new release.

Thank you, and best wishes for a lifetime of love and laughter. Oh, and don't forget to dance like no one's watching, every now and then.

Meda

Ride With My Heart
A Southland Romance Book 3

Maddie Baker's date morphed into an octopus when the clock struck midnight. Between the tequila and the beer, celebrating her divorce was turning into *Invasion of the Booty Snatcher*.

The roaming hands belonged to hometown boy and former Arena football player, Ricky Dalton. Granted, she should have stopped drinking hours before, but she also should've been safe on the little dance floor at Mason's Jar Bar.

The watering hole was owned and operated by a family friend named Mason, and it was apropos that the beverages, from draft beer to mixed drinks, were served in Mason jars. Having lived so long in Atlanta, Maddie loved the ambiance of the country bar with wooden floors, walls, and bar. The smell of sin, booze, and cigarette smoke permeated the air. A little sawdust on the dance floor and a local band playing southern rock made it a second home for anyone looking for a good time.

Accepting a date with Willow Creek's most eligible bachelor had seemed like a good idea when the final papers arrived in the mail. But by one in the morning, Maddie regretted her decision and her anger toward her ex-husband grew with each grope. It was Mark's fault she was in this position. No woman should have to endure being fondled against her will.

Every time Maddie removed Ricky's hand from her rear end, his other hand snuck down to the other cheek. She should have expected as much from a former receiver.

Gritting her teeth, she put her hands on his chest and pushed. She might as well have tried to push through a brick wall for all the good it did. The son of a bitch chuckled and pulled her closer.

Temporarily trapped in his grip, long-suppressed panic began to surface. Everything she knew to do flew from her buzzed brain. The knowledge returned in a slow motion whirlwind, and just as she'd decided on a course of action, another variable came into play.

"May I cut in?"

Ricky's hands loosened as Maddie looked to see if she had a savior or another horn-dog lookin' to score. Her shoulders sagged as relief flooded her.

"Heath." Her voice pitched higher than normal as she shoved away from Ricky and threw her arms around Heath's neck.

Ricky tugged her arm. "Get lost, guy. The lady is with me."

Ignoring her date, Maddie held on to her old friend's arm for dear life. "I haven't seen you in forever." Really, it had only been a year and a half, but who was counting?

"It has been a little while. I heard you were back in town." Heath squeezed her hand. "How 'bout that dance?"

"Maybe you didn't hear me the first time." Ricky stepped between them. "Maddie is *my* date."

They looked like two linemen squaring off, both massive muscle heads over six feet tall.

Maddie eased between them and put a hand on

Ricky's chest. "Don't be jealous of Heath. He's like my brother." She nodded toward the bar. "Now, go get us a couple of shots while I dance with my friend." *Whew. In-charge Maddie was back.*

Ricky narrowed his eyes a split-second before he shrugged and meandered off in the direction of the bar.

Heath moved in and placed his hands on her waist. "I'd say you've had enough to drink."

"I know." She covered her mouth to suppress a burp. "'Scuse me, this inebriation is gonna hurt like hell in the mornin'."

"What are you doing with Ricky Dalton? That guy's a creep, Mad." A tiny crease rested between his brows.

From her position, looking up past his dimple into his ice blue eyes, she wondered if he'd always been so beautiful. The answer was *yes, always, and even more so now.* "I know, right? Pickings are slim in Willow Creek. I wanted to move on, and he asked me out. I swear the man's got ten hands."

"Do you need me to take you home?" Heath asked.

Maddie looked for Ricky at the bar and found him chatting it up with Loose-Lips Linda. *Thank God for small favors.* For a split second, Maddie's manners warred with her good sense. *Screw that.* Politeness got a lot of women in trouble.

"I don't think he'd notice if I disappeared," Maddie said. "I'd appreciate the ride, Heath. I'm definitely safer with you."

"I wouldn't be so sure about that, Maddie-cake. You're unattached, and not a little girl anymore."

He wriggled his eyebrows as he looked her over. She smacked his chest, even as heat surged to places that hadn't been warm in a while. One thing she knew for sure, this man would never, ever hurt her. At least, not on purpose. "You're such a kidder. Come on, let's blow this Mason jar."

Also Available from Meda White

Play With My Heart
Southland Romance Book 1

Southern musician and closet geek Liz Baker enjoys her quiet life. While in Los Angeles helping her brother with a house project, the simple life gets complicated when British television actor Ian Clarke walks into the picture.

Ian enjoys his celebrity status in Hollywood and is determined nothing and no one will get in the way of his plans for success on the big screen. He never counted on meeting a woman like Liz, but she's the only one who can help him with a personal problem.

Forced into close quarters where priorities and cultures clash, an intense attraction catches them both by surprise. Secrets, old lovers, and the paparazzi threaten their new dreams and a chance for love could be lost forever.

***Play With My Heart* is the 2014 BTS Red Carpet Award Winner in Contemporary Romance.**

Dance With My Heart: A Southland Romance Book 2
Ride With My Heart: A Southland Romance Book 3
Fool With My Heart: A Southland Romance Book 4

Spring Fling
A Southern College Novella

Kellyn Crenshaw wants to make it to college graduation without becoming another notch on the belt of a fraternity boy. A boy exactly like Pace Samson. Forced into close proximity because their roommates are dating, Kellyn sets out to prove she's resistant to his charms.

Pace never figured himself for a one-woman man until he spends time with Kellyn. She's different, and he can't get her out of his mind. She's also aware of his reputation, and it may keep him from the one girl who makes him want to change his ways.

When Pace and Kellyn fake a fling on Spring Break to help their friends, Kellyn may discover she isn't immune to Pace after all. They'll each have to decide if what's between them is just a fling or if there's a chance their feelings are real.

Fall Rush
A Southern College Novella

Embry Harris is desperate to turn things around her senior year of college. She's determined to make more responsible choices and rid herself of the stigma plaguing her. But because of her job and the hot bartender who goads her into making impulsive decisions, it isn't going to be easy.

Stede Bennett's mission since returning from his overseas tour is to get his degree. The last thing he needs is a spoiled sorority girl distracting him. Being a Marine taught him many things, except how to handle a beautiful woman in constant need of saving.

Protecting Embry from the jerk threatening to ruin her reputation is how Stede begins to lose his heart. Being empowered by Stede's words is how Embry starts losing hers. If the schemer responsible for pushing them together gets his way, they could lose their chance for happiness.

Winter Formal
A Southern College Novella

Life is going according to plan for Sibba Douglas until she gets blackmailed. Her future dream of being a doctor is threatened unless she can help a spoiled fraternity boy do well on the MCAT.

Nash Lincoln knows he needs to settle down and focus on his studies, but academics have taken a back seat to social events, and he's coasting by on little sleep and lots of pills. The distraction of a tutor he's admired from afar isn't helping matters.

Substance abuse leads to tragedy and draws Sibba and Nash closer together. But it may also be the thing that tears them apart.

Christmas Give
A Holiday Novella

Eva Walker returns home to Georgia for the first Christmas since her husband's death. She's missed her family, but is afraid the void left by her husband will make it unbearable.

Between losing his job as an NFL defensive back and losing his wife to the star quarterback, Adam "Mack" Riggs has had a rough year. Looking for a change of pace, he visits an old college friend for Christmas.

The attraction between Eva and Adam is instant, and so is the laughter. Enjoying life again feels so good for both of them. Simple Christmas wishes unite with a shared holiday tradition, putting them on a path toward healing and acceptance. A path that could lead to a future, if only their pasts would remain where they belong.